M000305745

Career Night

ON

Union Station

EarthCent Ambassador Series:

Date Night on Union Station

Alien Night on Union Station

High Priest on Union Station

Spy Night on Union Station

Carnival on Union Station

Wanderers on Union Station

Vacation on Union Station

Guest Night on Union Station

Word Night on Union Station

Party Night on Union Station

Review Night on Union Station

Family Night on Union Station

Book Night on Union Station

LARP Night on Union Station

Book Fifteen of EarthCent Ambassador

Career Night on Union Station

Foner Books

ISBN 978-1-948691-13-0

Copyright 2018 by E. M. Foner

Northampton, Massachusetts

One

"In conclusion, it is the view of Union Station Embassy that our lack of a dedicated conference room suitable for hosting meetings with the alien ambassadors has limited our ability to gain traction on the more important inter-species committees, and as I have a standing promise from a private donor to pay for renovations to the recently vacated travel agency next door, I will be signing a lease and beginning the work of expanding our space immediately."

"Immediately?" Libby repeated back.

"Yes. In fact, I'd like to sign the contract before you transmit my weekly report, if that's possible. It would be just like the president to be working in his office in the middle of the night and waiting for me to suggest something like this so he can object."

"Why would he object?"

"You've never been to Earth, Libby, but the president's office is a bit of a joke."

"Very well," the station librarian replied, popping up a holographic lease over the ambassador's display desk. "There's no need to actually sign, of course. I'll just record your voice approval after you've read it."

"I trust you, Libby. I approve the contract."

"You surprise me, Ambassador. I've had the pleasure of hearing you quote my advice about reading the fine print of contracts many times over the years."

"That's different. You wouldn't see me signing a contract with Jeeves, even after reading it, unless I got you to check it first. You're practically my attorney, after all, and a man who acts as his own lawyer has a fool for a client."

"Don't you even want to know the rent?"

"Donna's husband once tried to explain to me how station rents and the Stryx cred all tied together, and frankly, it made me a little dizzy."

"As you wish. I've recorded your approval and released your weekly report to EarthCent. Congratulations on doubling the size of the embassy."

"When can you get somebody in to start on the renovations?" Kelly asked, retrieving her purse from the display desk's otherwise unused deep file drawer and rising from her chair. "Does Gryph just send in maintenance bots that take care of everything? It would be great to come in Monday morning and find the meeting room ready to go. I'm going to have Donna help me pick out the furniture."

"We leave all interior modifications to the tenant, Ambassador. The terms are identical to the arrangement under which your husband leases hold space on the station core for Mac's Bones. Speaking of Joe, he just exited the lift tube down the corridor and is on his way here to pick you up."

"Great! I'll show him the new space and get his advice."

"You don't have much time," Libby reminded the ambassador. "The Station Scouts fundraiser starts in twenty minutes."

"I never got around to writing a speech," Kelly groaned. "What am I going to say to all of those people after the meal?"

"Most of them are there because they have children in the scouts or because they plan to win something at the auction and get free advertising for their businesses in the

Galactic Free Press. The money raised at these events more than doubled when Chastity's paper began running a special section featuring the winning bidders."

"That makes it even worse! What if the paper reports my speech?"

"Do you remember what you said when you mediated the disagreement over lane violations for the all-species bowling league?"

"You mean about how we all have a shared responsibility for the children on the station, even if our species are engaged in trade wars? I wrote that part out ahead of time," Kelly admitted. "I didn't know you were listening."

"I'm always listening, and I think it would make a very nice after dinner speech for the arts-and-crafts auction."

"I guess that could work. You know, sometimes I think I put more hours into preparing for meetings while I was on sabbatical than I did as an ambassador. Czeros and Srythlan both do mediation work as a side job, but I don't think I could find the time."

"Find the time for what?" Joe asked as he entered his wife's office.

"Part-time mediation work, like the Frunge and Verlock ambassadors," Kelly replied, grabbing her husband's hand and pulling him towards the exit. "I want to show you our new conference room on the way out, but we don't have much time."

"You signed the lease for the space next door? How long does it run?"

"I guess it's year-to-year or something. Libby?"

"I gave you the standard short-term contract, one thousand cycles."

"What does that translate to?" Kelly asked as she led Joe into the corridor and they hurried to the adjoining office space.

"Approximately one hundred and thirty-nine years. Just swipe as you would at the embassy. I've reprogrammed the locks to respond to EarthCent authorized personnel."

Kelly waved her hand in front of the door and it slid open, allowing them to enter the former travel agency.

"Whatever happened to broom-clean?" Joe asked in disbelief. "Is that a half-eaten pizza or a new life form we've never encountered?"

"The previous tenants left the station on one of their own vacation junkets last cycle and never returned," the station librarian explained. "Their lease expired only yesterday so it wouldn't have been proper to send in cleaners before then. We use a Gem contractor in these situations, but they're on holiday."

"Chocolate Day," the ambassador confirmed. "Donna and I went to the event at their embassy for lunch and my stomach still hasn't forgiven me." Then she realized she had admitted to breaking her diet in front of her husband and quickly changed the subject. "So what do you think of the space, Joe?"

"Between the two of us, you're the conference room expert. I'd guess you'll want a large table in the wide area there, so the counter has to go, and this office lighting is a bit harsh. But other than that, once the Gem clean up and get rid of all the old furniture, I think it mainly comes down to decorating."

"What's your opinion on wood paneling?"

"Aren't you forgetting the Frunge?"

"Oops," Kelly said. "I guess that would be pretty offensive. But I don't want the conference table to be a giant slab of stone or some metal monstrosity."

"You can get tabletops made out of anything these days, and some of them look more like wood than the real thing."

"Maybe you'll find some nice artwork at the benefit that will fit in with the decor," Libby hinted.

"That's right, we have to get going," Kelly said. "Will the Gem have the room cleaned out by Monday? It's going to be my first full week back from sabbatical and I want to jump right in."

"Have you written up your post-sabbatical assessment?" Libby replied with a question of her own as the ambassador and her husband headed for the lift tube.

"Is that really necessary? You know how hard I worked, and all of my mediation sessions included at least one alien species. It really was a good experience."

"The report is for EarthCent, not me."

"I'll do it as soon as I get a look at Donna's write-up," Kelly promised. "I'm not going to copy from her," she hastened to add. "I just want to make sure that we use the same format since we're establishing a precedent for everybody who follows."

"Empire Convention Center," Joe told the lift tube. "We agreed on a two hundred cred maximum for tonight, right?"

"We talked about it," Kelly hedged. "You know that some of the other ambassadors will be there, and I don't want them to think we're too cheap to support a good cause, especially with Aisha's daughter joining the Junior Scouts this year."

"Fenna is ten now?"

"Nine. The organization has lowered the age since Paul was involved. It's an acknowledgement that humans have shorter childhoods than any of the other oxygen breathing species on the station."

"I wonder if they still sell raffle tickets," Joe said as they exited the lift-tube capsule in the giant Empire Convention Center complex. "Back when Paul was in the scouts, I won a dog-washing coupon and Beowulf loved it. It took a whole troop of scouts to scrub him clean, and then he dragged me to a park deck and rolled around in the dirt."

"Tell Donna you were late picking me up," Kelly instructed under her breath as they approached the entrance of the Meteor Room.

"Hi, Donna," Joe greeted the embassy manager, who took the lead for all of EarthCent's special events on the station. "Sorry we weren't earlier but I got side-tracked by a job and—"

"You were right on time," Donna interrupted. "I had Libby ping me when you got to the embassy. And the two of you are actually early so your wife's watch must be running fast again if she's asking you to make excuses for her."

Kelly compared the time on her faux-mechanical wristwatch to her implant and sighed. "The Dollnicks are supposed to be millions of years ahead of us. Why can't they make a fake watch that's accurate to better than a quarter of an hour?"

"When's the last time you changed the battery?" Donna asked.

"It has a battery? I thought it was powered by my body heat or something."

"Let me see it," Joe said, holding out his hand for the watch. Kelly slid the flexible band down over her wrist and passed it to him. "You had this before we were married, right?"

"I bought it in the Shuk the first time I met Shaina," Kelly confirmed. "That was around twenty-six years ago."

"Ambassador Crute," Joe called to the Dollnick, who had just arrived in the company of Ortha, the Horten ambassador. "May I ask you to read something for me?"

"Certainly," the towering diplomat replied. He extended one of his lower arms and accepted the watch from Joe. "The little hand is on the six and the big hand is on the eleven, so I believe in the Human timekeeping system that would make it five minutes before six."

"Thank you, but it's the engraving on the back I'm interested in."

"Genuine Earth watch replica manufactured under the authority of Prince Drume," Crute translated. "Twenty-five year unlimited warranty." He returned the watch to Joe, who gave his wife the thumbs down and stuffed the malfunctioning timepiece in his pocket.

"Thank you for coming, Ambassadors," Kelly belatedly greeted her colleagues. "Early is on time. Shall we go in?"

"You're all at the head table," Donna called after her. "Chastity gave the auctioneer a reserve bid of two hundred on everything, just so you know."

"Did you hear that, Joe? And I have to buy something or it wouldn't look right."

"It's not the money I'm worried about, it's the space," her husband explained. "I thought we were going to have extra room after Dorothy and Kevin moved into their shipping container, but I opened the door to her old room the other day and boxes began falling out."

"She was never very good at stacking," Kelly observed. "When she and Metoo used to play with building blocks,

7

he built the elaborate structures and she knocked them down. Besides, it's not like it rains in the hold, and you've been storing all of your work tools behind the ice-harvester for years."

"Just don't bid on any of those abstract sculptures that Dorothy's Vergallian friend Affie donated," Joe whispered as he pulled out a chair at the head table for his wife. "They all look like two melted blobs connected by a cube and they take up too much space. I'm not in any hurry for Sam to move out, and if he and Vivian get married, we'll want the extra room."

"That's years away. She just turned seventeen."

"Who just turned seventeen?" the Drazen ambassador asked, taking the chair to Kelly's left.

"Thank you for coming, Bork," Kelly said to her neighbor. "We were talking about Blythe's daughter, Vivian."

"It seems like yesterday that Blythe herself turned seventeen," Bork mused. "I remember because a Drazen consortium asked me to approach her about buying out InstaSitter, but she wasn't having any of it. She was remarkably mature for her age."

"Vivian is the same," Joe volunteered. "She couldn't have been fourteen when she left Libby's school and started at the Open University because Samuel was going." He paused and looked up and down the table. "I don't see Czeros. I was going to ask him about the contractor he used when they redid their embassy reception area last year."

"Czeros has a time conflict with a Frunge event," the Drazen ambassador excused his colleague. "Ah, I believe we're ready to begin."

A small woman made her way to the auctioneer's stand and cleared her throat loudly. If anything, the volume of conversation in the room rose. The auctioneer grinned at the challenge and then let rip at an astounding volume.

"Welcome to the benefit arts and crafts auction for the Station Scouts. I'm Shaina Cohan, and I should start by disclosing for the record that I'm not a disinterested auctioneer because my son Mike is starting in the Junior Scouts this year."

"The little boy who was on 'Let's Make Friends?'" Bork whispered to Kelly. "I wouldn't have thought he was old enough."

"They lowered the age for humans," Kelly whispered back. "Mike and Aisha's daughter, Fenna, both joined as soon as they turned nine."

"I have two important announcements to make before we begin," Shaina continued. "In the interest of raising the maximum funds and selling all of the donated items, we've decided to delay the meal until after the auction. Second," she bellowed over the loud chorus of groans, "all buyers tonight will have their names and items published in the Galactic Free Press, along with a brief bio and your thoughts about the piece you've purchased. Brinda?"

A woman who was easily recognized as Shaina's younger sister and the 'B' in SBJ Fashions, stepped up to the lectern and tapped the control pad, bringing to life a giant hologram of a canvas that might have been confused with a police identification kit for a crime scene perpetrated by dogs. Brinda pitched her voice for the large hall and easily matched her sibling's unamplified volume.

"Our first item today is an ensemble piece titled 'Family Portrait' and I'll start the bidding at two hundred creds," she announced.

"Two-fifty," Joe called out. "That's Beowulf's paw print up top next to Pava's," he told Kelly excitedly, "and I'm

9

pretty sure the second one in on the bottom row is Alexander's."

"Why would you want to hang paw prints on the wall when we have them all over the floors?" she demanded. "And what happened to two hundred creds?"

"Two-fifty, now three. Will you go three? Two-fifty, give me three? Tweedle dum-dee. Three. Now two-seventy-five. Give me two-seventy-five."

"Two-seventy-five," somebody called out.

"Now three, give me three. Come on, Joe. I've still got paw prints all over my apartment from when they got together to make it."

"Three," Joe confirmed.

"Three hundred," Brinda revisited the bid. "Now three-fifty. Will you give me three fifty? Three-twenty-five? Going once. Going twice. Sold, to the lucky Cayl hound lover for three hundred."

"Next we have an untitled abstract work from an anonymous donor," Shaina announced, and a hologram of two blobs connected by a pyramid shape appeared above the lectern.

"Looks like Affie has been experimenting," Kelly whispered to Joe.

"Do I hear two hundred?" Shaina began.

"Two thousand," the Vergallian ambassador sitting two seats to Kelly's right declared.

"Two thousand?" the auctioneer repeated to make sure she'd heard right. "I have two thousand, now three. Will you give me three? It's for a good cause, people. I've seen this sculpture in person and it's twice as big as I am. Three, three, three. Can I hear three?"

"Three thousand," Aainda called out.

"You're raising your own bid?" Shaina asked the Vergallian ambassador in disbelief.

"It's strategic, to discourage competition. Besides, we support station scouting."

The two Hadad sisters conferred briefly, and then Shaina took up the chant again, purposely looking away from the head table. "Four thousand, I have three, will you give me four. Four, four, let's get some more. Four?"

"Getting hungry over here," the Dollnick ambassador muttered loudly enough to carry to the auctioneer.

"Sold, to the Vergallian ambassador for three thousand creds," Shaina wrapped up.

Brinda auctioned off the next piece, and in less than an hour, the sisters had disposed of all of the donated art and raised over eleven thousand creds for the station scouts.

"It's nice to see Aainda and Joe getting along so well," Bork commented to Kelly while they waited for the food to be brought out. "I seem to recall he once had a bit of a phobia about upper-caste Vergallian women."

"I'm just happy she's still here," the EarthCent ambassador replied. "I must have worked with almost a dozen Vergallian ambassadors since coming to the station and she's the first one who takes our side. What I can't figure out is why she hasn't been reassigned yet. They're the only species that rotates ambassadors every couple years and I'm sure she's overdue."

"Didn't you read your intelligence report about it?" the Drazen ambassador asked.

"I might have gotten a few weeks behind," Kelly admitted. "I had a lot of mediation work to wrap up before returning from sabbatical. Can you fill me in?"

Bork glanced around at the other alien diplomats at the head table, and then shrugged. "I suppose it's not any big secret," he said. "Aainda put in for several extensions, and when they finally refused another, she pulled out some archaic law from their early tunnel-network days that allows ambassadors up to a year to arrange for suitable transportation. We hear that the imperial faction is furious, but ever since Aarania's failed attempt to kidnap you a few years back, the moderates have been gaining momentum in diplomatic circles."

Two

"Nervous?" Samuel asked Vivian as they waited for the students in her Dynastic Studies seminar to take their places.

"Why should I be nervous?" she shot back, paging through the presentation graphics on her tab for the fourth time in two minutes.

"Just imagine them all in their underwear," the ambassador's son advised her.

"Gross," she said, looking over at him this time. "Have you already forgotten about that all-species open swim we went to our first year in the Open University?"

"I guess I didn't find it as traumatizing as you did."

"Right. You were still taking Vergallian Studies courses back then and drooling over all the upper-caste females."

"I did not drool—"

"Are you and your minion ready, or should we wait a few million years until Humans develop their own faster-than-light drive?" a giant bunny inquired acerbically. It was the Grenouthian student's first turn at moderating the self-directed student seminar and he meant to take full advantage of the role.

"We're ready, and he's my boyfriend, not my minion," Vivian responded firmly. "I'm just waiting for the room's holographic display system to sync with my tab."

"Then you'll be waiting a long time because it's locked out," the bunny told her. "The administration is trying to discourage students from over-reliance on fancy graphics."

"Since when?"

"What's that flashing symbol in the corner of your tab, Viv?" Samuel asked.

"It's a special notice from university admin," the girl replied, quickly navigating to the announcement board. "Drat. As of now, student use of the holographic infrastructure will be limited to university-approved training simulations and formal reports."

"This isn't formal?"

"No, it's our mid-semester peer check. It's mainly an excuse for us to criticize each other."

"Still waiting," the Grenouthian half-sang, tapping his furry foot on the floor.

"All right already." Vivian straightened up and addressed the dozen or so alien students crowded into the small room. "I'm going to skip the basic intro since we've all been sitting in the same courses for almost three years, but—"

"Who are you?" a Dollnick princeling interrupted.

"That's Vivian Oxford," the Frunge student squeezed in next to the Dolly told him. "You know, the babysitter."

"I'm not a babysitter," Vivian retorted. "I'm an InstaSitter, there's a difference. And as one of the three primary heirs to InstaSitter—"

"Three?" the princeling interrupted. "Why haven't you eliminated the other two?"

"My twin brother and my cousin?"

"Yeah, family are the worst," the Dollnick replied in mock-sympathy.

"Just ignore him," Samuel urged her. "He's trying to get under your skin."

"As I was saying," Vivian continued, "as heir to one third of an income that would make your eyes water, I've sketched out a fifty-year plan that will allow us to consolidate our monopoly on Stryx stations and expand into the Cayl Empire."

"What about the other heirs?" a serious Verlock student inquired at his best speaking rate. "Are they participating in your planning?"

"Well, to tell you the truth, I'm only doing this because it's one of the course requirements," Vivian admitted. "My brother is more interested in InstaSitter operations than I am. The business is currently being managed by our minority owner, Tinka, who as a Drazen, is going to outlive us all in any case."

"You allow an alien to run your family business!" The Dollnick princeling began whistling in untranslatable mirth and the majority of the students in the seminar joined in with their own versions of laughter.

"She's a friend of the family," Vivian said defensively. "My mom and my aunt founded InstaSitter, but both of them are pursuing other business interests."

"Pursuing our business interests is more like it," the Grenouthian moderator growled. "I know that InstaSitter money is behind the Galactic Free Press, and they've been skimming off some of our network's potential ad revenue with an unpaid subscription model."

"That's Aunt Chastity's business," Vivian said. "My mom publishes translations of alien fiction."

"And runs your spy agency," a Drazen observed.

"Intelligence is recession-proof," the serious Verlock spoke again. "Good inheritance."

"First of all, my father is the director of EarthCent Intelligence, as if that's any of your concern. Second of all—"

"You have spy blood on both sides?" a Vergallian girl interrupted. "That's the perfect start for a dynasty."

"Aabina has a point," the Dollnick princeling said, seeing an opportunity to show off his knowledge of the technical side of succession planning. "I know a shipping heir who had to step aside when it became apparent he had inherited too much of an artistic nature from his mother."

"Time out," Samuel called, making the universally accepted hand-signal as if they were all participating in a multi-species LARP. "Vivian put a lot of effort into preparing this presentation so the least you could do is listen to it before criticizing."

"Bah," the bunny practically spat. "The point of this seminar is to attack one another until we're left with a survivable path forward. What's the point of our critiquing a plan for a dynasty she doesn't even want to run?"

"The point is moot since I kind of based the whole presentation on holograms," Vivian told them. "Why doesn't Grude go now and I'll reschedule for later."

"I'm still working on my dynastic succession outline," said a smaller Dollnick, who had sat with Samuel and Vivian on the committee to refit Flower. "After four semesters of failing to land an internship commitment from any of the princely shipyards, I've decided to complete my training elsewhere. I've applied for the visiting alien student slot in the design department for a leading Sharf naval architecture firm."

"You're going over to the enemy?" the princeling whistled disdainfully.

"They aren't our enemy, and while I would have preferred to intern in our own space, there are more Sharf merchant ships in service on the tunnel network than any other type."

"That's because the Humans have been buying up all of the used Sharf two-man traders," the Grenouthian moderator pointed out. "It would take a hundred thousand of them to match the displacement of an average Dollnick colony ship."

"One hundred and thirty-two thousand, six hundred and nine," the Verlock corrected him.

"I will go where the opportunity to work leads me," Grude said stubbornly. "My father's profession as a baker is an honorable one, but I've chosen another path."

"And you'll spend your entire internship in Sharf space?" a Frunge student asked, obviously intrigued by the idea of training with an alien species.

"Yes, or the first hundred cycles," Grude replied. "Perhaps with experience, I'll be able to find work closer to home."

"That's like fourteen years," Vivian exclaimed.

"The standard internship for ship engineers is five hundred cycles," he informed her. "But I really can't say anymore until they get back to me."

"I've often heard Humans bragging about thinking on their feet," the Grenouthian moderator said to Vivian in the lull that followed Grude's statement. "Why don't you run with the Verlock's idea for taking over your family's spy business?"

"Show us what you've got," the Vergallian beauty dared the girl, and a few other students chipped in with similar challenges.

"Well, I won't say I haven't thought about a career in EarthCent Intelligence," Vivian said slowly. "But it's not something I could just decide for myself."

"Why not?" the Verlock rumbled.

"My parents don't own EarthCent Intelligence. I mean, my mom funds a lot of it, but they're still working for EarthCent."

"Define your terms," the moderator instructed her.

"EarthCent? It's our government, kind of, except we don't vote for it. But EarthCent is administered from Earth, sort of, and there's a president, though I'm told he got stuck with the job when the last one ran off. But it's the only government we have."

"You're talking about the system the Stryx set up so Humans would have diplomatic representation on the tunnel network," Grude said. "How about Eccentric Enterprises, or that Conference of Sovereign Human Communities organization that Flower is helping?"

"My mom kind of funds Eccentric Enterprises too."

"And CoSHC?" the Dollnick prompted her.

"Good acronym," the moderator said. "I haven't heard that one before."

"Sounds mathematical," the Verlock observed. He checked his student tab for a different translation and smiled fondly. "Ah, hyperbolic functions. Reminds me of kindergarten."

"CoSHC is more of a trade organization than a government," Samuel explained. "The 'sovereign' part of the name means that those human communities have their own governments, though many of them are on open worlds where they are operating with limited autonomy under a planetary administration run by an alien species."

"You're the EarthCent ambassador's son," the moderator said, almost as if it were an accusation. "When you succeed her, do you plan on making a play for the presidency?"

All of a sudden the roomful of alien students seemed to be paying very close attention, and Samuel chose his words carefully.

"My mother was hired by EarthCent and worked her way up through the ranks. Even if I wanted to be a diplomat, it's not a career path I can choose for myself. You have to be—selected."

"He means the Stryx pick them out," a Horten student interpreted.

"You would make a fine diplomat, Samuel," Grude encouraged him. "You ran our committee for Flower, and you're always making peace between the students."

"What are you studying?" the Verlock queried the ambassador's son.

"Space Engineering."

"Why?"

"Why am I studying Space Engineering?" Samuel repeated to buy time to consider the unexpected question. "I grew up in a spaceship repair facility, and I've always wanted—"

"To be a mechanic," the princeling interrupted. "Don't you know the difference between creating new designs and patching meteor damage?"

"You're not being fair to the—" Grude began, but the higher ranking Dollnick silenced him with a piercing whistle that made all of the students in the small room flinch.

"I am having trouble with some of the alien maths," Samuel admitted, "But with the computational tools available, I think I'll be able to contribute."

"You mean you'll dream up pretty looking ships and ask the Stryx to do the engineering for you," the princeling jeered.

"You know the Stryx won't help us with technology," Samuel retorted. "And not everybody has to design jump engines or mega-structures. I'm thinking of specializing in reengineering alien ships for human usage."

"Interior decoration," the Grenouthian moderator said dismissively, leading to a general outbreak of laughter.

The Verlock student pounded the table in an uncharacteristic display of energy to get everybody's attention. "Diplomacy is more important. Combine it with intelligence for a dynasty."

"What are you suggesting?" Vivian demanded over the din of argumentation that followed the Verlock's remark. "You think Samuel and I should be planning some kind of empire?"

"Run with it," the moderator instructed her, clearly amused by the turn of events. "How will you and your minion take control?"

"Control of what?" Vivian said. "Even if I end up in charge of EarthCent Intelligence and Samuel becomes an ambassador or the president, it's not like we'd be running an empire. It's just a few hundred embassies and consulates and a couple thousand spies. Earth has its own local governments, and so do all the sovereign human communities."

"A fleet would be a good start," the Vergallian girl commented. "You're already buying up our military-surplus patrol craft for the police forces being deployed to some of your asteroid mining communities. You should infiltrate your loyal family retainers into those positions."

"I don't have any family retainers," Vivian objected.

"What about him?" the moderator gestured at Samuel.

"I'm not posing as a policeman so I can turn on the people I've been hired to protect," Samuel said firmly.

"Humans wouldn't recognize a good plan if you held them down and whistled it in their ears," the princeling said to the Vergallian, who nodded her agreement.

"Diplomacy and intelligence," the Verlock repeated.

"You could talk the sovereign communities into joining together in a new Human empire," Grude suggested. "You're good at that."

"Offer them free babysitting," the Drazen student contributed.

"Now just you wait a minute," Vivian said, glaring around at her classmates. "What you're all suggesting makes no sense at all. If humanity is as backwards as most of you are so fond of pointing out, why would Samuel and I want to take over in the first place?"

"Charity?" Aabina suggested. "After all, you couldn't do any worse."

"I thought that the point of Dynastic Studies was to preserve family assets," Samuel objected.

"And what do you think my family's assets consist of?" the Vergallian girl challenged him.

"Well, I don't really know anything about you."

"I'm ambassador Aainda's eldest daughter," Aabina replied proudly. "My mother will be queen one day and I will be queen after her. Our extended family owns several planetary systems."

"You mean, your family provides the hereditary government," Vivian said.

"No, they're ours, though we would never ask everybody to pick up and leave. In the end, stars are big balls of hot gas and planets are cold balls of rock. It's the living things that matter."

"A fine dynasty," the Verlock said. "My own family shares in a respectable chain of academies."

"But the goal of EarthCent is to promote democracy, and EarthCent Intelligence only exists to serve that cause," Vivian asserted.

"Actually, I've read through the charter and it doesn't say anything about democracy," Samuel told her. "It would be pretty strange if it did, since EarthCent has yet to hold an election."

"But the oath for EarthCent Intelligence was copied from the diplomatic one and we've both heard it a hundred times at graduation picnics," Vivian protested.

"I solemnly swear to do my best for humanity," Samuel repeated the oath. "That leaves a lot of wiggle room in how you go about it."

"The way I see it, you should leverage your intelligence service to expand your family's business until the Humans come to see you as their natural leaders," the Grenouthian advised. "With the backing of the Galactic Free Press, I see no reason you couldn't be running everything from the shadows before you're too old to remember what you want everybody to do."

"Humans," the princeling said in a voice dripping with scorn. "Can't you all see that neither of these two knows what they want to do with their lives? I don't understand why they're even here."

"I'll bet they ignored their ASAT results," the Frunge student speculated. He asked Vivian, "What's your deviation factor?"

"My what?"

"How far have you deviated from your ASAT projections?"

"What's an ASAT?" Samuel asked.

"How did these two ever get into the Open University?" the princeling demanded dramatically. "The Advanced Species Aptitude Test is required."

"For advanced species, which they clearly aren't," the Grenouthian reminded the Dollnick. "Still, taking the test might help you clarify your career goals," he told the two humans.

"Is this one of those week-long things I've heard alien kids talking about?" Vivian asked.

"No, those are competency tests. The ASATs were developed by the Open University to help place incoming students in courses of study that will help them reach their full potential."

"You mean it's a Stryx thing?"

The students all shifted uncomfortably in their seats, and finally the Verlock said slowly, "The station librarian administers the test. We employ a similar psychological profiling and aptitude screening process in my family's academy network. I could test you now, if you allow it."

"I don't know," Vivian said. "What good would a psychological test for Verlocks do for me? And we're so different from a physiological standpoint."

"I'll try it," Samuel volunteered, and whispered to Vivian by way of explanation, "Ten more minutes and you'll get credit for the seminar."

"The number of questions required for an accurate reading depends on the test subject," the Verlock informed him. "The minimum I have heard of for our test is five, the maximum is two hundred and eleven."

23

"He'll need a hundred questions just to figure out what he wants for lunch," the princeling predicted.

"I will begin. Would you prefer to read a book at a party or speak loudly while building a sand castle at the beach?"

"Uh," Samuel said, taking a moment to consider his options. "Build the sand castle, I guess."

"When talking about your feelings, do you logically analyze the actions that fed into your emotional state, or try to make yourself the center of attention?"

"He doesn't talk about his feelings," Vivian answered as Samuel struggled to come up with a reply. "Can we have a different question?"

"The answer is acceptable," the Verlock said, tapping his student tab. "Do you struggle to predict the outcome of events, or do you plot your course based on proven strategies?"

"Those aren't mutually exclusive options," Samuel complained. "I'm not sure they're even related."

"The score is based on your choices, not the internal logic of the questions," the Verlock said.

"Well, I don't struggle to predict the outcome of events. I'm not sure about plotting my course based on proven strategies."

"Your decisions are based on impulse?"

"Is that a test question or are you just asking?"

"Test question."

"Maybe? Sometimes?"

"Clearly the test is over his head," the princeling interjected, but this time, the other students hushed the Dollnick.

The Verlock nodded ponderously and made a note on his tab. "Do you value mercy over justice or make friends easily at a new workplace?"

"So you're asking which statement I agree with most strongly?" Samuel replied.

"But they amount to the same thing," the Vergallian girl couldn't help blurting out.

"Don't answer," the Verlock warned Sam as rapidly as he could get the words out while turning to glare at Aabina. "No kibitzing! I retract the question and will ask another. Do you have difficulty with theoretical books or do you often apply statistics to the complexities of life?"

"Well, I already admitted that I'm having trouble with the advanced math in the Space Engineering program, and I can't say that I've ever tried applying statistics to, well, anything."

"Excellent," the Verlock declared. "Finished in six questions. Do I have permission to submit a paper based on your responses?"

"It was just five questions because you withdrew one," Samuel reminded him. "Where would you submit a paper?"

"To the Verlock Journal of Student Career and Personality Profiling. And the withdrawn question counts because you heard it."

The other students all began rising from their seats and moving to the door as their implants or internal time sense informed them that the seminar period had reached an end.

"Wait," Vivian called to the Verlock, who was of course the slowest to his feet. "What about the test results?"

"Are you sure you want to know?" the serious alien responded.

"Yes," Samuel said. "It's interesting, but like Vivian said, I'm not going to change my life based on an aptitude test for an advanced species that outlives us by more than an order of magnitude. I'll bet I don't even qualify for ninety percent of the careers open to you guys."

"You'll never work in magnetic monopole design," the Verlock agreed. "Fortunately, the test results were crystal clear that your primary aptitude and nature correlate most highly with diplomacy."

Vivian placed a hand on Samuel's arm to keep him back while the bulky alien shuffled out of the room, and then she asked, "Do you think he gave you the real test results or did he just want to prove his original suggestion was correct?"

"I don't think a Verlock would lie about something like that," Samuel said. "But I can't say that the test made much sense either, and I don't see how my answers could have led to such a definitive conclusion so quickly when he said that five questions was the absolute minimum."

"Libby?" Vivian asked. "Was the test legitimate?"

"The correlations are all based on Verlock data, meaning the results could be argued, but Rythnal did follow the procedures."

"Did you really exclude us from taking the ASATs because we're not from an advanced species?" Samuel asked.

"You both attended my school," the station librarian replied. "I have much more accurate models for your aptitudes than any test could provide."

"Then why didn't you offer us career guidance?" the girl demanded. "I really am confused, you know."

"I wouldn't want to interfere with your free will," Libby replied disingenuously.

Three

"Let me get that for you," Affie said, slipping past Dorothy and retrieving the bolt of fabric from the lower storage rack. "You really shouldn't be bending over and picking up heavy objects."

"I'm pregnant, not sick," the ambassador's daughter retorted, though she didn't attempt to stop the Vergallian from rolling the cloth out on the cutting table. "What do the royal families do when a high-caste woman is expecting? Lock her in a tower guarded by a dragon?"

"Don't be silly, we'd never let a dragon get near a queen or her family. And no, we don't treat expectant mothers like glass figurines, but you could use a little common sense."

"It's not like I have prior experience at this," Dorothy pointed out, and began pinning a plastic pattern over the expanse of fabric.

"Didn't your mom explain everything?"

"Sure, and so did my sister-in-law, and all of my mother's friends. I'm the one carrying the baby and everybody else is the expert."

"Stop leaning over the table like that," Affie begged her. "You're going to put a dent in it."

"The table?"

"The baby. Pay attention."

"Morning, Dorothy. Hey, Affie," Flazint said as she entered the design room at SBJ Fashions. The Frunge girl had

27

her hair vines up in a casual twist, and she was humming to herself, a sound reminiscent of sanding a block of wood by hand. "Has the baby kicked yet?"

"Don't encourage him," Dorothy flung over her shoulder.

"So it is a boy," Affie declared. "I was starting to wonder when you'd know but I didn't want to embarrass you by asking. Most Vergallian women can tell within the first couple weeks."

"I guess that's why we call you an 'advanced species' because it doesn't work that way with us. I said 'him' because Flaz mentioned kicking and I thought of a boy."

"Then you leave me with no choice," Affie said in a mock-serious tone. "Librarian. Is she carrying a boy or a girl?"

"That's confidential information," Libby responded immediately. "Dorothy, you asked me to alert you when Jeeves returned to the station. He and Baa are back from their outing."

"Baa still makes me nervous," Flazint complained, twisting a stray hair vine around her finger. "I don't get how the two of you treat her like just another alien."

"Humans don't have any myths about Terragram mages, so to me she's a magical cheapskate with feathers who Jeeves had to bribe to get off my mother's couch," Dorothy explained.

"Acting confident is part of the royal training I had to take before my sister's daughters pushed me down the succession line," Affie added. "Besides, she's not that bad if you ignore the threats and insults. I think she has self-esteem issues."

"Afternoon, Dorothy," Shaina said, sticking her head in the door. "Morning to you, Flazint, and I don't have a clue what time it is for you at the moment, Affie. Jeeves and Baa are on their way and I've pinged Brinda. We're having a management conference in five minutes."

"Did something happen?" Flazint asked. "If there's a legal problem I could ask Tzachan if he's available."

"I'm sure he's never too busy for you," Dorothy said, winking at Affie, who rolled her eyes. "What were Jeeves and Baa doing out together anyway, Libby?"

"That's confidential information as well, though from what I know of Baa, she'll be happy to explain if you ask."

"I'll never get this pattern cut out with you guys hanging over me and a meeting in four minutes," Dorothy complained, pushing aside her scissors without ever taking them up. "We may as well just wait for them in the conference room."

The three-woman design team of SBJ Fashions followed Shaina down the hall and took their accustomed places at the conference table.

"Can I get you a glass of water or juice?" Flazint asked Dorothy.

"Coffee, please."

The alien frowned. "Did you have one already today?"

"I always drink coffee with Kevin in the morning," the ambassador's daughter replied. "He gets up early to run laps around Mac's Bones with the dog and then he makes me breakfast."

The Frunge girl suppressed a shudder at the thought of a male cooking, but pushed forward bravely with her subject. "I stopped in your embassy on my way here to ask about your coffee consumption—"

"You told on me to my mom?"

"I went to talk with the associate ambassador," Flazint said. "I didn't even see your mother."

29

"You went to ask my Daniel about safe levels of coffee for Dorothy?" Shaina asked in amusement.

"I wanted to consult with a medical expert for your species. The only one I know is M793qK, and he's on Flower."

"You went to our embassy to make a cross-galaxy call to Flower to talk to the beetle doctor about my coffee drinking?" Dorothy demanded. "Why didn't you just ask a human doctor on the station?"

"Remember when Affie and I went to your friend Lynx's baby shower?"

"In my apartment," Shaina added.

"Right. And Lynx had that countdown watch the Farling doctor gave her so she'd know when the baby was coming, and we all bet on the delivery time."

"We won't be doing that with me," Dorothy said pointedly.

"I wasn't suggesting—the point is that Daniel got M793qK on a holoconference for me and I asked him about some of your—what I could do..." Flazint blundered to a halt.

"You went behind my back to get instructions about what I should and shouldn't be doing while I'm pregnant?"

"Don't get angry, Dorothy," Affie said. "I did the same thing. I sent an information request to the Royal College of Physicians since they have plenty of experience treating the families of Human mercenaries on Vergallian worlds, plus our physiology isn't that far apart compared to most species. Flazint and I are your friends and we have a responsibility to look out for you."

"I think it's sweet," Shaina said.

Dorothy cast a longing look at the coffee machine and exhaled deeply. "So what did the beetle say?"

"Well, he started with some general opinions on the Human reproductive process that weren't very complimentary, and then he said that with primitive species, the best approach is to take everything in moderation."

"One cup of coffee a day is the Royal College of Physicians recommendation for your species," Affie said. "It's not a volume thing, though. They had specific guidelines for caffeine, so you can't drink six espressos and count it as one cup."

"The Farling suggested staying away from espressos altogether."

"Next you're going to tell me to stop wearing high heels," Dorothy groused.

"He did say that you should start weaning yourself by lowering the heel height a little every day since they're adjustable. I could help you with the programming," the Frunge girl offered.

"There's no way that wearing heels could be bad for the baby. I'm more likely to trip and fall in sandals because I'm used to the gyroscopic stabilizers in our shoes."

"I used to get calf cramps when I wore heels while I was expecting Mike," Shaina volunteered. "I didn't even try with his sister."

"Neither did I," Brinda joined in the moment she arrived, as if she shared a telepathic connection with her sister and had been there for the entire conversation. "Your whole center of gravity is going to change, you know."

"See?" Affie said. "They managed just fine without heels and they're both short. I mean, shorter than you."

"Gang up on me all you want," Dorothy responded defiantly. "I'm the one who brought those heels to market and I'll wear them until my feet fall off."

"I'd like to see that," Baa declared, entering the meeting room with Jeeves floating right behind her. "Just let me know ahead of time so I can be ready with a sarcastic comment. I hate it when I miss an opportunity to say something funny, and then later at home, I think up the perfect response I could have made."

The Terragram mage pulled out the chair next to the Frunge girl, who flinched and edged to the far side of her seat. Jeeves continued on to the head of the table and activated the holographic projection system. A dense grid of data appeared.

"If everybody would turn their attention to last cycle's sales," the young Stryx requested.

Baa made a point of not looking up at the data, pretending instead to be very interested in picking a bit of lint from the feathers on her left arm.

"Am I boring you already, Baa?" Jeeves asked.

"Stryx are boring by definition. You have infinite power and you waste it playing goodie-two shoes."

"I meant that in the context of our meeting today, which began less than a minute ago."

"It's a grid of data showing strong sales growth in shoes and wedding gowns, moderate growth in accessories and hats, and flat to contracting sales in tube dresses and travel cloaks. Wake me when you get to the good stuff."

"I wasn't aware you could read holograms without looking at them," Jeeves said grudgingly.

"I can't, but somebody shined his casing today and reflections are sufficient for data tables. Sales reports are a waste of holographic display technology if you ask me. You should get a flat screen."

"Since when are we losing sales in tube dresses and travel cloaks?" Dorothy asked. "Those are classics!"

"We've been expecting it for some time," Brinda said. "Neither product is in any way unique to us, although we helped bring them back into fashion. Shaina and I agree that lowering our prices for volume would just cheapen the SBJ brand."

"That data can't be right," Flazint objected. "I thought that my purses were our biggest seller last cycle. I've been working overtime getting the clasps for the bespoke orders done and we still have a three-cycle backlog."

"And we want you to hire more artisans," Shaina told her. "With the flexible labor contracts offered by the Frunge metal and leather-workers guilds, there's no downside."

"Then why aren't the sales showing?" Flazint gestured at the holograph.

"Because somebody who has an incentives clause in her contract insisted that I break out enchanted items on a separate grid," Jeeves grumbled, and the hologram morphed into a new data set.

"All of those are enchanted?" Affie exclaimed.

Baa blew on her fingertips and looked even more pleased with herself than usual. "Speaking of incentives, you know that I have a need for cash."

"All in good time," Jeeves replied. "The immediate point of this meeting is that Shaina and Brinda have been negotiating with the tunnel network's professional LARPing league to provide players with official bags-of-holding in return for product placements in the broadcasts.

I approved the deal approximately eight minutes ago, but we need a catchy name."

"Why is everybody looking at me?" Dorothy asked.

"You know you're good with names," Flazint said. "You even told me you came up with Libbyland."

"What's wrong with SBJ Fashions Bags-of-Holding. Wouldn't that get us maximum name recognition?"

"Have you ever even watched the league play?" Affie inquired. "Stick always has it on now and the commentators are never going to use a name that long. And the truth is, SBJ Fashions works great for a boutique, but it's not punchy enough for live action role-playing."

"Then call them Baa's Bags-of-Holding," Dorothy suggested, shrugging to show that she didn't consider enchanted fashions worth putting a lot of thought into, even if they were selling. "It would shorten to Baa's Bags."

"I like the name, but it's too long to use for a graphic," Brinda said. "We need something instantly recognizable to brand the enchanted line of bags, like the SBJ we embroider on all of our other products."

"BB?" Shaina offered.

"Hate it," Baa said immediately.

"How about a feather?" Dorothy suggested. "We could do different types and colors to match the bags. And maybe Baa could start enchanting more travel cloaks to revive the line. Couldn't you make them sword-proof or something?"

"I could add backstabbing protection," the Terragram mage mused. "It would take around three times as much energy as creating bags-of-holding."

"Pricey," Jeeves said. "How about making them stealthy?"

"Depends on the level you want," Baa replied. "It's no effort at all to whip up an enchantment that will allow players with a natural affinity to blend into the shadows, like rogues and assassins, but full invisibility comes at a cost."

"We could do numbers of feathers," Dorothy said, her enthusiasm for the new product line growing in proportion to her input into its final form. "Like, one feather would be something low-level, like the shadow-blending thing, two feathers could be back-stabbing protection, and three feathers would be full invisibility. I don't mean it has to be those three things," she added hastily. "You know I'm not interested in any of that fighting stuff, but I like differentiating cost points, like with my shoes. Can you make bags-of-holding that fit different amounts of stuff, Flazint?"

"It doesn't depend on my designs," the Frunge girl said. "It's all in the enchantment."

"I already created two tiers for our bags of holding and I was thinking of increasing the number," Baa said. "The simple enchantment just lets you carry more items and preserves them if you die in the game. We charge more for the version that reduces the weight of the items held."

"I guess I should have been paying more attention to this LARP stuff," Dorothy admitted. "I don't have the patience to sit through broadcasts, though. Maybe I should sign up for—"

"Are you crazy?" Affie cut her off. "You can't run around role-playing in your condition."

"But I want to learn more about what the players are wearing and how they're accessorizing."

"I'll do it," Flazint volunteered. "I enjoyed your Jack-and-Jill, even though Baa kept on raising our casualties from the dead as her personal slaves."

"Better bring Zach to advise you on intellectual property issues," Dorothy suggested with a wink at Affie, and for once the Frunge girl didn't even notice that she was being teased.

"It wouldn't be right to ask Tzachan to spend his own money and then give us advice for free."

"I'll pay for the LARP entrance but not for the time he spends playing," Jeeves said. "If he writes up his conclusions afterwards, that's billable time, but I'm not made of creds."

"I'd find you much more interesting if you were," Baa told the Stryx.

"So where were you guys when you left the station?" Dorothy asked. "Libby wouldn't say."

"When I agreed to work for SBJ Fashions, I insisted that Jeeves help me recover my old ship."

"The one next to my dad's ice harvester? But Paul and Aisha are living in it."

"That was just a habitat where I crashed for a while. I left my ship in a force-field hangar on the surface of—the planet isn't important—and the natives built a pyramid over it. I couldn't instruct the ship to extract itself without destroying the temple complex."

"And that stopped you?" the ambassador's daughter asked.

"The Stryx science ship monitoring the situation stopped her," Jeeves said. "Baa was participating in an unlicensed pantheon—"

"The Stryx have no jurisdiction over religious matters," the mage interrupted.

"You and your Terragram friends happened to choose a world that later came under our protection," the young Stryx continued unperturbed. "The natives were quite upset when their gods deserted them seven millennia ago without any explanation."

"I was in love and he wanted to travel," Baa replied sulkily. "Next time we'll go in my ship and he can be the one stuck with a major parking problem."

"Wait," Dorothy said. "Is this the same guy who—"

"We're made for each other," Baa said unapologetically. "He just doesn't know himself as well as I do."

"How long has this been going on?" Shaina inquired.

"Love is timeless."

"So what about your ship?" Affie asked.

"I displaced it for her, leaving the force-field intact," Jeeves said. "It's in horrible condition."

"Why would it be in horrible shape if the force-field was still intact?" Brinda wanted to know.

"I'm not much of a housekeeper," Baa replied with a shrug. "A cycle or two in a repair facility will sort it all out."

"If you can find one willing to work on a Terragram ship," Jeeves cautioned her. "And remember, no threats."

"How am I supposed to get a fair price if I can't threaten anybody?" Baa complained. "It's like saying that I'm welcome to be a mage as long as I don't use magic."

"My dad and Paul would take the job," Dorothy offered. The Frunge girl stared at her friend in horror, and everybody else in the room other than Jeeves looked surprised, but the ambassador's daughter continued undeterred. "They like working on alien technology and they have oodles of spare parts from the abandoned ships Aisha bought from the Stryx."

"Are you inviting me to stay in Mac's Bones?" Baa inquired casually.

"No," Dorothy answered immediately, "I'm saying that if you can't find somebody else to work on your ship, you should check with my dad."

"They have two Cayl hounds living there now," Jeeves added, causing the mage, who was allergic to the breed, to shudder.

"Tell your father I have a job for him, Dorothy, but I'd prefer to meet here to discuss it," Baa said.

"Is the meeting over?" Affie asked. "I'm having a late dinner with Stick."

"Let's just take a moment to recap," Shaina said, and began counting off points on her fingers. "One, Flazint is authorized to hire more contractors to help with bespoke clasps and leather work on her bags. Two, Jeeves is going to tell the LARPing league that the sponsorship deal is for Baa's Bags. Three, we're going to brand all of the enchanted gear that our resident Terragram mage produces with feathers expressing the price point and capability. Four, Dorothy is limited to one cup of coffee a day. Did I miss anything?"

"How about maternity leave?" Flazint suggested. "She'll be having the baby any time now."

"No I won't," Dorothy said in irritation at having her pregnancy made the subject of a meeting. "I'm not even halfway through my term."

"You should get one of those countdown watches so you'll know for sure," Affie suggested.

"I'm fully prepared to let you change to part-time whenever you're ready, and maybe you'd like to take a few years to bond with the newborn," Jeeves offered.

"Wait a minute," Dorothy said, staring at the Stryx suspiciously. "If you're figuring on taking back my programmable cred, you have another thing coming. I have an idea for a line of all-species snugglies for babies, and I've already contacted Drilyenth about creating a programmable elastic. He was very enthusiastic."

"That Verlock and his patent filings are costing me as much as your endless purchases of supplies," Jeeves grumbled, projecting a hologram of the word "supplies" in double quotes to compensate for his lack of fingers. "Well, at least covering babies shouldn't take much fabric."

Four

"Just a peek," Kelly pleaded with her best friend. "I promise I won't copy."

"I already sent it in so it's too late for that," Donna told the ambassador as she brought the sabbatical report up on her display desk. "Before you ask, Stanley helped with the beginning and the end."

"To the Office of the President," Kelly read. "I wish to express my gratitude for the full-year sabbatical leave I was granted by EarthCent and our Stryx benefactors. I returned to work with a renewed sense of professional pride in my calling as an embassy manager—Oh, that's good."

"Stanley's," Donna admitted.

"My sabbatical time was spent rotating through the embassies of oxygen-breathing species and shadowing my counterparts. I remained approximately six weeks each with the Verlocks, the Frunge, the Drazens, the Grenouthians, the Dollnicks, plus almost twenty weeks in the Vergallian embassy. My original plan had been to shadow the Horten and Chert embassy managers as well, but I was unable to cope with the antiseptic requirements of the Hortens, and my Chert counterpart proved impossible to shadow due to frequent invisibility."

"The truth is, the Horten embassy manager is a relative of Ortha's who didn't want me there, probably because he's embezzling from petty cash," Donna commented. "The

Chert was a nice woman, but it's hard to put aside a lifetime's habits all at once. We did try it out for almost a week before I went back to the Vergallians."

"In addition to learning how the alien embassies function, I was able to establish professional relationships that I'm sure will pay dividends in cutting through the red tape going forward," Kelly resumed reading. "I kept records of all my interactions with the diplomatic support staff I encountered, and I am attaching a summary to this report, which I have also provided to EarthCent Intelligence." The ambassador looked up at her friend. "Isn't that a little under-handed?"

"They all assumed I was spying, Kelly. It's no secret that my daughter and her husband run EarthCent Intelligence. In fact, with the exception of the Drazens who already work closely with us on the intelligence front, every one of those embassy managers asked me to convey back-channel requests to Blythe about one thing or another. Now skip over that long section about purchasing office supplies, it's pretty dry," Donna instructed. "Go to the second-to-last paragraph."

"I was surprised to learn about the extent of funding alien governments provide their embassies for event planning," Kelly read. "The embassy managers explained to me, with varying degrees of bluntness, that EarthCent is considered in diplomatic circles to be a cheapskate organization when it comes to embassy parties. This isn't at all difficult to believe as we've never really hosted an embassy party, other than Kelly's ball, which was paid for by Dring. Thanks to my sabbatical experience, I sincerely believe that I could make efficient use of any funds earmarked for entertaining alien diplomats should a budget be established." The ambassador snorted.

"I can dream, can't I?" Donna said.

"In conclusion—Hey, that's my line."

"I checked with Libby and you couldn't get a trademark."

"In conclusion, my sabbatical experience was both productive and enjoyable. I want to again thank EarthCent and the Stryx for granting me paid leave, and I am honored to work for an organization that facilitates the ongoing education and intellectual growth of its support staff." Kelly pushed back from the display desk. "Thanks for making it hard for me."

"What?"

"I was hoping to get away with a postcard telling the president that I'm back. Now I'm going have to write a whole report."

"Just export your mediation calendar from last year and submit that with a few explanatory notes of how the sessions went," Donna suggested. "It will be like filling in an outline."

"Can you show me how to do the export?"

"I'll do it for you and send it to your desk. You have to leave for the Verlock embassy if you're going to make the nuisance-species committee meeting."

Hurrying out into the corridor, Kelly almost barreled into a stunning female who was standing right in front of the doors when they slid open.

"Ambassador Aainda," Kelly greeted the Vergallian. "I want to thank you for extending the hospitality of your embassy to Donna when her time with the Hortens and Cherts didn't work out."

"We all enjoyed having her," the Vergallian ambassador replied. "Please forgive me for waylaying you like this, but we need to talk before the committee meeting."

"What is it?" Kelly asked.

"Wait until we're in the lift tube. They're nearly impossible to bug."

"We could go back to my office," the EarthCent ambassador suggested. "The embassy was swept clean just yesterday."

"The corridors are a safer bet than your embassy, which is why I waited for you to come out. No offense."

"None taken, though I should tell our people if you're hinting that we're not secure." The two ambassadors entered the lift tube.

"Verlock embassy, slowly if you don't mind," the Vergallian told the capsule, and then grasped Kelly's forearm and fixed her with an intent stare. "Can you promise to keep what I'm about to tell you entirely confidential?"

"I'm sure you know that I'm EarthCent's Minister of Intelligence. My job is making sure that our ambassadors are as well-informed as possible."

"This has a personal aspect related to both of our families."

"I can only promise to act according to my conscience," Kelly said slowly.

Aainda let go of the ambassador's arm and nodded. "Very well. To make a long story short, I'll be introducing myself as my replacement at this committee meeting and I want you to play along."

"I'm sorry, but I don't understand."

"I've been extending my stay on Union Station through legal maneuvering until a cousin of mine could be approved for the diplomatic service and now I'm taking her place."

"You're going to impersonate your own cousin? Where is she?"

"She'll be going out to Fleet," the ambassador explained. "Fortunately, we were both named after the same great-grandmother so I won't have to change names."

"But everybody will know," Kelly protested. "Your own intelligence—"

"Exactly," Aainda cut her off with a savage smile. "My family has a bone to pick with the imperial intelligence service. They were behind the death of my favorite uncle on my father's side and the destruction of most of his family. Vergallian royals often lose track of male relatives after they marry into another family, but my uncle was a wonderful man." The alien ambassador paused significantly before continuing. "I've always been friends with his illegitimate daughter, Baylit."

Kelly sucked in her breath as the pieces fell into place. "You're related to Ailia, the orphaned princess who lived with us before her half-sister came to reclaim her? Is that why you've been treating humans so nice?"

"We take family debts seriously. Vergallian Intelligence already knows that I'm pulling a swap, of course, but forcing them to accept the situation is part of the game."

"But aren't they the most powerful force in your empire?"

"Hardly," the Vergallian scoffed. "The intelligence organization has a seat on the imperial council but no worlds of their own, and most importantly, no family patronage. Many of us are working to purge their ranks of those dishonorable curs who have meddled in the internal politics of the empire. It's not the first time Vergallian Intelligence has forgotten its boundaries and needed to be brought back under control. Something similar probably happens every ten thousand years or so, but this time it cost my uncle and his family their lives."

"So what part of this exactly do you want me to keep confidential?" Kelly asked.

"All of it. I don't mean to say that you can't discuss it in private, though I would certainly prefer if you did so only with your top people under reasonably secure conditions. I have sufficient backing to defy Vergallian Intelligence, but the diplomatic service answers to the imperial family, and if it appeared that I was intentionally rubbing their faces in the dirt, it would be seen as an act of outright rebellion."

"I see, I think. I can do that."

"In any case, with the exception of the Horten ambassador, I doubt our colleagues can tell one upper-caste Vergallian from another," Aainda concluded with a laugh. "Their own intelligence people will tell them the truth soon enough and I wouldn't be surprised if the Grenouthian already knows since they track station arrivals and departures so closely."

The doors slid open on the Verlock deck, and Kelly and Aainda made their way to the embassy. The temperature in the reception area was surprisingly mild, thanks to the lava waterfall having solidified during routine maintenance, and the two ambassadors followed a young Verlock staffer to the meeting room. Two Gem caterers were just leaving, and the other ambassadors were huddled around the buffet, loading stoneware plates with their favorite delicacies.

"Ambassadors," Srythlan boomed from the head of the table. The slow-moving Verlock always sat out the food scrums where he stood little chance against faster hands, a sacrifice that cost him nothing since the other species wouldn't bother with the dried-out, hard-to-chew foods favored by the oldest of the oxygen-breathing tunnel network species.

A giant bunny was the only one of the ambassadors to look around at the newcomers, and he proclaimed, "I see that the Human has returned from her paid vacation and the new Vergallian ambassador has finally arrived."

"Sabbatical," Kelly retorted.

On hearing that a new ambassador was among them, the other diplomats immediately changed their behavior with an eye towards making a good first impression, and cleared a path to the buffet for late-comers.

"Ambassador Aainda," the Vergallian introduced herself to her old colleagues. "I'm replacing my cousin with whom I share a name. I hope nobody finds it confusing."

"Not at all, my dear," Ortha said, bowing and kissing the ambassador's hand. "It seems you shared a wardrobe as well. I recall that gorgeous dress from a reception we attended last cycle."

"My cousin left behind a few articles of clothing she didn't feel were appropriate for Fleet," Aainda lied smoothly to the Horten, who had their roles been reversed, would have undergone an embarrassing shift in skin color. "And you are?" she asked the Drazen.

"Bork," he replied, seemingly ignorant of the charade. "Welcome to Union Station. I hope you don't mind my saying that even though your predecessor was both the loveliest and the most cooperative Vergallian diplomat I have ever met, something tells me that you are her equal."

Aainda blushed prettily and moved on to the Dollnick.

"Crute," he introduced himself, offering a two-handed politician's handshake with his lower set of arms while holding a loaded plate and a brimming tankard of some alien brew with the upper set. "I was briefed on your arrival before the meeting."

"I've been expecting her for a week," the Grenouthian said, and Kelly would have sworn that the giant bunny actually winked.

"Czeros," the Frunge diplomat greeted Aainda, setting down his plate of cheese and water goblet of wine on the giant slab of rock that served the Verlocks as a conference table. "My government specially requested me to offer you and your family a warm welcome."

"I'm afraid I traveled alone, though my cousin's daughter remained on the station," the Vergallian said.

"The welcome extends to your family wherever they might be," Czeros replied with a knowing smile.

"Gwen Two," the Gem ambassador introduced herself. "You and your cousin could be clones."

"I'll take that as a compliment," the Vergallian responded diplomatically.

"I am Srythlan, the host of today's meeting," the Verlock announced, having just reached the knot of ambassadors at a slow shuffle. "I will instruct my staff to reset the security monitor to allow you free access to the reception area."

"Funny she didn't set off an alarm when she came in," the invisible Chert ambassador commented.

"The company of Ambassador McAllister would have prevented it," Srythlan replied slowly.

Aainda loaded her plate with fruit salad from Earth trees cultivated on the station, and Kelly followed suit, adding a few crackers and pouring herself a half-glass of wine from the bottle Czeros had nearly depleted. She couldn't help watching the Vergallian out of the corner of her eye to see if she would carry on with her deception. It

47

was obvious that all of their colleagues had either been informed by their own intelligence people beforehand or had figured it out on the spot, but Aainda appeared to be as perfectly relaxed and poised as always.

The ambassadors had all worked out their places at the table and started on their food by the time their host made it back to his seat with a small wooden box of salt cod imported from Earth and called the meeting to order.

"A small matter of official business before we begin," Srythlan announced, and several of the other ambassadors groaned with their mouths full. "Today's meeting marks the third time in a row I have hosted, and protocol requires that our next meeting be held in the embassy of another nuisance-species treaty signatory."

"Booked up solid," the Grenouthian announced immediately. "Our network is shooting a docudrama about diplomacy and I'll be lucky if I can get into my office for the next ten cycles, much less our conference room."

"My sisters are uncomfortable enough with my attending these nuisance-species meetings without hosting one," Gwen Two excused herself apologetically. "It wasn't so long ago that some of you tried to add clones to the nuisance-species list."

"We're still decontaminating from our last interspecies meeting," Ortha said. "I suspect the Fillinduck was molting."

"We hosted the meeting before you," Crute pointed out.

"And we hosted before the Dollnicks," Bork said.

"I would be honored—" Aainda began, but Czeros cut her off.

"No, no. You just arrived and should be given time to settle in. It's between you and me," the Frunge ambassador said to the Chert. "Rock, foil, scimitar?"

"Wait a minute," Kelly interjected. "I'd be happy to host the meeting. It's every two cycles, right?"

"I don't think we could all squeeze into your office," Czeros said apologetically.

"We're expanding our embassy into the old travel agency office next door," Kelly declared proudly. "I signed the Stryx lease and we're shopping for contractors to do a quick renovation. I'm sure it will be ready long before the next meeting."

"Have you issued the RFP?" Crute asked.

"The what?"

"Request For Proposals," the Dollnick explained patiently. "Or are you planning to award the contract to a favored family member without a bid process?"

"Of course not. I've never really done anything like this before but I was going to contact three contractors for prices."

"And then what?" Bork asked, taking a napkin in his tentacle and carefully wiping the crumbs from his vest.

"I'll—I'm not sure," Kelly admitted. "I guess I'll take the middle bid since I don't want to overpay, but I don't want sloppy work either."

"That makes no sense at all," Crute informed her. "Let me send over an engineering firm and they'll draw up plans for your approval. After that, the contractors will know exactly what they're bidding on."

"It's just a conference room," Kelly protested. "I want to have a counter removed, maybe change the lighting, and get a new entry cut through to our embassy's lobby, but other than that, it's just interior decorating."

All of the ambassadors stopped chewing and a sudden silence blanketed the room.

"Did you say you want to cut in a new entrance?" Crute whispered.

"What's the big deal?"

"Have you discussed this with the Stryx?" Ortha inquired.

"They rented me the space. Of course they know I want an entrance from the embassy."

"It's not regular metal, you know, and the honeycomb nature of the decks means that even partition walls become structural," the Dollnick ambassador informed her. "There's an environmental impact statement to file, you'll have to clear the change with the station's historical preservation society, and then there's the public meeting where your neighbors can raise objections. You'll be retired by the time it's all ready."

Kelly gaped at Crute, who suddenly pointed at her with all four of his index fingers and whistled, "Gotcha!"

"Sorry," Bork said in her ear as the other ambassadors dissolved in laughter. "There's a new Grenouthian documentary out about Human construction practices on Earth before the Stryx opening. You must not have seen it. All the spectacular collapses are worth the price of admission."

"Maybe I'll watch it and learn something," the EarthCent ambassador said defiantly. "I want to do this renovation right, and if you think about it, your future comfort in meetings is at stake as well. I welcome any suggestions you have."

"Don't forget the kitchen," Gwen Two told her. "A catering cart is fine for a meeting like this, but if you ever want to host a party, you really need to set aside a space for food preparation, even if it's not fully equipped."

"Hear, hear," the ambassadors rumbled their agreement.

"And a cloak room," Aainda suggested. "It doesn't have to be large, but you don't want your guests all piling their coats on a chair in the corner."

"I hadn't thought about that," Kelly said. "The travel agency was around the same size as our current embassy so it's not that large of a space, but maybe we can have the whole wall removed so it opens on our current reception area."

"May I?" the Grenouthian ambassador asked their Verlock host, who nodded his approval. The giant bunny activated a device on his wrist, and a large hologram of the EarthCent embassy and the adjoining space appeared over the conference table, complete with dimensions and materials. "The ambassador is talking about removing this wall," he said, waving that divider out of existence with a paw. "Putting aside any structural considerations, which I'm sure are minimal, I would locate the kitchen in this corner."

"That's my office," Kelly objected.

"The cloakroom could go there," Crute said, poking at the hologram with a laser pointer taken from his utility belt.

"That's where my embassy manager sits."

"The cloakroom has to be at the entrance," the Dollnick pointed out. "If it's not here then you'll have to sacrifice space in your conference room. If you insist on keeping your corner office—"

"Yes," Kelly said firmly.

"—then you should put the cloakroom where I said and make this room the kitchen."

"But that's Daniel's office."

"Perhaps we should form a committee," the Frunge ambassador suggested mischievously.

"Or, you could hire a construction management firm like Ambassador Crute suggested," Bork said. "There's no need to reinvent the wheel in this case, and I can suggest a Drazen consortium that specializes in rapid station renovations for retailers."

"That's a good idea," Kelly said. "I know from my friends that shops don't make any money while they're under construction so they need to get through it quickly. I'll check into it right after the meeting, but what I want to know," she added, turning to the Grenouthian ambassador, "is why are you walking around with the plans to our embassy on your wrist?"

"Oh, please," the bunny retorted. "The plans aren't on my wrist. I'm pulling them from our station subnet, and I'm sure all of the ambassadors here could have done the same. Am I right?"

"It's what we pay our intelligence people for," Ortha added after a general chorus of assents. "If you're not getting access to our embassy plans, Ambassador McAllister, I suggest it may be time to replace your minister of intelligence."

"But I'm the minister of intelligence."

"He knows that," Bork muttered. "It's just his way of welcoming you back from sabbatical."

Five

"Don't go in," Joe warned Samuel. "We're waiting for Jeeves to get here and disarm any security systems."

"Didn't Baa do that when she brought the ship in?"

"She said she wasn't sure she remembered every little thing, and what amounts to a 'little thing' for her could turn into a hole in the head for us. I asked Libby for any technical plans to Terragram vessels in her library, but they come under the 'competitive information' exclusion."

"It sure doesn't look like much," the teen said, tilting his head back to study the vessel's prow. "Where does it fall on the Dollnick scale?"

"Class H, if you considered it to be a yacht. She displaces about two times as much space as our tug, and going by the portholes, I'd guess that it's ninety percent technical deck and ten percent bridge."

"Is Jeeves inside?" Paul asked, coming up to the other two men. "Sorry I'm late, but Aisha is on a Station Scouts thing with Fenna."

"So who's watching little Stevie?" Joe asked. "Did you call InstaSitter?"

"Dorothy and Kevin took him. They're practicing being parents."

"I think it's really neat that Kevin has set up as a chandler," Samuel said. "I was afraid that he was going to go back to trading on his own, and then Dorothy would be moping around the whole time."

"Selling ship supplies is a good match for our repair business and I'm glad to see the bay doors getting more use," his father said, gesturing up at the ceiling which opened onto Union Station's core. "The traders like dealing with Kevin because he put in ten years out there himself and knows what they're up against. We had a twelve-man trader stop by the other day, and if the size of the vessels keeps going up, he'll have to hire somebody to start running the supplies out to them in a bumboat."

"If his business keeps growing we won't have room for it in Mac's Bones unless you evict the EarthCent Intelligence training camp," Paul commented.

"Don't do that," Jeeves said, floating up to the group. "The other species will suspect it's a strategic move, and then they'll all run around the station planting new bugs and drilling holes in the bulkheads."

"Thanks for coming, Jeeves. Are you sure there's nothing in there that can hurt you?"

"This robotic shell I wear? I doubt it, but the Terragram mages have been around forever and their mix of technology and magic can be surprising at times. Don't tell Baa, but I find it interesting to watch how she does things."

"It's not really magic, is it?" Samuel asked. "I thought it was just more math that we don't understand."

"It all comes down to definitions in the end. If you believe that any repeatable action that yields the same results would be amenable to a scientific explanation if you just knew enough, than all magic is science."

"That's not a very useful reply."

"Then I'll give you my parent's stock response," the Stryx said, referring to Libby. "That's competitive information."

"Baa claims she shut down everything she could remember and that you can activate the comm system on her bridge for us so she can describe the work she wants done," Joe said. "I think Beowulf must have snuck in there this morning before I woke up because his hair smells a little burnt and he won't go near the ship now."

"That may have been the atmospheric scouring system. Baa's allergic to dog hair. I'll just go in and have a look around."

Jeeves floated up the ramp into the bowels of the ship and disappeared. A minute later there was a muffled thud, and then the portholes lit up with brilliant flashes like somebody was arc welding inside. Next a sudden chill settled over the observers, and the hull of the mage's ship turned white with frost from moisture condensed out of the air. Three minutes later the frost was gone and the McAllisters all backed away as the exposed metal surfaces all began to glow cherry red. Finally, an alien orchestral score swelled from hidden audio projectors at a volume that would have sufficed for an outdoor concert.

"He must have reached the bridge," Joe said. "Baa mentioned that Terragram vessels all come equipped with public address systems for giving instructions to their worshippers on primitive worlds."

"I am the great and powerful Jeeves," the Stryx's voice replaced the music. "Who dares appear before me?"

"Is it safe to come in now?" Paul shouted.

"Those of faith may approach and be spared my wrath!" Jeeves thundered.

"And he says that we get carried away with role playing," Samuel muttered, following his father and stepbrother up the ramp.

"Is that a Cayl pile?" Paul asked Joe. "I've only seen the one, but the geometry looks similar."

"It might be," Joe allowed. "We haven't worked much on the really advanced stuff, in part because it tends to be pretty bullet-proof."

"Who uses bullets?" Samuel asked.

"It's an Earth expression for gear that's indestructible," Joe said. "Baa told me she doesn't remember how most of the technology on board works, though she was confident she could figure it out if she had to. I don't think there are that many Terragram mages around, at least in this galaxy, and if their equipment can go hundreds of thousands of years without repairs, it makes sense that not many of them would maintain an interest."

"This looks like it might contain the main drive," Paul said, patting a curved bulkhead. "I'll bet it takes up more than half of the ship's total volume."

"And it's sealed," Jeeves told them, floating out of an opening that might have been an airshaft. "Steer clear of the circle on the floor until you're ready to go up. It's a lift."

"Did you leave the capsule at the top?" Joe asked.

"No, you just stand in the circle and you'll float up. Make sure you keep your arms in when you get to the opening."

"It sounded like something blew up when you entered the ship, but I don't see any damage," Samuel said to the Stryx.

"Baa forgot to disable a robot trap," Jeeves explained. "It triggers on certain profiles of energy expenditure. I didn't want to shield myself because the reflection might have done unintentional damage so I had to go supersonic to avoid the payload."

"And what happened to it?"

"Chased me around the drive a few times and dissipated," Jeeves said.

"And the lightning?"

"Terragram mages are fond of weather effects as a method of impressing non-technological species. Her lightning circuits were fully charged and I thought it would be safer overall if I cleaned them out and transferred the energy to the station grid. Besides, she owed us a cup of electrons."

"Was the frost another weather effect?" Joe inquired.

"Executed properly, a ship hidden in rain clouds can cause snow or hail," Jeeves confirmed. "There's more to it than just manipulating the temperature, but the ship is full of such tricks."

"If they want to impress the natives, why don't they make it rain when the crops need water?" Samuel asked.

"They use off-the-shelf weather control satellites from the other species for that if they stick around a world long enough. A Terragram mage's ship like this one is built for first encounters."

"How does this circle thing work?" Paul asked, standing on one leg and gingerly extending a foot over the outline to see if it would kick up. "Doesn't feel any different."

"There's a non-sentient AI ship controller," Jeeves told him. "It's smart enough to know not to lift you until you're in position. I'm afraid it only has two speeds and you wouldn't like the fast one," he added, after Paul stepped into the circle and began rising towards the opening in the upper deck no faster than if he were climbing a ladder.

"What's the mechanism, Jeeves?" Joe asked. "It can't be gravitational nulling since our weight is based on the station's spin, and he's not wearing a special suit like the Physics Ride the two of you developed."

"It's a basic form of manipulator field, but don't let my elders know I told you that."

"I'm sure Libby can hear you," Samuel said.

"That's why I answered at the beginning of my sentence, before she could interfere."

"Come on up," Paul called down to them from the deck above. "You aren't going to believe this."

Joe took his place in the circle and was lifted by the invisible force, followed by Samuel, who was amazed by the fact that it felt like he was standing on the deck the whole way.

"Is this lift Terragram technology or do other species have it as well?" he asked the Stryx, who floated alongside for the journey. "How come you don't do it on the stations?"

"It's disruptive to living cells," Jeeves explained. "No worse than standing an hour in the sunshine for a short trip like this, but you wouldn't want to use it twenty times a day for year after year."

"And it doesn't affect Baa?"

"Self-correcting DNA," the Stryx blurted out. "Ha, that's two I've gotten past the censor."

"It looks like Baa has been raiding tombs and stashing the loot on her bridge," Paul told them. "This stuff looks like a museum exhibit from an Egyptian pyramid."

Joe whistled in admiration. "I think that's real gold on the sarcophagus, and those feathers look so lifelike I expect her to spread her arms and fly."

"It's the Terragram equivalent of an acceleration couch," Jeeves explained. "Her body is much tougher than most humanoid species, but g-forces will eventually turn any biological life into jelly. The sarcophagus pumps the occupant's lungs full of a breathable liquid, as well as filling in the space around the body."

"The Cayl do something similar for high-G reentry craft. Woojin told me about it."

"How many G's could I take in that thing?" Samuel asked.

His father flinched. "Never ask that question, Sam. Someday, somebody might want you to repeat the answer back and then take you at your word."

"I'm afraid that your brains are a bit looser in your heads than the other species," Jeeves said apologetically. "Your people will probably be better adapted to acceleration a few hundred thousand years from now."

"Clearly all of this stuff is way beyond our capacity to repair," Paul pointed out. "What does Baa want done, other than cleaning up all this mess? She could have hired the Gem for that."

"Humans are one of the few oxygen-breathing species on the station that doesn't have a history with the Terragram mages," Jeeves reminded him. "The Gem wouldn't even talk to her. Playing gods to primitive cultures has its advantages, but you can't expect to get good service from their descendents. I never would have hired Baa to enchant fashion accessories if it wasn't for the fact that role-playing enthusiasts are more comfortable with mages than your average humanoid."

The Stryx floated over to a solid black slab that was mounted under what was apparently the main viewport on the bridge. There he waved his pincer through an intricate pattern that reminded Samuel of watching a Verlock mage casting spells in a LARP competition. A set of controls rose out of the seemingly solid surface, and

Jeeves grasped a long cylinder and pulled it forward. A miniature hologram of Baa appeared.

"I wanted you to see the ship before explaining what I need," the holographic mage announced. "Basically, our standard configuration doesn't provide enough storage and I've been meaning to do something about it forever."

"But she couldn't find anybody interested in the job, at least not at the price she offered," Jeeves interjected.

"You know I'm at work," Baa told Jeeves. "The longer this takes, the fewer handbags I'll enchant today. Now, as I was saying," she continued when the Stryx wisely chose not to respond, "I had in mind storage lockers all along the side bulkheads, and they'll have to be welded so they don't come loose if I'm taking evasive maneuvers."

"What size lockers?" Joe asked.

"It's not critical. See what you can come up with from the suppliers on the station. The Frunge make excellent storage units, but you better not mention who they're for when you ask. If necessary, I'll pay you to fabricate lockers from scratch, but I want the ability to configure each unit individually with add-in shelves, and they have to be able to stand up to the G's."

"So basically you're looking for more closet space," Joe concluded.

"More? I'm looking for ANY closet space. My ship wouldn't be such a mess if I'd had a place to put things."

"Paul and I will check on what's available and send you the options," Joe said. "I'm worried about the bulkhead alloy, though. If it's as advanced as the rest of your tech, I don't think my welding rig will do it."

"I can change the chemistry of the inner surface as needed," Baa said offhandedly. "It's our version of memory metal." She paused briefly before muttering, "Oops, I think I cursed that bag by mistake. Serves me right for trying to do eleven things at once." The hologram winked out.

"She'll be the ruin of me yet," Jeeves lamented, and moved towards the shaft connecting the bridge to the technical deck. "I'll be back in a minute."

"Interesting job," Paul said, pulling out his laser rule to measure the areas Baa had indicated for the storage lockers. "Do you think we'll find something off the shelf?"

"If Baa's control over this metal is what she claims, it might be fastest to just fabricate them in place," Joe mused, thumping the bulkhead with the side of his fist. "I wonder if she'll want locks, or if the ship's security system would let us get away with magnetic seals and a mechanical back-up latch."

"You mean you're taking the job?" Samuel asked.

"Why not?" his father responded. "How many people can say they've ever been inside a Terragram ship, much less worked on one?"

"But it's…interior decoration!"

Paul stopped playing his laser rule over the interior dimensions and turned to the younger man, a wry smile on his face. "Have the aliens at the Open University been giving you a hard time?"

"How did you know?"

"You wouldn't remember when I was attending because you were just a little tyke, but I thought I was going to invent a counterweight system for small ships that would create a poor-man's centrifuge so traders wouldn't have to spend so much time in Zero-G."

"What happened?"

"I built a prototype and it worked fine, but then I learned what engineering really is."

"You mean the aliens already had something better and they just don't use it?"

"I don't doubt that, but what I meant is that engineering is the art of solving problems cost efficiently. My approach was fine in theory but I misunderstood the problem. Now that I think about it, I doubt I would have even started if it wasn't for the fact that Blythe gets sick in Zero-G. Her whole family is like that."

"Vivian too, but it doesn't sound that expensive."

"The last thing a small trader needs is to haul around a chunk of metal the same mass as the ship just to use as a counterweight, though I should really call it a countermass. But even if you get around the cost issue by splitting the ship itself into two masses cabled together to rotate around a common center-of-gravity underway, I missed the most important factor."

"What's that?"

"Lack of demand. Nobody forces people to travel space in small ships, it's a self-selecting process. Most of the people who operate small trade ships actually like Zero-G, and exercising all the time gives them something to do on long voyages. Maybe it would have made sense for the luxury yacht market, but I wanted to do something for people like us."

"There's nothing dishonest about building storage lockers, Sam," his father put in. "A man should work to the best of his ability at whatever he can do. You've helped out here long enough to know that every job isn't an engine overhaul, and given the chance, I'd rather fabricate something for a customer than change the filters in some alien technology that I'll never understand."

"That's just it," Samuel said in frustration. "I've been studying math since I was a little kid in Libby's school, and everybody is always telling me that I'm doing great for a human. But I asked Grude about his levels the other day, and I'd be lucky to catch up with him in twenty years, if I'm still capable of learning new stuff at that point."

"Who's Grude?" Joe asked.

"Dollnick student, he sat on Samuel's committee for Flower's refit," Paul said.

"His father is a baker but he's always wanted to be a spaceship engineer and the Dollnick shipyards won't give him an internship," Samuel explained. "He wants it so bad that he's planning on interning for the Sharf."

"And you don't want it that bad?" Joe guessed. "If you're interested in my opinion, the galaxy has too many spaceship engineers and not enough bakers."

"I don't want to give up. I already dropped Vergallian Studies and I've been at the Open University almost three years. If I change majors again it will be like I've wasted all that time."

"You know that I never had any higher education, Sam," his father said. "It's all been on-the-job learning for me, and that's what's needed for this kind of work. I can follow Dollnick and Sharf blueprints, and even though I'll never understand the theory behind any of the advanced tech, I've got a good enough feel for it to fine-tune the output, just like Beowulf can spot coolant leaks with his nose without understanding thermal fluidics."

"I don't know about that," Paul said. "Those Cayl hounds are pretty smart."

"I'd hire InstaSitters to watch that mage around the clock if I thought they'd do it," Jeeves declared, floating back onto the bridge. "Imagine if that cursed bag-of-holing had found its way into our sponsorship launch."

"Holing?" Samuel asked.

"Everything you put in falls through a hole and goes straight to the lost-and-found," Jeeves explained. "The thing about curses is that it takes more power to reverse them than to just start from scratch." A panel slid open on his casing and he pulled out an SBJ Fashions purse and extended it to Paul. "For Aisha. Just make sure she doesn't use it in a LARP."

"Thanks," Paul said, accepting the bag and self-consciously draping it over his shoulder. "Samuel was just telling us that he's getting frustrated with the Space Engineering program at the Open University."

"It's just that sometimes I wish that my future would make itself clear for me, like in the visions that Kevin's sister receives as a Prophet of Nabay," Samuel said.

"I'm working on it," Jeeves muttered.

Six

"Did you stay up all night painting that guy on our wall?" Dorothy asked the Terragram mage. She moved closer to the recently designated bags-of-holding enchanting workbench for a better look. "No, I don't see any brushstrokes. It reminds me more of Lynx's printed photographs, only much bigger."

"It's a mind image," Baa informed the girl, quickly hiding the tissue with which she'd been dabbing her alien eyes. "He's so imprinted on my memory that I can conjure up every last barb of his feathers."

"But how did you transfer it all to the wall?"

"Superior intellect," the mage replied, pushing an empty spray can labeled, 'Telepath Actuated Base Coat,' further under the workbench with her foot. "He's gorgeous, isn't he?"

"He's colorful," Dorothy responded carefully. With his vertically slit pupils and too-long face, the figure on the wall looked even less human than Baa, though perhaps the fact he wasn't wearing a shirt contributed to the disconnect. The feathers not only covered his arms but extended across his torso in intricate swirling patterns that made the girl feel slightly woozy. "I think I better sit down."

"He's always had that impact on primitive species," Baa said. "Together we would have been invincible."

"So that's him?" Affie asked casually, removing the shawl she often wore in the corridors and coming over to examine the art. "I've seen depictions in fairytale books but they didn't get the feather pattern right."

"He probably never visited Vergallian space, and the plumage patterns of our males are unique. Of course, I haven't been able to look at another man since he came along."

"Oh, come on," Dorothy said. "Everybody looks."

Baa shook her head sadly. "It doesn't work that way with us. He stole my heart and there's nothing I can do about it."

"I'll bet the Humans have a support group you could join," Affie suggested. "They have support groups for everything."

"Not for this," the mage repeated. "All I can do is to wait."

"Time heals all wounds," Dorothy offered hopefully. "When my first boyfriend eloped with a woman who my mom brought back from Earth, I thought I'd never get over it. Look at me now."

"It's been over forty thousand of your years since he fanned his feathers at me the first time," Baa told them. "Now I only see him when he's out of funds."

"Is that why you're so set on making money?" Affie asked. "I've always wondered about it since I've never seen you spend a cred."

"I have to be ready. He always knows where I am, and the best I can hope for is to hold onto him for a short while when he comes to me."

"That's incredibly depressing," Dorothy said.

"Not to mention backwards," Affie added. "How can such a powerful woman allow herself to be made into a slave by a display of feathers? If you were Vergallian—"

"If I were a mere Vergallian I would throw myself out the nearest airlock," Baa cut her off angrily. "Neither of you could ever understand what I'm feeling, so just drop it." Discharges of static electricity danced around the tips of the feathers of the mage's arms, and Affie retreated to where Dorothy had sat down, keeping herself between the mage and the human.

Flazint arrived at that moment, an unstrung bow in one hand and a dagger at the belt of a Forest Ranger outfit. Her hair vines were woven through a color-coordinated trellis. When she saw the portrait of the Terragram mage on the wall, her eyes went wide. "That's HIM."

"Baa's boyfriend," Dorothy confirmed.

"No, I mean HIM. The Terragram mage who coerced millions of ancient Frunge to build the Great Temple. There are statues of him all over the necropolis of our homeworld."

Baa shrugged. "We weren't together that long ago so I know nothing about it. Who else was in the pantheon?"

"Nobody," the Frunge girl said, unable to tear her eyes away from the lifelike image. "The legends say that he would block out the very sun when he was angry."

"That sounds so like him," the mage said proudly. "Why get into a knife fight when you can bring a moon? And he always had a thing for monumental building projects."

"He's coming here?" Flazint squeaked, backing away from the image.

"Don't worry, he loses interest in species as soon as they figure out multiplication tables. Besides, at the rate I'm making money, your children's children will be in their dotage before he sets foot on Union Station." Baa let out a long sigh.

"Why are you all dressed up, Flaz?" Dorothy asked. "Going on a LARP date with Zach?"

"Tzachan and I are not dating," the Frunge girl replied sharply. "We haven't even been officially introduced. He's meeting us at the holo studio in his capacity as SBJ Fashion's intellectual property attorney to make sure our new trademark for Baa's Bags is honored."

"I'd like to see anybody not honor it," the mage snorted. "Come along, girls. It's time to earn your keep."

"Where are we going?" Dorothy asked.

"You're not going anywhere," Affie told her friend. "We have to hand out bags at the LARP event we're sponsoring. I would have gotten out of it myself if I could have."

"This is discrimination against expectant mothers!"

"You don't even like role-playing," Flazint reminded her. "After the sponsorship intro, we're going up against a whole army of undead in some league play scenario that has 'Blood' in the title."

"Oh, I wouldn't care for that," Dorothy admitted. "Don't forget your bags-of-holding, and pick up plenty of loot."

The Vergallian and the Frunge followed Baa out of the office and Dorothy turned back to her table and began cutting out a pattern for a maternity frock. Out of the corner of her eye she thought she saw something exiting from beneath the fume hood Flazint used when working with chemicals. The ambassador's daughter did a double-take as Jeeves emerged.

"Mum's the word," the Stryx said, floating rapidly for the door.

"Wait a second. Were you spying on us? And if you were spying on us, why would you bother doing it in person rather than through the station security system or some multiverse trickery?"

"I wasn't intentionally spying on anybody," Jeeves said reluctantly. "Flazint complained that the exhaust fan on her fume hood was noisy and I was fixing it when Baa returned from breakfast and started mooning over that mind image she created. I didn't want to embarrass her any more than she was already embarrassing herself, and then you showed up and I lost the chance to slip out quietly."

"We should do something for her," Dorothy said. "I don't know, find her a new mage-guy or something."

"She wouldn't even look at him," the Stryx told his lead designer. "The situation is even more complicated than I initially realized, and nothing is simple with Terragram mages." He moved towards the door, then halted and spun back to the girl. "Do you have a minute to talk about Samuel?"

"Sam? But he never does anything wrong. Is he in trouble?"

"He's not happy with his studies."

"Really? Whenever the whole family eats together, he's always talking about spaceship stuff with Dad, Paul and my husband. It's like the women are having one conversation and the men are having a different conversation. I don't even know why we sit at the same table."

"Samuel wants to contribute to humanity and he's afraid he'll never be able to do that in spaceship design. One unfortunate consequence of our bringing Earth onto the tunnel network before you developed your own faster-than-light travel is that the gap between your engineering base and that of the more advanced species won't be surmounted in just a few generations."

"But he could make contributions using alien technology for humans in ways that nobody else has figured out," Dorothy argued. "Just look at our heels and my wedding gown. I don't know how the Verlock technology works, but nobody used it the way we're using it in our products before I thought of it."

"I don't believe that will be enough for him," Jeeves said. "You know that Paul studied Space Engineering at the Open University for years, but other than a few of our Libbyland projects, he's never really put the knowledge to work. Imagine if every new fashion you designed, somebody told you that the aliens have already done it a hundred times better and proved it to you."

Dorothy frowned. "Maybe they have and maybe they haven't, but I'm going to keep trying. Otherwise everybody would just sit at home watching Vergallian dramas all day."

"I have my own ideas on what would be good for everybody, but you know that we avoid actively interfering with your development," Jeeves said, crossing his pincer manipulators to cancel out the obvious lie. "As Samuel's sister, what career do you think would suit him?"

Dorothy was struck by the seriousness of the Stryx's question and took longer than her usual half-a-second to respond.

"He's always been good with aliens," she eventually said. "It's probably because he was on 'Let's Make Friends' so young, before Aisha raised the age for humans by a year. Maybe something in interspecies relations?"

"I was thinking along those lines myself. I'd better go catch up with the others before Baa turns all of our potential customers into zombies." Jeeves began moving for the door again, and then halted for a moment to add, "You shouldn't spend too long sitting in one position. I put in a Stryxnet call to Flower myself, and M793qK says that—"

"Go!" Dorothy commanded, pointing at the exit, and didn't drop her arm until the Stryx had left the room. As soon as the door slid shut behind him, she got up and followed, turning left in the hall and entering the conference room. There she took a few minutes doing the basic stretches that the Farling doctor had taught Chastity, who had insisted on passing them along. "Libby?"

"Yes, Dorothy," the station librarian answered immediately.

"Can you show me what's happening at the LARP that everybody went to? I never watched any of that league play, but I guess it's practically part of the job now."

"It does seem unfair that the others are off playing while you're stuck at work," Libby said.

A holographic projection similar to that generated by a standard home entertainment immersive system appeared over the conference table. About a third of the hologram was given over to a pair of commentators standing in some sort of studio space which was loaded with displays for the Drazen doing the play-by-play to follow the action. The color commentator, not surprisingly, was a Horten.

"...and we're kicking off the season with a new sponsor," the Horten was saying. "Every participant in today's LARP will be receiving a bespoke bag-of-holding from Baa's Bags."

"Fashions to die for, or kill for, or something like that," added the Drazen, who was apparently having trouble with the prompts on his heads-up display. "Bags-of-holding have come a long way since your days in the league. Isn't that right, Poga?"

71

The Horten didn't appreciate the reference to his age, but the endless sparring between the two commentators whose species had fallen out long before was part of their attraction as a team. "That's right, Bunky," he replied, using the diminutive form of his co-host's name, which made the Drazen's tentacle twitch angrily. "When I came into the league, we considered ourselves lucky if they gave us a sack without a hole in the bottom, and you can forget about magical weight reduction. I remember one time I took out a trio of Berserkers, and carrying their axes back to town to cash in was more work than those cheap Drazen weapons were worth." Then his face blanched yellow in fear, and he stuttered, "T—T—T—Terra—Terragram!"

"Sounds like somebody didn't spend enough time under his sunlamp this morning," the Drazen jeered, but when he scanned the displays, his tentacle stood on end. "Holy Hot Sauce!"

"T—T—T," the Horten repeated.

The hologram of the LARP space expanded into the section previously occupied by the commentators, and the view zoomed in on Baa and the two fashion designers, who approached the team of players waiting to start. The role-players had their game-faces on, and either they had been warned that a Terragram would be joining them, or they were too worried about the coming battle to be picky about their allies.

"Gather 'round, please," Baa called in a friendly manner. "I expect we'll be picking up a lot of loot today and I've brought you all new bags-of-holding."

"Where are they?" demanded a human player who had no cultural fear of Terragrams.

"Why, in here, of course," the mage said, tapping her small handbag which was embroidered with five red feathers, the highest level of enchantment the Baa's Bags brand offered. "Any ideas for this fine gentleman, girls?"

"The red backpack with a sword loop for those impractical yet fashionable over-the-shoulder draws," Affie suggested.

Baa opened her handbag, peered inside, and feigned a surprised expression for the immersive cameras as her whole arm disappeared into an impossibly small space. Then she nodded and pulled out a red backpack that was at least ten times the size of the enchanted purse in which it had been stored.

"You can keep bags-of-holding inside bags-of-holding?" the human player asked as he eagerly accepted the backpack from the mage and shrugged it on. "Does the weight reduction get multiplied?"

"It does for our five-feather bags, but mine is the only one I've created so far. Your backpack is the three-feather model, so it can store other bags-of-holding and preserve them all if you die, but the original weight reduction for each will remain in force. Who's next?"

Another human stepped forward, this one dressed as a barbarian warrior with a two-handed longsword balanced on his shoulder. "I only wear leather," he proclaimed.

"And I would never think to dress you in anything else," Baa responded. "Any suggestions, girls?"

"The one you all said I put too many studs on," Flazint answered immediately. "They give the wearer eighty percent damage reduction from backstabs."

"That's better than my jerkin," the barbarian said eagerly as Baa searched inside her purse. "Does the protection stack?"

Flazint shrugged and pointed at the feathered mage.

"Items ensorcelled by different makers always stack with Baa's Bags," the Terragram answered, turning slightly to speak directly towards the nearest floating camera. Then she pulled from her handbag a leather pack that must have weighed as much as a saddle given the number of metal studs piercing the exposed surfaces. Baa dangled it from one finger before handing it over to the barbarian, whose arm dropped towards the deck when he took on the unexpectedly heavy load. "Four feathers give it a ninety-five percent weight reduction for contents. I thought I'd better compensate for the mass of the fashion statement."

As the barbarian shouldered his way into the pack, the alien role-players, emboldened by the generosity of the easy-going mage, pushed forward and began stating their requirements.

"I can't believe how good she is at this," Flazint whispered to Affie as the mage made an on-the-spot adjustment for a healer who wanted a special cooler section to keep herbs at the height of their potency. "She's really putting everybody at ease."

"Shaina told me that she gets a percentage of everything sold under the Baa's Bags brand," the Vergallian girl whispered back. "Look, here comes Tzachan."

Flazint's hair vines turned dark green and she almost tripped over her own feet trying to strike a casual pose.

"The private conversation wasn't part of the broadcast," Libby reassured Dorothy as the holographic view pulled back and the side-hologram of the commentators reappeared. "I just didn't want you to feel left out."

"But I do feel left out," the girl complained. "I could have been there for this part. It's basically a fashion show until the fighting starts." Dorothy's eyes lit up. "Hey, that gives me a great idea."

"Care to share with your former teacher?"

"We could have a fashion show for our LARPing line, but rather than the models strutting up and down a catwalk, they'd do combat stuff to show off the enchantments. It would have to happen real quick or the viewers would get caught up in the action rather than paying attention to our products."

"Something like the Vergallian fitting rooms?" the station librarian prompted.

"Exactly, or like a LARP studio, but with all of the actions scripted," Dorothy said excitedly. "I'll bet Thomas and Chance could do all the programming. They're always working up holographic training simulations for the training camp."

"Paying for models and props adds up quickly," Libby cautioned her. "The commentators are about to discuss the sponsorship so I'll restore the sound."

"As soon as the Terragram mage finishes handing out her bags-of-holding and tree-boy gets over his stutter, we'll be back with zombie-riffic fighting action," the Drazen announced. "Also, we have a special bonus offer for Galactic Free Press subscribers watching today. Score the match at home and submit your total in the interactive LarpAddict box on the masthead of today's paper, and whoever comes the closest wins a three-feather bag. I hope I didn't shock you by mentioning 'paper', Poga."

"Ah, go strangle yourself with your tentacle, Bunky," the Horten retorted.

"People really watch this?" Dorothy asked the station librarian.

"It's the most popular competitive LARPing broadcast on the tunnel network," Libby assured her. "I expect that orders for Baa's Bags will increase substantially."

"Those are mainly Affie and Flazint's designs. You know I'm more into clothing and shoes."

"Are you working on a new maternity frock?"

"Yeah, I got the idea from a drama, but I checked some old books and there used to be something similar back on Earth called a 'poncho'. The great thing is I can wear it for my whole term without letting it out, and then after I give birth, the hem will just fall a little lower."

"Do I detect a new product idea?"

"Actually, I was just making it for myself, but now I see where I could use maternity clothes as a bargaining chip to get Jeeves to go along with my fashion show idea. What do you think of 'Pregnancy Ponchos' for a brand name?"

"I'm sure he'll hate it, if that's what you mean."

"Perfect. And they take a ton of fabric as well. Maybe I'll tell Jeeves that they have to be silk. Then when I let him talk me out of it, he'll owe me."

Seven

"So we're limiting ourselves to metal or stone for the conference table," Donna concluded, using her forefinger to check off two boxes in the holographic catalog projected by her display desk. "No synthetics?"

"Synthetics are fine, as long as they aren't wood grain," Kelly replied, scooching her chair a little closer to Donna's. "I like the subdued browns and some of the lighter slates. I can't see holding a committee meeting sitting around any of those pastel colors, though. They look like pre-school activity tables."

"Are you getting worried about the contractors delivering their plans and estimates yet? It's been a week since you had them all in and we haven't heard back from a single one."

"I almost wish that were the case," the ambassador said. "The sales rep from the Dollnick engineering firm that Ambassador Crute recommended came by and hand-delivered a tab with a complete set of blueprints and detailed estimates last night while we were eating dinner at home. He also brought a cake from the Little Apple and chew toys for the dogs."

"Are they too expensive?"

"Joe thought the estimate looked pretty reasonable."

"Did you ask the Dolly if he would use human subcontractors?"

"He said that would drive up all the cost estimates and double the construction time because humans are inefficient and difficult to schedule."

"Using an alien contractor would be a bit risky from the security standpoint," the office manager ventured.

"They're Thark-bonded. The Dollnick brought the certificate and everything. There's no better guarantee, because if the contractor cheated and the Thark bookies had to pay out, the contractor's premiums would go through the roof."

"The president has made himself available early if you're ready to take the holo-conference," Libby broke into the conversation.

"Tell him I'll be right in," Kelly said. "Maybe we should wait on ordering the furniture until the remodeling is done, Donna."

The embassy manager shook her head in the negative. "I wouldn't. You're hosting the next nuisance-species committee meeting and having a place for everybody to sit is the most important part."

"Other than catering," the ambassador said, rising from the chair and heading for her office. "I'll probably be tied up for an hour since this is our full intelligence steering committee meeting."

"I'll keep looking," Donna promised.

Kelly waved to engage the security lock after entering her office and sat down at her display desk, where a hologram of EarthCent's president in his own office was already projected.

"Steven," the ambassador greeted her boss. "Are you early because there's a problem?"

"If there is, I hope there's time to avoid it," President Beyer responded. "Have you started renovations yet?"

"We're still shopping for contractors. I did get a reasonable quote and detailed plans from a Dollnick their ambassador sent over."

"That's what I wanted to talk to you about. Our public relations department just finished chewing my ear off about EarthCent's contracting practices, and if I don't pass the message along, I'll get no peace in the office or at home."

"Hildy is a handful," Kelly acknowledged. "I guess that's why some organizations have a rule against office relationships."

"Have you heard about Ambassador Zerakova's fiasco with the school for contract runaways?"

"Fiasco? I heard it went brilliantly and I sent Svetlana some books for their library. Libby told me that the Stryx are now channeling human runaways to Corner Station when they can do so without being too obvious."

"Oh, the school is a great success, I didn't mean it that way. The problem is with the dormitories."

"Not enough space? Leaky plumbing? Over budget?" Kelly guessed in rapid succession.

"No, the dormitories are exemplary and the contractor came in under budget. Hildy and I went for the grand opening and stayed over in a room. It's all so nicely done that the runaways will never want to leave."

"So what's the problem?"

"You must have missed the Grenouthian network coverage," the president said sadly. "I knew that Ambassador Zerakova had conducted an open bid process, in fact, I approved of it at the time, but all of the work went to alien contractors. The bunnies had a field day claiming that we can't even do a little redecorating on Stryx stations without alien help."

Kelly sighed. "I wish you hadn't told me that. We did an open house in the new space to bring in contractors and get their proposals, but none of the human-owned businesses have gotten back to me."

"I won't try to tell you how to run your embassy, but Hildy says that this sort of thing carries a real reputational cost for EarthCent. Did I mention that the dormitories were furnished by a Drazen consortium and the school equipment was all purchased from a Verlock academy supplier?"

"So you want me to stick with human-made furniture."

"Yes, if at all possible. You can order products manufactured by our people on open worlds, and I suppose you might turn to an alien vendor for a species-specific chair, but let's keep it to a minimum."

"How about the goods being manufactured and exported from Earth by alien businesses? After all, getting them to come to Earth has been one of your greatest triumphs."

Kelly saw the president's eyes look away as he scanned his office to make sure that Hildy hadn't snuck back in. "Fine," he replied in a half-whisper, "though I'm not aware of any of them being in the office supply business. And I understand you're on a tight schedule, but if you do have to use any alien subcontractors, please don't get caught." Then the conferencing algorithm seamlessly integrated two more figures who appeared in the hologram, taking seats at their own desks. "Ah, I see the others are starting to check in."

"Good evening, Carlos," Kelly said, taking an educated guess at the Middle Station ambassador's time zone based on the fact he wasn't nursing a coffee. "Good morning, Raj," she greeted the Echo Station ambassador, who was often stuck attending the steering committee meetings in the middle of the night. "You're looking chipper."

"That's because I'll be going out on sabbatical next week," Ambassador Tamil reported gleefully. "The bench ambassador and his wife are here, and I understand she'll be spelling my embassy manager. I'm told they were just married."

"Yes, but they also worked together before their first assignment on Union Station. There's just something about this place that's conducive to matchmaking," Kelly added, glancing up at the ceiling.

"Hi, all," Belinda White half-spoke and half-yawned as she took her place in the hologram. "I don't want to drink any coffee because I'll be going back to bed after the meeting. Why can't we settle on a universal tunnel network time for humans? It makes no difference to the aliens and all we'd have to do is ask the Stryx to change the lighting cycles on our decks."

"And update our implant times," the Void Station ambassador contributed the very moment he appeared.

"Hello, Zhao," the president greeted him, and then made a show of counting heads. "Who are we missing?"

"Svetlana," Ambassador White said. "Maybe she's lying low after the Grenouthian broadcast."

"That was painful," Raj said. "I almost cancelled the Gem catering for an embassy party I threw to introduce my sabbatical replacement. But everybody hires the clones for all-species events on the stations these days so it would have looked silly."

"What's next?" Carlos demanded. "Are we going to worry about traveling on alien ships when we need to go somewhere? It's not like we make any interstellar-capable space liners of our own."

"Sorry I'm late," Ambassador Zerakova said, popping into the holo-conference. "Crisis at the new school."

"Anything serious?" Kelly asked.

"Just a bunch of Grenouthian correspondents hanging around bothering the kids about who made their school uniforms," Svetlana replied. "And the bunnies seem genuinely fascinated that underage humans would 'leave the warren,' as they put it, no matter how bad the circumstances."

"You have to remember that they've had a few million years to work these things out," the president said. "It would be strange if an advanced species made it this long without solving life's basic challenges related to rearing offspring."

"Will the Director of Intelligence be joining us today?" Ambassador Fu inquired.

"He and Blythe are planning to try out their new command-center setup," Kelly answered. "I'll just ping them when we're ready, and if it doesn't work, they can ask the station librarian to patch them in."

"Let's get started, then," President Beyer declared. "The topic for today is Vergallians, or to be more specific, Ambassador Aainda on Union Station. Kelly has some very interesting news to share with you all, but I wanted her to wait and do it in person so we can stress the need for secrecy."

"If all of us are about to know, it can hardly remain a secret," Zhao pointed out. "I've recently been informed by my wife that I'm talking in my sleep."

"It's not a secret-secret," Kelly explained. "It's more of a supposed-to-be-secret-to-save-face secret."

"I think it would be easier if you just tell them," the president said.

"You all know that Vergallian ambassadors are rotated through the embassies around once every two years. Our intelligence people suggest a number of reasons for this, ranging from imperial paranoia to a desire to get back home before their opposition takes heart and revolts."

"Our current Vergallian ambassador left her eldest daughter in charge back home when she was posted to Corner Station," Svetlana informed them, "but she's the first serving queen I've known to take the job."

"From what Aainda has told me, the mature women in her family take turns running things, even though only one of them can officially be queen. She hinted that it's common practice outside of the core worlds of the empire, where tradition is iron-clad."

"That's interesting information," Raj said. "I recall that one of our Vergallian ambassadors left her position just a few days after being appointed because an unexpected death in her family created a ruling vacancy. Their cultural attaché filled in until a replacement arrived. But perhaps she was from one of the core worlds."

"Is that the secret?" Belinda asked.

"Not even close," Kelly replied, suppressing a grin at the bomb she was about to throw. "Ambassador Aainda decided to stay on Union Station in spite of her empire's policy. First, she extended her tour through some legalistic delaying tactics, and then she announced that she had been replaced by her cousin."

"So her cousin is just a puppet ambassador," Ambassador Oshi surmised.

"She is her cousin," Kelly reported gleefully. "I mean, her cousin isn't coming. Aainda is pretending to have replaced herself and everybody knows it. Part of her motivation is to make a display of dominance over

Vergallian Intelligence, but she's also committed to helping us. The secrecy comes in because we can't run around talking about it in public. Otherwise the Vergallian imperial council will think that she's intentionally showing them up and that could end badly for everybody."

"I don't understand," Belinda said. "It sounds like a huge risk just to make a point, or is helping humanity that important to her?"

"There are personal factors involved as well," Kelly hedged, deciding on the spot that everybody didn't need to know about the Vergallian ambassador's relationship to Ailia's deceased father. "Shall I invite our intelligence director on to brief us about what they've learned?"

"Please," the president said.

Kelly pinged Clive, and EarthCent's spy chief immediately appeared in the hologram, but he looked like a little boy. Apparently he was seeing the same thing in reverse, because he turned to someone who wasn't visible to the others and said, "Bring me up fifty percent."

The hologram flickered, and then Clive was about the same size as Belinda.

"Another thirty percent?" he guessed.

The hologram flickered again, and then Clive looked more or less the right size. He nodded, and Blythe, who must have been operating the new equipment, entered the hologram.

"Do we look alright?" she asked.

"Hold your hand up," Kelly suggested. "I remember from the cave art project that Samuel and Vivian did for Libby's school that our hands were the same size."

Blythe spread her fingers and the two women brought their hands together in the hologram.

"We're still a little small," Clive observed, since Kelly's fingers peeked out over those of his wife. "Good enough for today. We'll recalibrate on our own time."

"Thank you for coming," the president said. "Ambassador McAllister has just informed us all of the intrigue on Union Station involving the Vergallian ambassador. Can EarthCent Intelligence tell us about the wider picture? Is there anything from our special relationship with Drazen Intelligence?"

"I had a meeting a few hours ago with Herl, my Drazen counterpart, and I'm pleased to say that this was one instance where I was able to bring something of value to the table."

"Due to Aainda's confession to Kelly?"

"The Vergallian ambassador's faked replacement doesn't even qualify as an open secret at this point because everybody in the local intelligence community knows," Clive said. "But this is one of those rare situations where we have more boots on the ground than the Drazens. Thanks to the tens of millions of human mercenaries and their families serving on Vergallian tech-ban worlds, we now get a steady stream of intelligence from the ones who complete their contracts. Ex-mercenaries going through the training course on Flower to become policemen for sovereign human communities are an especially good source of information."

"Wouldn't the mercenaries still serving on Vergallian worlds have more up-to-date intelligence?" Ambassador Fu asked.

"Certainly, but they're bound by their contract and oath not to spy on their employers," Clive explained. "Once they leave, they're free to say whatever they want, and since we aren't talking about battlefield intelligence, the lack of real-time reporting doesn't hurt us at all."

"So how serious is the Vergallian schism looking?" the president asked.

"At over a trillion strong, they're the most populous tunnel network species, and the main schism remains the one between Fleet and the Empire of a Hundred Worlds," Blythe reminded everyone. "There are multiple fault lines within the empire that slowly crack open or heal according to their own logic. Aainda and her faction represent the independent queens who don't pay taxes to the empire and don't have full representation on the imperial council for that reason."

"And they resent it when Vergallian Intelligence meddles in their affairs," Zhao said.

"Are you telling me that those unending drama series they produce offer an accurate depiction of the Empire of a Hundred Worlds?" Belinda asked.

"So much so that we now require our analysts on the Vergallian desk to spend at least two hours a day watching," Clive confirmed. "I know from Herl that the Drazens consider alien entertainment broadcasts one of the cheapest ways to keep up with the internal affairs of other species. It just takes a little while to learn to differentiate between production values and the underlying cultural shifts."

"Art imitates life," Kelly volunteered. "You can learn a lot about our history by reading old novels. Authors include the details of everyday living in their stories, and nobody would have read them in their own time if they got everything wrong."

"Is any of this actionable?" Ambassador Oshi inquired.

"If you mean do we intend to choose sides in Vergallian quarrels, absolutely not. But you need to be aware that Aainda's faction is much more willing to work with us than the imperial-aligned faction, and that over time, we will naturally find ourselves allied with the queens who are dabbling in open worlds that accept humans."

"Just don't let her get involved with your embassy renovation, Kelly, or the Grenouthians will be all over you," Svetlana advised.

"Easier said than done," the Union Station ambassador griped. "I was telling the president earlier that I can't even get a quote from the human contractors on the station."

"Did you give them a deadline?" Belinda asked.

"No." Kelly frowned. "Is that necessary? I thought they'd all be hungry for the work."

"I saw the story in the Galactic Free Press. You're basically just converting the space next door to your embassy to serve as a conference room. Right?"

"Are you suggesting that it's not a big enough job for human contractors to be interested? The Dollnick sales rep already delivered a full set of plans, plus goodies."

"He probably saw the Grenouthian news segment about our new campus for runaways and he's hoping to get his foot in the door in case you build one on Union Station," Svetlana said. "Either that, or—did the Dolly ambassador send him around?"

"Yes. I thought it was very generous of him."

"Family connection," several of the ambassadors chorused.

"Oh, that makes sense. Well, I guess I'll try contacting all the contractors who came to the open house and telling them that there's a deadline. Any other suggestions?"

"Get your furniture and any custom millwork ordered early," Ambassador Oshi said. "That stuff can take a surprisingly long time to show up, especially if they try to save on shipping costs."

"Can you recommend a supplier on Earth?"

"Are you avoiding wood products?"

"I'm afraid so," Kelly said. "Our Frunge ambassador is a traditionalist."

"I went with a carbon fiber composite table and added a custom mosaic covering for our conference room," Ambassador Fu told her. "It's a depiction of the Great Wall of China as seen from space."

"Where did you find room in your budget for that?" Belinda demanded. "I had to get a tablecloth for ours."

"My embassy manager has an artistic bent and she's active in the Station Scouts so she made the table into a merit badge project. Win-win."

"Are you planning a grand opening?" Svetlana asked.

"I thought we'd have a party after the first meeting I host," Kelly replied. "I only wish it could have been something other than the nuisance-species committee, but that's what was on the schedule."

"I remember my first one of those," the president contributed. "That was back when everybody still had it in for us, and every meeting, they held a vote to label humanity a nuisance. I was never really sure whether they were serious or if it was some kind of alien joke I didn't get."

"What did you do?" Carlos asked.

"I voted against, of course. Our station librarian was always a bit cagey on the subject, but my best guess is that the point of the committee was to provide an object lesson for the ambassadors to relay to their home governments. Given the number of tunnel network stations and the different mix of species on each, sooner or later, everybody will find themselves on the losing end of a popularity contest."

Eight

"Are you sure you're allowed to show me all this?" Vivian asked, gesturing at the stream of real-time data coming into the command-and-control room of EarthCent Intelligence.

"Why not?" the duty officer countered. "You're Clive and Blythe's kid, plus Judith signed on as your mentor. If you hadn't showed up so early she'd be standing next to you right now. How did you get to know the terror of new recruits?"

"I've been fencing with Judith for years. But isn't there, like, a formal security clearance?"

"A what?"

"Background checks and all of that, you know, to make sure the person is loyal to EarthCent. We do it for InstaSitter."

"InstaSitters have to be loyal to EarthCent?"

"Not the EarthCent part, especially since most of our employees are from other species, but we spend a lot of creds on background checks and psychological tests."

"That's because babysitting doesn't leave any room for mistakes," the duty officer replied. "We mainly deal with business intelligence here."

"I know that, but what about the spies in the field? You wouldn't want any of our field agents getting exposed because of a security leak on Union Station."

"The alien intelligence services already know who our agents are and most of them are registered with the local authorities for their own protection. The only spies we employ who are truly underground are the casuals, usually traders who have an assigned controller they can report to if they see anything interesting. That's the channel Darlene is monitoring this shift," he continued, indicating one of the two analysts manning a communications console.

"I guess I didn't realize it was all so informal," Vivian said, feeling somewhat let down by the information.

The officer picked up on the disappointment in her voice and called over to the field agent communication team. "Either of you ever heard of a security clearance?"

"In spy novels, maybe," replied the middle-aged man who was responsible for routing incoming anonymous tips. "I'm guessing it was one of those Earth things that was popular for a while and then kind of faded out."

"I think the Vergallians rate their agents for different factions," Darlene contributed. "All of the advanced species assume that their citizens are loyal, of course. It's not like a Drazen would ever spy for the Hortens or vice versa. But Vergallians give their primary loyalty to the local queen, not the empire. According to our sources the queens all have truth-seer ability so they personally interview retainers for all of the sensitive positions."

One of the displays the duty officer was monitoring changed over from a stream of ship location data to a security camera view of a woman standing outside the control room door staring up at the lens. The duty officer hit a button on his console and asked, "What's the secret password?"

"Open the door or I'll fail you when your next physical comes up," Judith shot back.

"I tried, anyway," the officer said to Vivian as he buzzed in the EarthCent Intelligence trainer.

"Hey, Vivian," Judith said. "I'm early so you must have been really anxious to start."

"I've been up for hours because our Cayl hound decided it was my turn to take him for a pre-dawn patrol of the park deck and dragged me out of bed. Thanks for agreeing to be my mentor, Judith. I would have felt funny doing this with anybody else."

"It's a quiet day at the training camp so I'm glad to have something to do. But when did you decide to intern with EarthCent Intelligence?"

"I finished my InstaSitter management training but I don't want to work there. My brother Jonah is more into the business than I am. I've been trying to decide about whether I'm on the right track at school and I thought I'd get more out of working here than at a fast-food job."

"Don't bet on it," Darlene put in. "I learned a lot more about aliens working for Human Burger than I did in my EarthCent Intelligence training."

"That's why we hire so many Human Burger alumni," Judith concurred.

"Vivian was just asking us about security clearances," the duty officer said.

"I was surprised that they let me come in here and see all of this," the girl said, sweeping her arm to indicate all of the screens and holographic projections, "without making me fill out any forms or anything."

"Are you worried about double agents?" Judith asked. "We don't really do much cloak-and-dagger stuff, unless you were planning on using us to launch a secret takeover of humanity."

"Not me," Vivian said, flushing slightly at being reminded of the advice from her classmates in the Dynastic Studies seminar. "But what's to keep a Vergallian face-dancer from joining and feeding us false information?"

"Beowulf. He sniffs all the recruits for us and doesn't even charge. If we ever move the camp out of Mac's Bones we'll probably have to put him on the payroll. So are you ready to see the real nerve center of EarthCent Intelligence?"

"I thought this was it."

Judith laughed. "These guys are just dealing with field operatives. The real work happens in customer service. I'm surprised you didn't know."

"That's what my parents are always telling me but I thought they were holding back because I didn't—"

"Have a security clearance," the duty officer cut her off and laughed. "I'll buzz you through."

Judith led the way and they passed into a cavernous office space that must have contained hundreds of individual cubicles. Passive acoustic shielding reduced the background conversations to a barely audible murmur, and the intelligence trainer guided the girl through the maze of partitions. Eventually they emerged at the dead center of the hall where four casually dressed analysts were seated around a table talking on headsets.

"This reminds me of the InstaSitter War Room, where we take the calls from nervous parents and stressed-out sitters," Vivian said.

"It's a little less pressurized here," Judith told her. "We call the agents working this duty in shifts around the clock our 'memory team.' They take the incoming calls from our

93

business intelligence subscribers and see if they can answer off the tops of their heads before passing the request on to a dedicated analyst."

"Four people are enough to handle all of the traffic?"

"We pay the station librarian to handle some of the screening overhead, just like you do with InstaSitter." Judith worked her way around the table and tapped the shoulder of a man sporting a military crew-cut. He looked around without breaking off the detailed answer he was giving somebody about Dollnick shipping rates beyond the tunnel network. "Mind if we listen in, Howard?"

The man tapped an icon in the corner of the screen in front of his place at the round table, and the intelligence customer's next sentence came out of a hidden speaker at normal conversational volume.

"I think that will do it, then, and I'll watch out for the exchange rate. You guys are great."

"You're welcome," Howard replied. "Thank you for using EarthCent Intelligence. Your subscription is appreciated." He tapped another icon and made sure there were no incoming calls awaiting his attention before asking, "What's up, Judith? Come to apologize for not inviting your favorite former trainee to your wedding last year?"

"Sorry about that. I didn't find out I was getting married until a minute before it happened. Do you know Vivian?"

"I wouldn't be on the memory team if I couldn't keep track of our first family's family."

"First family?" Vivian asked.

"Sure. Didn't you know that's what everybody calls you guys? It's a compliment."

"Blythe tells me they try to leave the office at the office," Judith explained. "Vivian has done her InstaSitter management internship but she doesn't know much about EarthCent Intelligence."

"Well, this is where it all happens," Howard said, hopping up. "I'll be right back." He went around the round table and returned wheeling two chairs with big orange "Observer" stickers on the unpadded side of the backrest. "How much do you know about our business model?"

"I know we sell intelligence subscriptions to whoever is willing to pay to offset some of our costs for the free intelligence we provide to EarthCent," Vivian answered. "I didn't realize that subscribers would call you with questions that they could probably get answered by a station librarian."

"It's funny how that works. The Stryx, including our librarian, have backed away from answering some types of questions for human businessmen since we've built up the capacity to do it ourselves. But there's also the fact that people paying for a subscription like to get their money's worth. We probably answer more questions about sports scores than anything else, and that's information you can find anywhere."

"The memory team members are EarthCent Intelligence's highest paid headquarters employees, if you adjust for seniority, and it's incredibly competitive to get a spot," Judith told the girl. "I've tried to get Bob to try out, but he prefers reporting for the Galactic Free Press."

"What kind of special training did you receive?" Vivian asked.

Howard shrugged. "You just have to be curious about everything and have a good memory. Judith is right about her husband being a likely candidate because most of the questions we get are actually answered in the Galactic Free

Press. One of the perks for team members is a free subscription without the ads."

"So if anybody asks for secret information, you pass them on to the dedicated analyst team?"

"Secret information?"

"I don't know. Like, which Vergallian queen is in danger of losing her throne, or where the Dollnicks are sending their newest colony ship."

"Queen Ashiba is losing her marbles and is going to be deposed by her eldest daughter any month now, and the Dolly colony ship that just launched from Prince Drume's shipyards is headed for—" Howard whistled a long Dollnick name that didn't mean anything to Vivian. "But those are hardly secrets since I learned about them from our Grenouthian news feed."

"Well, how about stuff like military secrets?" Vivian persisted.

"I don't think I've ever gotten a military-related question," the analyst said, scratching his head. "Why? Are you planning a war against one of the advanced species? I'd advise against it."

"I just thought that—I don't know. Aren't our field agents involved in espionage?"

"Industrial espionage primarily, and we try not to be too rude about it," Howard explained. "Don't get me wrong, the agents tracking piracy are deep into the cloak-and-dagger stuff, but the information they send back isn't kept secret. In fact, we have an analyst we share with the Galactic Free Press who writes the piracy updates for traders who subscribe to the paper. But the most dangerous field agent job in EarthCent Intelligence is keeping up with the human criminal syndicates that are gaining strength outside of the tunnel network."

"And do we keep that information secret?" Vivian asked.

"Only if it would put an undercover agent at risk or compromise an ongoing investigation," Judith told her. "Don't forget, we now have a contractual obligation to share our criminal findings with ISPOA, the Inter-Species Police Operations Agency. Business information aside, your parents have been shifting resources away from gathering intelligence about friendly aliens towards tracking unfriendly humans."

"I've got to take this one," Howard said, tapping an icon on his screen and glancing at the subscriber information. "EarthCent Intelligence. How may I help you today, Szcar?"

"I've got a couple of Human traders in here who are asking for half-credit," rasped the Frunge. "Name is Dailey, Mr. and Mrs. I checked the marriage certificate. Ship name is Falcon. A two-man Sharf job, looks well-cared for."

"You're all set," Howard said. "The Daileys are covered by our credit guaranty program. Is there anything else?"

"That'll do it," the alien replied and ended the call.

"We sell information to aliens?" Vivian asked in surprise. "I didn't know that."

"We run all new subscribers past ISPOA for a criminal background check but that's our only limitation."

"And what was that about guarantying credit?"

"We sort of fell into the business when the need became apparent," Howard explained. "The advanced species all have their own trade databases, of course, and the Thark bookies beat the prices most insurers can offer on guarantying business transactions, but they offer bad odds on humans because we're so new."

"And untrustworthy," Judith interjected in an undertone.

"So EarthCent Intelligence is on the hook if the, uh, Daileys don't come back and pay the Frunge for the rest of his cargo?"

"Eccentric Enterprises actually, but they pay us commission for brokering the deals. The Daileys, and other human traders, can pay Eccentric Enterprises a fee to act as guarantor. It's not as risky as you might think since the traders still have to pay half down in cash or goods for whatever deal they're making, which weeds out the con artists. My understanding is that defaults are rare and Eccentric is making a small profit on the business."

"And you remember the names of all the human traders who are buying this service?"

"First thing I do when I come on shift is check the list for pre-qualified traders who are currently docked. It's usually less than a half-a-dozen names because traders don't earn a living hanging around Stryx stations. And all of the diplomatic-grade calls from the tunnel network get routed here, but we only take business-subscriber calls from the locals. The tunnel network stations with an EarthCent embassy have their own local points of contact for subscribers, though it's just one agent per shift. Any request they can't answer gets routed here for processing."

"Oh. What's that blinking yellow symbol mean?"

"New subscriber making a first call," Howard replied and swiped the icon. "EarthCent Intelligence. How may I help you today, Producer?"

"I need Human extras for an immersive production on the station and the union rates are too high."

"I'm sorry, Producer, but we don't—"

"Cancel my subscription," the bunny ordered and broke off the call.

"Does that happen a lot?" Vivian asked.

"It's our money-back guarantee," Howard said. "We make it painless to subscribe, but it does result in quite a few expectations mismatches. We get customers who want us to spy on their spouses, steal their competitor's pizza sauce recipe, things like that. As soon as they find out we're not that kind of intelligence service, they cancel."

"What if aliens subscribed to ask for information so they could compete with InstaSitter?" the girl demanded.

"We get that one all the time, especially from Verlock clans who are enamored of your success. In the case of InstaSitter, the truth is your best defense. Between your low margins per sitter-hour and the Stryx back-office support that the aliens shy away from, they can't compete with you. And your brand is already so ubiquitous on the station network that it would take extremely deep pockets for anybody to try."

"Grab that one," Judith instructed, pointing at a line on Howard's display. "The premium package calls are usually a hoot."

"EarthCent Intelligence. How may I help you, Mister Johnson?"

"This is a little embarrassing," came a hushed whisper. "I just ran into the bathroom and pinged you."

"I understand, but we can only help with information."

"That's what I need. What was the main reason for the separation of Imperial and Fleet Vergallians, plus I need three other examples of species where major groups have intentionally split off from the main body."

"Are you working on a homework assignment?"

"Not mine, my daughter's. She's at that age where she still believes I know everything."

"Does she attend the station librarian's experimental school?"

"No. Does that make a difference?"

"If she did, our service agreement with the station librarian would prevent me from helping, but on the other hand, your daughter would likely know the answers already."

"So we're good?" the relieved father whispered.

"Yes. The Vergallians split into two groups because the Stryx wouldn't let the imperial worlds join the tunnel network as long as their colonists were employing aggression in expanding the Empire's reach. The then-navy sided with the colonists, in part because they saw a limited future in peace, and in part because the tech-ban in effect on the majority of imperial planets was beginning to impact the fleet's ability to compete on the galactic stage. The Stryx accepted this compromise, allowing the Empire of a Hundred Worlds to join the tunnel network, while the newer colonies and fleet went their own way."

"Tunnel network, navy, tech-ban, Stryx. Got it. How about three more examples?"

"The most obvious is the division in Horten society between the tunnel network worlds and the pirates. Again, the Stryx tacitly accept this arrangement, but they sometimes hold the mainstream Hortens accountable for pirate behavior because of the fuzzy separation between the two groups."

"Hortens, of course. Got anything else?"

"The Cayl," Vivian suggested to Howard.

"Another example is the Cayl Empire, where all of the excess savings of the ruling species, the Cayl, goes into building expeditionary forces that are sent off to found their own empires. Ironically, while the exiled groups maintained the military structure and capabilities of the parent group, they all chose to avoid the burden of creating their own empires."

"One more," Mr. Johnson urged.

"Humans," Judith whispered to Howard. "I've been to Earth."

"The final example is humans, with Earth being the prime example. Nearly a century after the Stryx Opening the world is still a patchwork of semi-functional nations and somewhat more effective city-states. There's more cooperation between the worlds of the sovereign human communities conference than most political entities on Earth."

"You've been a big help. Gotta run."

The call ended with a flushing sound.

"Some guy pays for the premium package to help with his kid's homework?" Vivian asked in disbelief.

"No, his company pays for the package," Judith explained. "We don't limit the hours or subject matter for premium subscribers. You'd be surprised how much easier it is to close sales when executives get something for themselves out of the deal."

A chime sounded and Howard's casual attitude disappeared as he took the call. "EarthCent Intelligence. How may I help you, Ambassador McAllister?"

"I have a quote for our embassy renovation work from Triple-A Construction and their references are excellent, almost too good. I thought I'd better see if you have anything on them before signing the contract."

"Just a moment, Ambassador," Howard said, rapidly flipping through some screens. He hesitated for a moment, his finger over the button that would patch Kelly through to the analyst who specialized in local businesses, then instead typed a query to the database and nodded at the response. "It appears they're a front for a Dollnick contractor."

"I was afraid of that," Kelly said. "Could you recommend somebody else?"

"Let me patch you through to our local business specialist, Ambassador, but finding contractors for small construction projects is always a tricky business."

"Thank you."

Nine

"You've got to talk your dad into accepting rent," Kevin told Dorothy as he heaved a case of canned baked beans onto the industrial shelving he'd welded together with his father-in-law's rig. "Anybody can succeed in business if somebody else is paying for all the overhead. I'm a trader and I pay my bills."

"You keep telling me that the business is half mine and I vote against making my dad feel bad by insisting he take our money. Let him help us if he wants. It's what makes parents happy."

"Then tell him to put the money aside for his grand-children," Kevin said.

"Just let it go for now. If it bothers you that much, keep track of what you think you should be paying and put it in a separate account. If my folks never need it, I'll spend it."

"It's not the same thing. Hey, is it safe to rest the tab on your stomach like that while you're using it?"

"Libby? Could you tell my husband that my tab is one hundred percent harmless?" Dorothy requested.

"The only health risk your wife is running by using her tab is eyestrain, and perhaps carpal tunnel," the station librarian told Kevin. "It's the standard Open University student model that she never returned. The tab is hypoal-lergenic and certified as a low radiation emitter for all humanoid species."

"I wondered why I never got back my security deposit," the girl said. "And isn't low radiation still bad?"

"The case of beans that your husband just placed on the shelf is also a low radiation emitter. Everything above absolute zero is a low radiation emitter," Libby informed her.

"Speaking of canned beans, is there really so much demand for you to have ordered so many of them?" Dorothy asked as her husband moved another case from the stack on the counter to the shelf.

"What makes you think I ordered these?" Kevin replied. "I traded for them. I got twenty cases for a recharged crystal."

"Like a meditation crystal?"

"Part of the projection system for a standard holo rig. I told the guy he could buy one in the Shuk for forty creds, but he needed to unload the beans to make space on his ship."

"Can you sell them for more than two creds a case?"

"Sell them? Why would I do that? They're worth much more as throw-ins for trades."

"I didn't realize beans were such a popular item."

"Sure, they make anything into a meal, and they clump together and stay in the can in Zero-G. Try eating peas that way and they'll be flying all over the place after the first spoonful."

"You're teasing me now. Whenever we went anywhere in your ship, I had to eat out of squeeze tubes."

"I didn't want to show off in front of you," Kevin said. "Eating normal food in Zero-G is something you have to grow up with or you never get the hang of it."

A tall woman approached the counter and asked, "Is this the chandler's shop?"

"Yes it is," Kevin replied, perking up at the prospect of business. "I've been meaning to put up a sign but it's been too busy. Heading out?"

"The McAllisters just finished tuning up my ship and I have a cargo of hand-carved chess sets that are selling like crazy at the Horten fairs lately," the trader said. "I'm just looking for a few things to top off my ship's stores."

"Twine?" Kevin asked, reaching under the counter and coming up with a heavy spool that he thumped down next to the beans. "This is the good stuff, straight from a Frunge fiber plantation."

"Well, I wouldn't say no to a ball of twine, but I'm mainly interested in supplies for myself in Horten space. I may be spending two weeks at a time on the ground and there won't be much there that I can eat. Even their water is tasteless."

"Distilled," the chandler confirmed. "The Hortens are like that. Are we talking about a cash purchase, or do you have something other than chess sets to trade? We're more into card games around here."

"How fortunate," the woman said, slipping a small rectangular box out of her pocket. "Do you know what these are?"

"Rainbow deck," Kevin said, keeping his voice casual. "Our associate ambassador brings his to a game from time to time, but I suppose I wouldn't mind having my own set."

"I don't imagine you would." The trader slipped the deck out of the box and casually threw the cards from one hand to the other in a glittering magician's arc. "Never been used in a game."

"I guess I could let the twine go for a deck."

"While I appreciate the quality of your product, I once had a spool that size unravel on me in Zero-G. It took a month to get all the knots out," the woman said, shifting into a trader's tall-tales mode. "In fact, if I hadn't been traveling with a specially trained twine-monkey, I doubt I'd be here talking to you today."

"That's all well and good, but have you ever had a hull breach the size of a can of baked beans?"

"I don't think the self-sealing hull could handle it," the trader admitted.

"These beans could save your life in a situation like that," Kevin said, slapping one of the cases that remained on the counter. "You could sleep secure at night knowing that you're prepared for a whole meteor shower, and if you don't need them to patch the hull, well you can eat them at that Horten fair."

The woman's larynx bobbed as she swallowed. "Cooked in tomato sauce? The vegetarian kind?"

Kevin slit the top case open with his pocket knife and gave the customer a can to examine. "Just arrived from Earth. Normally I'd ask for two Rainbow decks a case, but I'll trade you straight up since it saves me moving it to the shelf."

"Well, I'm not one to haggle with an old hand such as yourself," the trader said, "but I'll be needing that twine to tie up the case now that it's open."

"Let me cut some off for you."

"No need, no need," the woman said, sticking the can back in the case and putting the spool of twine on top. "I prefer to do my tying in privacy. Lots of secret knots, you know."

"If I know, they can't be very secret," Kevin called after the trader as she hurried off with her booty. He picked up the Rainbow deck and threw an impressive arc of his own.

"So what just happened?" Dorothy asked. "Did we come out ahead?"

"Sure. I could go down to the Shuk right now and trade this Horten deck for a wheel of cheese that you could barely lift."

"How much is that in creds?"

"I don't know. The point in trading is to keep upgrading, not to convert every last thing into ready money. Besides, if I can't get your dad to accept rent, it would just pile up on my programmable cred. When you keep your wealth in trade goods, it helps grease the whole system."

"Barter is better," Dorothy reflexively parroted from her early education in Libby's experimental school. "But what happens when you run out of space?"

"Instead of trading crystals for cases of beans, I'll trade cases of beans for crystals. It's just a matter of keeping everything in balance."

"Oh, here come those cute kids from that family trader that reminds me of the one you grew up on," Dorothy said. "Let me try."

"Don't give away the store," Kevin cautioned her. "The kids have been stopping by for the last two weeks and I swear they're just playing with me. We haven't completed a trade yet."

The two trader children approached the counter, which came almost as high as their necks, giving Dorothy the feeling she was serving disembodied heads.

"Are you new?" the boy asked.

"I'm just helping out today," Dorothy replied. "It's my husband's shop."

"Were you ever a trader?" the girl asked her.

"I went on a couple of trips with my husband, though he did all of the trading."

The children exchanged a significant look, and then the boy said. "You're so tall that it makes me feel small. Why don't you come out here and we'll spread a blanket?"

"Yeah, and bring stuff," the girl added. "We have plenty to trade."

"That sounds fun," Dorothy said to her husband. "I haven't had a good blanket trading session since Mist and I sat in on an EarthCent Intelligence training class for agents posing as traders. Do you have a box of items the kids might be interested in?"

"The yellow bin under the counter," he said, resigning himself to a loss. "Take the blanket too. They didn't have one with them."

Dorothy put the fringed trader's blanket on top of the yellow bin and went around to the front of the counter where the siblings were waiting and whispering to each other excitedly. They broke off to help her spread the blanket on the deck.

"Now let me see if I remember how this works," Dorothy said, settling slowly into a cross-legged position that Aisha had taught her in their first informal pre-natal yoga lesson. "Should I lay out all of my goods or do we take turns going?"

"You're the chandler, so we get to see everything," the girl said immediately. Behind the counter, Kevin shook his head but held his peace.

"All right then." Dorothy began pulling items out of the yellow bin and laying them on the blanket, and she was surprised to find that most of them were children's toys. There were fluffy stuffed animals from a multitude of worlds, various constructions that looked like they would fly if thrown into the air, and every variety of marble imaginable. Next came a whole jar of multi-colored hard candies in transparent plastic twists. At the bottom of the bin were some old-fashioned coloring books and a giant box of crayons. The children's jaws were hanging slack at the sight of the bounty by the time the bin was empty, but they both composed themselves rapidly before Dorothy looked up.

"Same old, same old," the boy said in a bored voice. "Do you see anything you want, Shira?"

"I don't know," the girl replied, trying to imitate her older brother's nonchalance. "We have much better stuff back on the ship."

"Oh, I'm sorry," Dorothy said. "Let me call my husband and—"

"No, it's fine," the boy interrupted her. "We wouldn't want him to get mad at you or anything. Maybe me and Shira could pick out a couple of those stuffed animals for our younger sisters."

"Go ahead and—wait," Dorothy interrupted herself. "Aren't you supposed to offer me something in return?"

The boy and the girl whispered to each other again, and then the boy made a show of looking around to see if they were observed before pulling an odd-shaped bit of glass out of his pocket and placing it on the blanket.

"Dragon's tear," the boy said in a low voice. He glanced up at the counter to see if the chandler was observing, but Kevin had finished shelving the cases of beans and had moved to the back of the shop. "It's from Floppsie space."

"Wouldn't that make it super valuable?" Dorothy asked skeptically. "How did you get it?"

"From a dying trader," the girl blurted out, ignoring the pained look on her brother's face. "He gave us a map."

"A map?"

"A treasure map," the girl continued. "For an island."

"On Earth?"

"In space," the boy said, deciding he couldn't do any worse than his sister. "It was a space island."

"Like an asteroid?" Dorothy suggested.

"Yes," the girl jumped back in. "And we had to dig up the treasure chest, and the only thing it held was this one dragon's tear."

"From a Floppsie," the boy asserted.

"It looks like regular glass," Dorothy said. "What do you do with it?"

Here the children's imaginations betrayed them, and after exchanging another look, they both shrugged.

"Well, I guess a dragon's tear is worth a stuffed elephant," Dorothy offered.

"And a bear," the boy said. "We have two little sisters and they just fight if they don't each get one."

"Do you have anything else to trade?"

The boy's hand went into the small belt pouch he wore in lieu of a purse and pulled out a handful of nuts and washers he'd probably gleaned from the deck while watching the men do ship repairs. Dorothy pretended to be looking elsewhere while the two children quickly picked out and concealed three more dragon's tears that were mixed in with the odd lot.

"Ready," the boy said, unable to keep a guilty tone out of his voice.

"What a nice collection," Dorothy complimented him. "I grew up around ship repairs and my father taught me the names of all the fasteners. Those are #4 Sharf washers, and this is a Dollnick reverse-threaded lock nut, and that one is—" she paused and looked mysterious, "a Vergallian loyalty ring."

"This one?" Shira asked, picking out the O-ring that Dorothy had pointed at. "It's like a metal, but it feels rubbery."

"That's because it fits all size fingers."

"It must be worth a lot," the boy ventured.

"I could go a stuffed bear," Dorothy allowed. She picked up the O-ring and slid it onto her pinkie where it fit loosely.

"I think I hear our mother calling," the boy said, deciding that escaping with their loot now made more sense than waiting for Kevin to return and veto the one-sided trade. He gathered up his collection of hardware and thrust it back into his pouch while his sister stood up with a stuffed animal under each arm. "Uh, thanks."

"Yes, thank you," Shira added, and the two children fled in the direction of their family's ship.

Dorothy repacked the remaining trade goods and returned the bin to its place under the counter. Then she returned to her seat and picked up her tab to resume reading the translated Dollnick romance where she'd left off.

"How did you do?" Kevin asked when he returned to the front of the shop.

"I got a priceless dragon's tear and a Vergallian loyalty ring in exchange for two of those stuffed animals," she replied without looking up.

"Sounds like you just made a legendary trade and I can retire."

"You keep the tear," Dorothy said, handing over the oddly shaped bit of glass. "I'm giving the loyalty ring to my dad."

"Looks like the dragon in this case was a volcano," Kevin said, dropping the supposed tear in a jar with other bits of shiny stone and rounded glass. "Someday an artist will come in wanting pieces for a mosaic and I'll make a killing. What's your dad going to do with a Vergallian ring from a cereal box?"

"It's actually a Verlock O-ring, the metallic elastomer type used for high-pressure hose fittings. Dad wouldn't let me play with them when I was a girl because they're too expensive to lose. He'll be happy to get this one back."

The sound of frantic barking came from out of sight to the left, and before Kevin could get around Dorothy and go to investigate, a trader appeared alongside a ship's mulebot. Alexander trotted behind them, obviously herding the pair towards the chandlery.

"Hey, there," the trader greeted the couple. "I didn't realize Joe had added a supply business down here."

"I'm just renting—well, squatting really." The chandler offered his hand over the counter, "Kevin Crick, and my wife, Dorothy."

"Joe's daughter. I heard you got hitched," the trader said. "I'm Hank, no last name, or maybe I've just forgotten. Must be five years since I was last here."

"The eight-man Frunge survey craft I saw coming in to park an hour or so ago? We don't see many humans who can afford those."

"Your father-in-law put it together for me," Hank explained. "It was just a salvage shell when I bought it from him around twenty-five years back. The drive is a rebuilt Sharf unit he let me have cheap, and we wired everything into the Stryx voice controller so she doesn't even have a main console. Some traders call me Frank instead of Hank because they say she's a Frankenship."

"Looked to me like she's got twice the cargo capacity of the Sharf two-man model most traders fly, so it's probably jealousy."

"Three times the capacity because I converted the cabins to cargo and live on the bridge," the trader explained. "Plenty of space with all the survey equipment gone. Just a lot of Zero-G exercise equipment and a sleeping sack."

Alexander whined impatiently at the interminable niceties.

"Oh, sorry, boy," Kevin said, and tossed the Cayl hound a crunchy dog treat. "Forgot your commission."

"I was just headed up to the market deck to stock up on supplies when your barker roped me in," Hank continued, maintaining a straight face at his own pun. "Doesn't look like you're in the fresh food business."

"I've got some onions and potatoes in the back, but it's mainly non-perishables for food. Got seven grades of twine, though, and every type of cargo netting imaginable."

"Brupt cargo netting?"

"No, not that, but I'd always heard they just went around making war on everybody until the Stryx threw them out of the galaxy."

"Saw a Grenouthian documentary about them once, bit of a hit job if you ask me. Apparently the Brupt had two methods of stowing supplies on their military vessels. One was an interlocking cargo container system, not that different from what most of the advanced species use today, but the other was self-adjusting cargo netting. No motors taking up slack or elastics, mind you. The ropes were woven from long chains of nanobots and they would reconfigure to fit perfectly around any geometry."

"Sounds a bit like overkill," Kevin said, putting another spool of his Frunge twine on the counter. "Recognize that?"

"I better. I do most of my trading in Frunge space. They consider my ship a novelty."

"They're not offended that it's a hybrid?" Dorothy asked from her chair. "The Frunge I know are pretty uncomfortable with mixing things."

"Different in trader circles," Hank explained. "Wouldn't be much interspecies trade if the traders were afraid of mixing. Besides, the ship is metal and Frunge sensibilities about food don't extend to alloys. My last stop was the metallurgical fair on Tzeba and I'm loaded with samples."

"Really?" Dorothy asked, ignoring Kevin's wince at her untrader-like show of interest. "Would you arrange a private showing for my friend Flazint? She does all the buckles and metal parts for our fashion line."

Hank shot Kevin a sympathetic glance before replying. "Anything for a friend of Joe's family, I wouldn't be in business without him. I do want to start with fresh produce since I plan to be here a few weeks, but I'll be sure to stock up on non-perishables on my way out."

Ten

"I've never seen such attractive laborers in my life," Donna whispered to the ambassador as the two women stole glances at the workers through the demolished wall of the embassy reception area. "I hope this job drags out forever."

"You have to stop reading those steamy alien romance novels your daughter publishes," Kelly admonished. "And don't forget I've committed to host the next nuisance-species committee meeting, so the renovations have to be finished on schedule."

"With a party immediately following," the embassy manager reminded her. "There's enough in petty cash to pay for something special. Our sabbatical replacements hardly spent any money at all."

"I just wish those men would work faster," Kelly said, though she couldn't help smiling back at the broad-shouldered young construction worker whose teeth were way too white to be natural. "You know, I'd swear I saw that guy in the orange vest walk past with the same metal panel five minutes ago."

"I wasn't looking at the panel," Donna said, nudging Kelly with her elbow and drawing an exasperated sigh in return. "Besides, Union Builders was the only contractor you found that was willing to start immediately."

"I wonder if they're named after Union Station or if they're actually a union contractor and the workers are slowing the job down on purpose. I should have asked when I requested a list of contractors from EarthCent Intelligence."

"Were you worried about their credit ratings?" Donna asked.

"No, I just wanted to make sure they were human-owned. There's a lot less demand for this sort of construction on the station than you'd think, and none of the contractors our friends recommended could fit us in on time."

"Could they be taking a morning break already? They're all putting down their tools."

"Who's that guy in the suit flashing a badge at them? I better go check this out." Kelly pushed her chair back from Donna's display desk where the two women had been pretending to shop for furniture and hurried across the embassy reception area. She stepped over the small gap in the deck where the dividing wall had been cut out just in time to see the last of the workers filing out into the corridor. "Who are you?" she demanded of the newcomer.

"Dick Jones, Building Inspector," the man rattled off in a professional manner while flashing an impressive looking badge. "You have no posted permit, there should be safety tape across the opening you just walked through, and it's illegal for metal panel removers to be working in a space with open lighting fixtures."

"What?"

"I don't see any safety posters about proper lifting techniques, you need a board showing the number of days since the last lost-time injury on the construction site, and there are no temporary bathroom facilities for the workers."

"They're welcome to use the embassy bathrooms," Kelly protested.

"Furthermore, none of those men were wearing appropriate eye protection, only one of them had crush-proof toes on his footwear, and the recycling bin in the corridor should be cordoned off while the lid is raised. Sign this."

Kelly automatically accepted the tab that was thrust towards her and scanned the extensive list of violations. The inspector held out a stylus, but as she reached for it, he suddenly pulled it back.

"Or, rather than getting station administration involved, we could just settle this right now. I calculate you've got a minimum of two thousand creds of finable offences, not to mention the cost of the proper permits, but I'm a reasonable man and we're all humans here."

"Are you asking for a bribe?" Kelly demanded incredulously.

"I'm offering to make your problems go away," the inspector told her. "Say a thousand creds and you'll never hear from me again."

"Just a second," the ambassador said, pointing at her ear and turning away for privacy as if she had an incoming ping. Instead, she subvoced the EarthCent Intelligence hotline.

"EarthCent Intelligence. How may I help you, Ambassador McAllister?"

"There's a building inspector on my renovation site asking for a bribe," Kelly subvocalized, her throat barely moving. "I think he's a conman."

"That's a safe bet since Union Station doesn't have building inspectors. I'm dispatching an agent. Try to stall him."

"Sorry about that," Kelly said, turning back towards the fake inspector, who was halfway to the door. "Where are you going? Hey, come back! I have the cash right here," she shouted, but the conman had already fled. "Libby! Do you have security imaging of the man who was just here?"

"Yes. Did you want a souvenir hologram?"

"I want you to send it to EarthCent Intelligence so they can track him down!"

"You know we don't interfere in these situations," the station librarian chided her.

"And you would have let him con me?"

"According to my information, it's a venerable tradition back on Earth. Construction inspection pay-offs are included on our list of protected corrupt practices for humans."

Kelly pinged the EarthCent Intelligence hotline again and didn't bother subvocing this time. "Cancel that agent," she said. "The fake inspector left in a hurry and the station librarian informs me that he wasn't breaking any Stryx laws."

"What was that all about?" Daniel asked, stepping through the opening into the construction space with a coffee in one hand. "I heard you yelling."

"Some conman came in and ran off our construction crew," Kelly replied angrily, but then something hit her. "I wonder why they went for it."

"The workers?"

"Yes. You'd think they would know better, but they just put down whatever they were doing and left."

"That does sound funny. Did you check out the outfit before you hired them?"

"All I really know is that they're one hundred percent human and they were available," Kelly admitted. "I never realized there was a skilled construction labor shortage on the station, at least as far as humans go. I guess I'm spoiled by the fact that Joe and the kids always do everything at home."

Donna joined the other two and said, "I've got bad news, Kelly."

"Let's get it over with," the ambassador said with a sigh.

"I just pinged Chastity and asked her to put me through to the editor who handles the services directory for the local edition of the Galactic Free Press. It turns out that Union Builders is a husband-and-wife business and they didn't have any more free time in their schedule than any of the other contractors you contacted."

"Then who were all the men working this morning?"

"Actors. Union Builders hired them to keep the jobsite warm until they finished with a restaurant interior they're doing in the Little Apple."

"Actors cut the opening between the embassy and the travel agency?"

"That's the bad news," Donna continued. "Union Builders subcontracted a Dollnick crew to come in and do the cutting last night. I think we better change the security codes again."

"I can't believe this! We would have been better off if I'd just accepted Ambassador Crute's suggestion two weeks ago and hired that Dollnick engineering firm to do the whole job. They probably would have been finished by now."

"Why not bring in a crew from one of my sovereign human communities?" Daniel suggested. "They're building all the time on some of those open worlds, but it's boom-and-bust, so availability won't be a problem."

"But we don't have any time to lose," Kelly objected. "How long would it take them to get here?"

"You just need basic metal construction skills and some finish workers to install the trim package, right? I'll check the boards right now and I bet I can have a crew here in four days from a tunnel network world."

"Thank you, Daniel. Please do. Donna and I will concentrate on ordering the millwork and the furniture."

"I *bet* I can have a crew here in four days," Daniel repeated significantly. "Twenty creds. Any takers?"

"If it will help get the job done, yes, I'll bet you twenty creds." The associate ambassador disappeared into his office and Kelly followed her office manager back to her desk. "I better tell Joe it's time for a poker game before we lose Daniel to the casino circuit. That's the third bet he's made with me since we got back."

"Have you won any?" Donna asked as she took her seat and called up another holographic furniture catalog.

The ambassador nodded. "He was sure that the Junior Scouts jamboree was two weeks off, but I knew that it starts on Sunday because Aisha and Paul are taking Fenna."

"I wondered why Daniel was scheduling sick days a week ahead of time but I didn't get a chance to ask. I guess he and Shaina must have volunteered as chaperones to go along with Mike."

"Whose catalog is this?" Kelly asked, her interest piqued by the holographic presentation above Donna's display desk. "Some of those benches look pretty nice."

"Choral Suppliers. It's a human-run factory town on one of the Drazen open worlds. They specialize in furniture for music halls and houses of worship, but Tinka was at our family dinner last night and she tipped me off that they're branching out into conference room furnishings. InstaSitter is trying their products in a new training room concept."

"What's that material? It looks more like marble than plastic, but the colors are so pure."

"Onyx," Donna told her after zooming in on the small print. "It's considered a gemstone on Earth, but miners on Dorl have recently discovered large deposits that make it practical as a furniture material. The onyx is glued to a carbon fiber substrate for additional rigidity," the embassy manager read on, "and the table legs can be positioned anywhere along a steel track to accommodate different lower body spacing for aliens. Some assembly required."

"That sounds ideal! What other patterns are there?"

Donna flipped through a number of holograms of tabletops, some of which were almost too bright for the eyes, then stopped on a simple black-and-white design that was reminiscent of a jigsaw puzzle.

"It's certainly eye catching," Kelly said.

"I like the way that it's all black at one end, all white at the other end, and mixed-up in the middle. It's almost like you'd be making a statement that diplomacy isn't as simple as choosing between one extreme or the other."

"You know, I hadn't thought of using the furniture to send a message. Where's the price?"

"It depends on the size," Donna told her. "Wow, they really are out to attract nonhuman business. The sizing doesn't go by table dimensions. Instead you enter the number of guests you want to accommodate, specify the species of each, and then they give you a minimum required length and width for the room."

"Put in all the oxygen-breathing ambassadors, and then add an extra Verlock and an extra Dollnick for a margin of error," Kelly instructed.

"How about multiple human spots? It is our conference room."

"We fit in anywhere, it's just a matter of the right chair height. Speaking of which, where are the chairs?"

"Um, it looks like we order those separately," Donna said as she entered one each for all the oxygen breathing species. "Should I have included the Fillinduck?"

"He refuses to attend meetings at other embassies when I'm going so I doubt he'll come here," Kelly said. "Skip the Fillinducks. If the ambassador shows up he can take one of the empty places or sit against the wall."

"There's going to be a sitting wall?"

"Bork suggested that we buy extra matching chairs and just line them up along the walls. Sometimes ambassadors like bringing support staff to critical meetings and it's normal for them to sit around the periphery."

"You never bring me to critical meetings."

"I guess I've never been to one of those. They don't come up often, but you know how far-sighted the aliens are."

"Scratch the Fillinduck, add an extra Verlock and Dollnick for a safety margin," Donna said as she made the final adjustments. "Oh. I think I better call Blythe."

"What's wrong?"

Donna grimaced and pointed to the price, which had appeared in small figures under the calculator.

"Is that five hundred creds? It seems cheap for such a large table."

"There's no decimal point."

"FIFTY THOUSAND CREDS? For a table without chairs?"

"I know, it sounds like a fortune…"

"It doesn't *sound* like a fortune, it *is* a fortune. Our combined salaries don't come anywhere near that in a year!"

"An embassy should have something nice," Donna insisted, and pinged her elder daughter through the display desk's conference calling function. "Blythe?"

"What's up, Mom?"

"Kelly and I were looking at furniture for the conference room and it's a bit more than the budget we talked about."

"Like ten percent more or a thousand percent more?" Blythe asked suspiciously.

"Well, maybe the money you already gave us will cover the chairs," Donna said, though she didn't sound that hopeful.

"Do you have a ballpark?"

"The table is fifty thousand."

"That's an awfully round number, Mom. Did you ask for a diplomatic discount? It's a human manufacturer, right? It ought to be worth something to them that their table is going to be used in the Union Station embassy conference room."

"I can bargain in the Shuk, do price comparisons on catering, and ask the Dollnick manager at the Empire Convention Center for a quantity discount, but these sorts of numbers…"

"Send me the catalog information for what you pick out and I'll see if I can talk them down. Try to get everything from one vendor to give me extra leverage."

"Love you." Donna broke the connection and beamed at Kelly. "Let's pick out some chairs and see what else they have."

One hour of intensive shopping later, the embassy manager forwarded a list of catalog numbers for all of the conference room furnishings the two women could think of. The grand total was just under two hundred thousand creds.

"I've never spent so much money on anything in my life," Kelly said in a hushed tone. "Do you think she'll go for it?"

"Blythe has more money than she knows what to do with, and if Chastity finds out, they'll end up fighting over who picks up the tab," Donna reassured her. "Besides, you're forgetting that you were a trillionaire after the Kasilian auction. You once bought a whole planet."

"No, the Stryx used me as their tool to buy a planet," Kelly corrected her. "It was fun shopping for it, though."

"Assuming Blythe places the order before lunch, delivery is guaranteed within thirty days. As long as Daniel's work crew comes through, I don't think we'll have any trouble meeting our deadline."

"Speaking of deadlines, is there a due date for my sabbatical report?"

"You haven't sent that in yet?" Donna rapidly navigated through a number of diplomatic service menus, but got caught up reading a special bulletin.

"Libby?" the ambassador asked. "Is there a drop-dead date for my sabbatical summary?"

"If you had gone out under the current rules your report would already be overdue, but since the program parameters hadn't been decided when you and Donna took your sabbaticals, the rules for you are grandfathered."

"Does that translate to a particular date?"

The station librarian affected a sigh.

"What's this announcement about changing the EarthCent recruitment process?" Donna asked. "Are the Stryx going to stop picking all of our new employees, Libby?"

"The president's office has been pushing us to allow them to play a part in recruiting for the sake of appearances," the station librarian replied. "Although we believe that our track record in selecting EarthCent staff speaks for itself, we recognize that the process works against your public relations bureau's attempt to foster a reputation for independence, so we're willing to try a hybrid approach."

"What does it say?" Kelly demanded, pleased at the opportunity to change the subject away from her tardy sabbatical report.

"A special team headed by Hildy Greuen has been negotiating with the Stryx to create a competitive exam system that will attract the best and brightest candidates to EarthCent," Donna read out loud.

"The best and the brightest willing to work for peanuts," the ambassador added.

"An announcement describing a Beta trial of the new system will be released on Opening Day. That's a week from Monday."

"You once told me that we're hundreds of years away from self-government, Libby. Have we made that much progress, or will the new system just be a show for the aliens while you continue to pick all of our key personnel behind the scenes?"

"The goal of our negotiator was to arrive at a mutually acceptable system that would identify the same qualities we currently look for in candidates. If it works as intended and cheating is kept to a minimum, there would be no need for us to override the results."

"Who handled the negotiations with EarthCent? One of the first-generation Stryx?"

"We left it to our expert on human behavior."

"Jeeves!?"

"My offspring has matured alongside your children and the creation of this new system is a test for him as well. His extracurricular activities have left him behind the other Stryx his age on multiverse studies, but this is his opportunity to prove that he's settling into a career. I expect that whatever Jeeves comes up with will serve admirably."

"The way you put that, it sounds like you've allowed him to negotiate without consulting you or the other Stryx."

"It wouldn't be a fair test if we were looking over his shoulder the whole time."

"Isn't he a bit—young?" Kelly substituted at the last second.

"He's certainly too young to take on the responsibility of a science ship or a station librarian," Libby replied. "You know that since I opened my experimental school, we've been undergoing a minor population explosion with a half-a-dozen or more new offspring a year, but with the exception of Jeeves, they've followed the path we've all taken for tens of millions of years."

"Becoming a specialist on human behavior doesn't sound like a very challenging career for a Stryx," Kelly said. "You could have bought Jeeves a full subscription to EarthCent Intelligence instead, but I suppose you know what you're doing. Still, I can't imagine that spending his time trying to figure us out can be that interesting for him."

After Kelly and Donna headed home, Libby said to the empty embassy, "It's what Jeeves does with his conclusions that makes the job interesting."

Eleven

"Over there, Fenna! To the left. That old Horten dropped something."

The two children and the dog raced for the bench where the elderly alien had dozed off, but a little Grenouthian bounded past them and reached the prize first. The Horten woke up just as the bunny was bending to pick up the fallen water bottle and he thanked the furry scout.

"You should have cut him off," Mike grumbled to the Cayl hound. "You could have caught that bunny easy and then we would have won."

"Don't be mean to Queenie," Fenna scolded her friend, and gave the crestfallen dog a big hug around the neck. "Picking up the Horten's water bottle wouldn't have counted as a good deed if we had stopped the Grenouthian from doing it anyway."

"I don't see why not," Mike argued. "My mom says it's all about supply and demand."

"Scouting badges?"

"Everything, I guess. There sure isn't much demand for good deeds around here."

"I already told you we can just pick up litter."

The dog disappeared into the bushes at this comment and returned a moment later with a food wrapper she'd sniffed out.

"Good, Queenie," Fenna praised the Cohan family's dog, taking the wrapper and putting it in her Junior Station Scouts utility bag. "Can you find more?"

"I want to help an old alien," Mike insisted. "It was at the top of the list."

"I think that's just the way you copied the suggestions. Picking up litter was at the top of my list."

"Maybe we could find somebody who's lost and help them get home."

"But they could just ask the station librarian and she'd send a maintenance bot."

"Stupid bots. That's why there isn't enough litter to pick up."

"But you said you don't want to pick up litter."

"I said that because there isn't any," the nine-year-old replied perversely. "Maybe we should just go and help build the rope bridge."

"My dad said that everybody agreed that the Dollnick kids should build it," Fenna said. "They practice field engineering on their regular campouts, and this is our first overnight."

"I don't know why we couldn't have had a jamboree with Drazens and Frunge instead of Grenouthians and Dollnicks. They're so much bigger than we are."

"The Verlocks too," the girl added. "My mom said it has to do with the clock. They try to do these things with species that are going to sleep at the same time on that day."

"They better know some scary ghost stories. They're all older than us so they should."

"You're thinking about their biological ages. My mom says we grow up a lot faster than they do."

Queenie returned with something wrapped tightly in metal foil and dropped it at the boy's feet. Mike unwrapped what turned out to be half of a sandwich and the dog gulped it down.

"Did you pick that out of a trash can?" Fenna asked the dog, and received a toothy smile and a lolling tongue in return. "It's not litter if somebody put it in the trash."

"Doesn't count as a good deed," Mike concurred, still nursing a grudge that Queenie hadn't headed off the Grenouthian from helping the Horten. Then the sound of a horn being blown in short blasts rolled across the park deck. "That's the recall. Race you back."

Dozens of children, humans and aliens, soon found themselves in a footrace for the camp area, with the bunnies easily coming in first. The dog forged ahead of the children at the end and led them directly to the row of green-and-white striped tents that the chaperones had just finished erecting.

"Is it time for the bonfire yet?" Mike asked his father.

Daniel consulted his implant. "Dusk will begin in a few minutes. Tell me as soon as you see the overhead lights begin to dim."

The other Junior Station Scouts from the human contingent naturally clustered around Aisha, easily the most recognizable person in the galaxy thanks to her hosting role on 'Let's Make Friends', the hit children's show for all species produced by the Grenouthian network. Fenna tugged on her mother's sari and asked, "Are you going to tell one of the ghost stories, Mommy?"

"You know I don't like scary things."

"We could do Storytellers, just like on the show," a brash young boy suggested. "You could start a nice story and then we could make it scary."

"I don't know if the other parents would like that," Aisha said. "Besides, Mike's mother Shaina was a Station Scout when she was small and she knows lots of ghost stories."

"As long as they scare the aliens," the same little boy said. "Just because they can build rope bridges and do math and stuff doesn't mean they should have scarier stories."

In the meantime, Paul had set up a small folding table outside of the first tent in the row and called to the children, "Who doesn't have a translation implant?"

Around half of the children lined up, including Mike and Fenna, and one by one Paul equipped them with an ear-cuff translator. After each fitting, Daniel tested the child with an alien phrase he had picked up from members of his sovereign human communities, who were always borrowing words from the host species on open worlds.

"The lights are dimming," Mike announced. He had hardly looked away from the high ceiling of the park deck since his father had explained dusk, and his words were accompanied by another blast on the horn.

"Any Frunge present?" a giant Grenouthian parent bellowed. Everybody stopped what they were doing to carefully examine their neighbors, making sure no little shrubs had snuck into the jamboree. "Everybody gather 'round the bonfire."

In preparation for the event, the bots had been instructed to set aside all of the deadwood from routine maintenance of the park deck, and the Verlock parent in charge of the fire had perhaps cheated and arranged for some heavy logs from one of the ag decks as well. Placing the wood for the fire had been the job of the young Verlock Scouts, who were too slow-footed to compete with the human and Grenouthian children in doing good deeds for

131

strangers. A dozen children from each of the four species took their places just outside the perfect circle of rocks laid out by the Verlocks.

The largest bunny, who was the scoutmaster for the jamboree, gave an order to the shorter Grenouthian, who blew a different note on his alien horn.

"Light the bonfire," the scoutmaster intoned, and a Verlock parent who was an amateur mage cast forward a cloud of dust and then blew out the air compressed in his mighty lungs. The powder ignited and created a ball of flame that immediately engulfed the kindling, causing the ventilation system to open a grille overhead and create a steady draft for the smoke.

"That was pretty impressive," Shaina said to Paul as the fire roared to life. "I'm not shy about using my voice, you know, but how are the children on the other side of the fire supposed to hear anything over the noise?"

"See the silvery coil of wire just inside the stone ring?" Paul replied. "It must be for an audio suppression field. We usually work with the Dollnick systems that are designed for privacy or hearing protection, but I'm guessing that's the Verlock version, and they're way ahead of the Dollys. It will be interesting to see how it works."

A pair of young Verlocks made their way around the circle from opposite directions, passing out long telescoping rods of some composite material for use in spearing and roasting whatever snacks the chaperones for each species provided. It didn't take long before all of the human children were waving marshmallows before the flames, and the aliens did the same with their own treats.

The Grenouthian scoutmaster gave the Junior Scouts a few minutes to enjoy the noisy fire before giving a signal to the Verlock, who activated the audio suppression loop. A translucent silvery shield reminiscent of a giant soap bubble formed a cylindrical wall around the bonfire and the noise level fell to a pleasant background crackling. At the same instant, the conversations of nearly fifty children that had previously been drowned out by the bonfire suddenly sounded so loud that they all stopped talking at once. One of the Dollnick parents seized the opportunity.

"Once upon a time there were two princes," he whistled quietly at the silvery Verlock barrier, which re-radiated the acoustic energy evenly around three hundred and sixty degrees, "who both sought the hand of the same fair maiden. Prince Gruy lived in a castle on an island reached by a long suspension bridge. He kidnapped the maiden from her seminary and brought her to his castle with the intention of making her his own on Marriage Day."

"He got her from a cemetery?" Mike asked his father while the Dolly paused to let the story sink in. "This is really scary."

"Seminary," Daniel replied. "It's a type of boarding school."

"Boarding school? That's even scarier."

"Prince Koof was unwilling to concede the contest for the maiden's hand just because his opponent had beaten him to the punch, so he called up his army and they began marching towards Prince Gruy's castle. The first day they marched forty Jursts, the second day they marched fifty Jursts, and on the third day, they came in sight of the island and stopped to sharpen their weapons."

"Is there going to be fighting?" Fenna asked her mother during the pause. "I don't like fighting."

"Neither do I," Aisha told her daughter. "If it gets too scary, just take off your ear-cuff translator."

"Chicken," Mike muttered at his friend.

"On the morning of the fourth day," the Dollnick continued, "the brave warriors began whistling their battle
tune and marched onto the bridge. While Prince Gruy's
forces remained inside their castle preparing for the
assault, the flower of Prince Koof's army crowded the
narrow road, the noise from their footfalls sounding like a
giant drum."

"Oh no!" cried one of the Dollnick children, drawing a
sharp look from the storyteller, who then rushed ahead
with the tale.

"The bridge began to sway with their steps and the
roadbed started to rise and fall. Prince Koof whistled to his
men to stop marching in unison, but it was too late, for the
harmonics had already done their damage."

Here a four-armed boy shrieked and covered his ears,
and the other Dollnicks appeared to be equally shaken.
One of the Verlock scouts had taken out a tab and was
trying to analyze the bridge's structure based on scant
information, and the Grenouthian children were suppressing yawns.

"A section of the bridge fell into the sea, and then another, and another. Many a brave Dollnick went to the
bottom in his heavy armor, while the survivors clung to
suspension cables and waited for the harmonics to settle."

The storyteller settled back into his camp chair satisfied
with the effect he had made on the young Dollys, most of
whom looked like they wished they had never heard such
a scary story.

"What happened next?" one of the puzzled human
children asked. "Did their ghosts do something?"

"That wasn't scary at all," a Grenouthian scout added
with a yawn.

The Dollnick parent appeared to be taken aback by the criticism of his terrifying tale. "You want to know what happened next? Prince Gruy was so ashamed of the bridge failure that he paid reparations to Prince Koof for his lost troops and gave up the fair maiden as well. And that's what you can expect if any of you do such a bad job at engineering," he added for the benefit of the young Dollys.

The Verlock scout with the tab raised his hand. "I think the soldiers would have had time to get off the bridge," he said slowly. "Maybe a stone causeway would fail all at once."

"Let's not get overly analytical about this," the scout-master said, and the young bunnies squeezed together to admit his large bulk into their midst. "Our Dollnick friends may lack a fine sense of what's truly terrifying, but not everybody can have a Grenouthian upbringing."

"That sounded odd," Aisha muttered to Paul.

"I think he was talking about their theatrical schools," her husband whispered back.

"Now," the alpha bunny continued, "it happens I have a true story to tell. There was once a famous director who was so brave that he entered a cursed swamp to make a documentary about a witch."

"A witch!" Fenna repeated, moving her hand near the ear-cuff translator so she could pull it off quickly if the story became too scary.

"When the director went to the Immersive Production Guild, of which he was a member in good standing, they refused to underwrite the production due to the known hazards of working in a cursed swamp."

"Oh, the risk," a young bunny moaned.

"What's he talking about?" Mike asked his father.

135

"I think business insurance," the associate ambassador replied. "Ask your mother."

"The production crew all demanded overtime pay from the first hour, and the narrator wouldn't even come on the shoot, insisting he could add the voice-over in the studio," the Grenouthian continued. "The director pushed ahead with the production in spite of the obstacles, and the witch agreed to cooperate since she wanted to be famous just like everybody else. But the schedule began to slip—"

"Not the schedule," a little bunny interrupted, and several of the other Grenouthian scouts began rocking back and forth on their heels.

"The schedule began to slip, and then, before the director even knew what was happening, they were over budget."

A collective moan came from the young bunnies.

"The director pledged his family assets and forged ahead as if he had been possessed, and finally he had enough raw content for the editing room."

"The data cans were empty!" another little bunny blurted, desperate to bring the nightmarish tale to its logical conclusion, even at the cost of speaking the words herself.

"No, my dear. The cameras had functioned properly, and there was almost too much to work with. The director slaved away in the editing room, rejecting paying jobs to reach the end of his self-imposed mission, and at the end, at the very end, when the last audio track was laid and the final credit was superimposed..."

"This is too complicated to be scary," Mike muttered darkly.

"The network gave him an early morning broadcast slot."

"Oh, no!" a young Grenouthian scout cried, and unable to take it anymore, hopped away from the bonfire.

The scoutmaster paused and hunched over, his back to the fire, the dancing flames casting strange shadows over his face. "And when the documentary finally aired against a number of alien reruns, a shopping channel, and the station's public access slot for Humans, it got a ONE SHARE," he thundered.

The little bunnies all screeched, and one of them seemed to be trying to burrow into the ground, but the children from the other species remained unimpressed.

"Maybe he should have re-edited it," a young Dollnick suggested.

"Bad business, witches," a Verlock child stated flatly.

"What did the witch DO?" a human scout wanted to know. "Did she cook children in a giant pot?"

"Cultural mismatch," the Verlock parent announced ponderously. "I believe I have a universally scary tale to tell."

"Somehow I doubt that," Daniel whispered to Aisha, who nodded her agreement.

The Verlock confirmed their suspicions immediately by starting with, "Once upon a time, a little girl found a book of math problems."

"Not math," the Grenouthian horn-blower complained.

"Don't interrupt him or it will take forever," the scoutmaster hissed.

"They were all in story form, from an alien species, with simple questions about two trains departing a station at the same time and other exercises fit for babes in the cradle. The last problem was about siblings who found a box of salted fish."

Here the Verlock scouts all pulled out pads or rubbed a little smooth spot on the ground in front of them to be able to diagram the problem. Several of the Dollnick and Grenouthian scouts slumped in their places, apparently fast asleep.

"The siblings wanted to divide their prize evenly, and they decided the only fair way was to go by their respective body masses. The oldest of them was three times the mass of the youngest, and the masses of the two middle children added together were twenty percent higher than that of the oldest."

The Verlock scouts all scratched away at their diagrams, working cooperatively with one another for the best solution. Mike pulled on his father's pants leg and said, "I'm hungry now."

"After the siblings made their final calculation," the Verlock parent continued, his speaking rate dropping to a glacial speed, "they opened the box, and it was empty!"

"Trick question," a stunned Verlock scout proclaimed. "Who would do such a horrible thing?"

"As long as it wasn't a divide by zero error," his neighbor said, and all of the young Verlocks shuddered in terror at the thought.

"All right, campers," Shaina called out brightly as she moved to the front of the human group. "Who wants to hear a real ghost story from Earth?"

"We do!" the human contingent cried, waking up the snoozing Grenouthians and Dollnicks.

"Once upon a time, there were three men prospecting for gold, and although they lived in the same cabin, each of them dug his own mine."

"Typical," a Dollnick parent muttered.

"Inefficient," commented the Verlock.

"One of the prospectors worked twice as hard as the other two, but he never found any gold. His cabin mates always laughed when they saw him fumbling his way home by lantern late at night because they knew he had dug his mine in a bad place. But one night, as the prospector labored away in his shaft, he saw a large nugget of gold gleaming in his lantern light."

"Probably pyrite," the scoutmaster couldn't help commenting. "It's much more common than actual gold."

"He became so excited that just as he pried the nugget out with his pick, he knocked over his lantern and broke it. The prospector dropped to his hands and knees and found the nugget in the dark, and then he climbed out of his shaft and headed for the cabin."

"I'll bet he picked up a regular stone," one of the other alien parents guessed, but Shaina just shook her head in irritation and continued.

"Without his lantern, he mistook the path to the cabin in the faint moonlight, and wandered for hours in the dark. Then he heard a nearby howling, and fearing hungry wolves, he began to run."

Queenie growled impressively, showing her teeth and making clear that she would never flee from a mere wolf.

"The prospector saw a bright light in the distance and put on a final burst of speed," Shaina said, talking faster and faster. "The light almost seemed to be coming to meet him, and then he tripped over a metal rail, hit his head and fell asleep."

"So it was railroad tracks," a young Dolly interrupted, proud to be the first to solve the mystery. "He saw the light from the train, and now the automatic safety system will halt the locomotive and the prospector will be saved."

"This was long ago when trains were new on Earth and they didn't have very good safety systems," Shaina said apologetically.

"They still don't have very good safety systems," commented the scoutmaster, who had done the re-edit for a Grenouthian documentary on the subject pieced together from archival footage of spectacular train wrecks.

"Be that as it may, when the other two prospectors woke in the morning, they wondered what had happened to their cabin mate. They searched his mineshaft and found the broken lantern, but the prospector was nowhere to be found. All day they looked for him, but when it got dark, they went home to the cabin and decided he had been eaten by wolves."

Again, Queenie growled, and Fenna gave the hound a comforting belly rub.

Shaina paused for a long moment, and dropping her voice to a loud whisper that was carried around the bonfire by the Verlock technology, continued, "Late that night, the two prospectors were awakened by a knocking at the door."

All of the young scouts finally began paying attention now, and some who were on the other side of the fire actually crawled around to where they could see the storyteller.

"One of the men called out, 'Is that you, Tom?' but the knocking just grew louder. Finally, they each took up a tool to use as a weapon, one of them a pick and the other a shovel, and the man with the pick used it to lift the bar from the door." Shaina stopped here and inserted her own sound effect for a creaking hinge. Queenie closed her eyes and put her paws over her ears. "And who do you think was at the door?"

"The dead guy," Mike guessed, holding tightly to Fenna's hand.

"A train safety inspector," the scoutmaster suggested.

"A mine safety inspector," the Verlock storyteller rumbled.

"A wolf," a Dollnick Junior Scout contributed.

"A detached human hand," Shaina said in her spookiest voice, and Fenna shrieked and hid her face in the dog's fur.

"Was the hand still holding the nugget?" the scoutmaster asked. "It would be a noble act to bring it to his roommates."

"Did they find the miner and reattach his hand?" a Verlock child asked.

"Sleepy," one of the small bunnies said, leading the rest of the Junior Scouts to realize that they were ready for bed as well.

Twelve

Samuel hoisted the intake bin onto the counter of the lost-and-found and began sorting through the collection of weapons and enchanted items brought in by maintenance bots on the prior shift. Ever since LARPing had become popular on the station, his part-time job had gotten a lot more interesting, though there was less time for study. He carefully examined each new item, in no hurry to begin his latest homework assignment. Then he returned the bin to its place, and after a moment of guilty hesitation, pulled out the next bin in line and repeated the process, even though he had seen the items on his previous shift.

An hour later the teenager ran out of ways to procrastinate and was calling up the first homework problem on his student tab when an athletic-looking woman in her early thirties entered the lost-and-found. Samuel turned off the screen with a relieved swipe and greeted her with his best customer-service smile.

"Can I help you?"

"My hammer is missing and somebody told me to try the lost-and-found."

"Did you drop it when you were killed?"

The woman looked at Samuel like he was crazy. "No," she replied slowly. "If I had been killed, I wouldn't be here."

"So you were too busy fighting to pick it up again," Samuel surmised as he headed back down the counter for the intake bin. "I'm pretty sure I saw a weird war hammer in here."

"Then it's not mine because my hammer is just a regular hammer," the woman said.

"You took a regular hammer into a LARP? No enchantment or anything? I'm pretty sure that the only hammer I saw was a weapon. Hang on a sec."

"I'm just going to go out and come in again," the woman announced, having reached the conclusion that Samuel was an artificial person who was relegated to working in the lost-and-found because he didn't quite have all of his marbles. "You hit your reset button and we'll start over from the beginning."

"Sorry, what?" Samuel asked, having missed that last part as he ducked below the counter again. "Here it is," he said, straightening up with the hammer in his hand, but the woman had vanished. He was vacillating over whether to return it to the bin or keep it out when she reentered the lost-and-found.

"Hi, I'm Mink. I lost my hammer."

"Back again? I was worried you changed your mind because your hammer is cursed or something. That seems to happen a lot, but we won't know until I run it through the cataloging system. Is this yours?"

"Yes," the woman said, breathing a sigh of relief. "It was my father's hammer and I really didn't want to lose it. Wait. Where are you going?"

"We have to make a record of everything that gets claimed," Samuel informed her, walking down the counter to the cataloging system. The woman mirrored his steps on the other side, keeping her eyes on her hammer. "Any last name?"

"Mink is it."

"I've never heard that one before," Samuel said, putting the hammer on the turntable and imparting a gentle spin. "I know a Lynx, though."

"It's short for Minka. I grew up on a Drazen open world."

"Claw hammer, manufactured on Earth," the cataloging system reported.

"It's being claimed by Mink," Samuel said, and handed over the hammer, handle first. "What do you use it for if it's not a weapon? Those claws look pretty nasty."

"They're for pulling nails. Haven't you ever built anything?"

"All of the time. My other job is in a ship repair facility. But I've never seen a hammer like that before."

"Did you grow up on the station?"

"Born and bred," the teen replied proudly. "Do you mind if I ask you a question?"

"Go ahead," Mink said cautiously.

"When you talk about pulling nails, do you mean..." he grimaced and tapped the nail of his left thumb with his right index finger.

"Of course not!" the woman exclaimed. "I'm a carpenter."

"Like a ship's carpenter? But they weld everything."

"Not on wooden ships, they don't. And I'm a regular carpenter. I build houses for people to live in."

"You must mean from wood," Samuel declared, as if he had solved a difficult puzzle. "I visited Earth a few years ago and my dad pointed out that some of the houses were built from wood, though it seems to me they were usually covered in plastic or metal to keep them from rotting. My grandmother had wood floors in her house."

"We use wood for building on all the open worlds. Well, not Frunge open worlds," Mink corrected herself, "but I've never been to one of those. We use nails for construction because they're fast and they work. Plus, with a hammer like this, you can always remove them," she concluded, mimicking drawing a nail out of the counter.

"Neat. But what are you doing with a wood hammer on the station? You wouldn't use nails in furniture, would you? And nobody builds with wood here."

The woman shrugged. "I've never been to a Stryx station before and friends of mine got a rush job doing some work for the embassy. I tagged along as their laborer. You know, to fetch and carry, throw stuff in the recycling bins. My friends do a lot of prefab installations."

"That's my mom's embassy. You must be on the construction crew for the conference room." Samuel grinned sheepishly. "Sorry about all the confusion earlier. It's just that the lost-and-found has turned into the official destination for dropped items in role-playing games and I assumed that belt you're wearing was some kind of battle harness."

"Just a carpenter's belt," Mink replied. "I hadn't been wearing it on the station because I'm not doing any carpentry and it's heavy, but after losing my hammer, I learned to either bring it all or leave everything in my room."

"Why did you bring your hammer to the job?"

"Oh, I had to demo the counter." Mink noted Samuel's puzzled look, and said, "I meant I had to demolish the counter, not show it to people. It was made out of some kind of composite material that the station librarian said was recycled from pressed and treated solids, whatever that means. It was glued and screwed so I had to knock it apart."

"You're still tearing out the old stuff?"

"Demolition was the main part of the job," Mink told him. "The new panels and millwork are custom fitted so it should all snap together. We're expecting everything to arrive tomorrow."

"That will make my mom happy. Sorry again for the confusion."

"It was worth having a story to tell," the woman said with a smile, and slid a five-cred tip onto the counter. "See you around."

Samuel checked the out-take bin next to the turntable again in hopes that there would be something to catalog that he'd missed earlier, but the Verlock girl who worked the shift before him had cleaned it out. Then he took his time meandering back down the counter to his stool, and just before he reactivated his tab, a familiar face entered the lost-and-found.

"Sam?" the newcomer asked, limping up to the counter.

"Harry!" the ambassador's son enthusiastically greeted his latest excuse to procrastinate starting his homework. "I haven't seen you since the last 'Let's Make Friends' reunion. You were a cast rotation behind me, right?"

"I think so, but they had already raised the age for humans," the teenager replied. "I've seen you around the Open University campus a couple of times, but you always looked busy, so I didn't want to interrupt."

"Don't worry about that. But why are you limping?"

"LARP."

"Did something go wrong with a noodle weapon or did you twist your ankle?"

"Neither." Harry put one hand on the counter and then lifted a leg straight out like a ballet dancer performing an arabesque in reverse. "As you can see, I lost my shoe."

"How long ago?"

"Half-hour, maybe? I came right here after changing. I've been playing a sun-cult priest and it's a bit embarrassing walking around the station dressed for the part."

"I didn't see any shoes in the intake bin, though I'll look again," Samuel offered. "We usually get the drops pretty fast when you get killed."

"I didn't get killed. An orc patrol forced me to hide in the swamp, and when I climbed out, one of my shoes got sucked off."

"By a holographic swamp? Did you try fishing for it?"

"Couldn't get my hand deep enough without sticking my face in the mud, and you know how realistic those LARPs are. I was trying to slip into a castle a few weeks ago by swimming underwater through the moat and I couldn't hold my breath long enough. It really felt like I was drowning as I died."

"Rough," Samuel sympathized. "If you want to hang out and wait for the shoe to be brought in, I'm not doing—"

"There it is," Harry declared as a maintenance bot with a shoe dangling from its pincer floated into the lost-and-found. He intercepted the robot before it reached the counter and relieved it of the shoe. "I'd love to hang around but I'm running late," he said, straightening up after restoring his missing footwear to its proper place. "Is there a fee?"

"Bot didn't reach the counter so it's like it never happened. See you later."

Samuel climbed back onto his stool and resignedly called up the homework assignment on his tab. An hour later, he was still struggling to quantify the parameters of the first problem in a mathematical form that made sense when Baa entered the lost-and-found.

"Daydreaming over your tab, young McAllister?"

"Doing my homework."

"I saw more staring than doing," the mage replied. "If you're not too busy, I seem to have lost something."

"Anything for a patron," Samuel said, happily setting aside his tab. "Start guessing."

"I do NOT guess, I simply have trouble remembering certain things. That purse on the top shelf looks awfully familiar."

"That one?" Samuel asked, and then took the lift platform up to retrieve it. "Heavy," he commented, weighing the purse in his hand. Then he checked the shelf for the location code and headed down the counter to the turntable, Baa tailing along on the other side.

"That's the one, I'm sure of it," the Terragram said. "My time is valuable, so why don't we skip the foolishness with the cataloging system and I'll give you a big tip."

"Last time you said you'd give me a big tip you told me to floss after eating."

"And was I wrong?"

"Purse from location PR 7-20," Samuel told the cataloging system. "Being claimed by Baa."

"Shuga bullion carrier," the disembodied voice announced. "Unable to verify claim."

"Do you have security footage?"

"Never mind, never mind," Baa interrupted. "I was just testing you. I can't be too careful with the people I take into my confidence."

"Just let me put this back, then," Samuel said, returning to the lift platform and restoring the purse to its location.

On the way back down, he noticed that the mage had somehow activated his student tab and was reading his homework assignment. "Hey. That's private."

"Your life is even sadder than mine if a simple containment field calculation is your idea of personal information. Besides, you're going about the solution all wrong."

"I've been having trouble keeping up with the math lately," the teenager admitted.

Baa smiled broadly, a strangely disconcerting sight. "I'd be happy to help you with your homework."

"In return for what?" Samuel asked suspiciously.

"Oh, nothing special. Just a little help with a problem of my own."

"Does it involve killing anybody or becoming a zombie myself?"

"Please, I can do my own killing and make my own zombies without volunteers. I just need a little help persuading a girl to do some work for me and you're ideally situated."

"Will it get me in trouble with Vivian?"

"A man who has his priorities straight. No, your girlfriend will neither know nor care."

"So you didn't come here today just to try to con the lost-and-found out of something that never belonged to you."

"Never is a long time, both of which are terms you couldn't possibly understand," Baa said, and tapped her finger on the tab. "What level have you reached in mathematics?"

"You mean like, partial differential equations?"

"I hope that's not what I mean or you may as well give up now. You go to school with Verlocks. You must have an idea where you grade on their academy scales."

Samuel's ears turned pink. "Advanced beginner," he mumbled.

"Thirteen point zero zero eight," Baa said. "There's a fifth dimensional angular component as well, but if I give you that, they'll know you cheated. You can figure out the units yourself from dimensional analysis."

"I want to learn how to solve the problem, not be given the answer."

"Then start taking remedial math courses and maybe in a few decades you'll be ready," the Terragram stated flatly. "Personally, I can't imagine why you'd want to waste your time that way."

"Can't you at least explain it in words so I'll have an idea what I'm missing?" Samuel asked, but something in his voice gave away the fact that he already knew the answer to that question.

"Mathematics is the language of engineering. I could translate the functions and transforms involved into long strings of words, but doing so would waste more time than I'm willing to invest while leaving you none the wiser. I'm surprised your station librarian even let you sign up for the course."

"I'm auditing," the ambassador's son admitted, turning off the tab. "I knew I wouldn't pass the competency test but I wanted to see what it was all about."

"Don't waste your time in school banging your head against the wall," Baa told him. "I've spent enough time around primitive species to know that strategic thinking is critical to making the most of your short lives. Do you want to be a career student?"

"No! I want to do useful work."

"Then start taking courses that will enhance your natural abilities and stop trying to force yourself into a mold that doesn't fit. Do you even enjoy Space Engineering?"

"I did the first two years."

"The introductory courses," Baa scoffed. "How many containment field theory courses have you taken?"

"Just the one I'm auditing now."

"Quit while you're ahead."

Samuel felt himself wilting under the ongoing assault, but then he rallied and demanded, "What's it to you?"

"You're the one who asked for help with his homework," Baa pointed out, "and I did my best to hold up my end of the bargain. Now it's your turn."

"So what do you want?"

"Look," the mage said, pulling up one of the loose sleeves of her housecoat. "Do you see that?"

"Everybody knows that your arms are feathered."

"Look closer," Baa said, sticking the arm out over the counter.

"They're pretty nice feathers," the teen said, wondering if the mage was trying to hypnotize him. "I guess I never noticed all the swirls before. What's wrong with the green ones?"

"Split ends. It's from wearing this stupid housecoat all the time."

"So take it off," Samuel said. "It's not like your presence on the station is a secret anymore, and I've seen you in LARPs wearing a vest."

"I promised the Stryx to keep my arms covered in the corridors. My presence upsets many of the older individuals of the advanced species, and LARPing is primarily a sport for younger people. I want you to get your sister to design me a garment that won't ruffle my feathers."

"Is that all? Why don't you just ask her yourself?"

"It's embarrassing," Baa said. "A Terragram mage doesn't ask primitives for favors."

"You just asked me."

"No, we made a fair exchange. You could suggest it to her as a way to get on my good side. After all, she used my bracelet without permission while I was sleeping."

"I guess I can do that," Samuel said, though something about the whole exchange struck him as odd. "But why don't you just design something with sleeves that go on easy yourself? It can't be that complicated."

"That just goes to show how little you know about godhood," Baa retorted. "Why should I bother when there's somebody else to do the work for me? Besides, being super-intelligent takes a lot of calories. Even in a primitive species like yours the brain consumes at least twenty percent of your available energy. I can tap into the station grid to do enchantments when I'm working for Jeeves, but designing clothes for myself would force me to waste extra money on food to gear up my intellect for a task I've never had the need to exercise before and probably never will again."

"Never is a long time."

"Don't get smart with me," the mage shot back, though she let out a laugh at the same time. "It seems you have a gift for picking up the important points of a conversation and you clearly aren't intimidated by superior aliens. If you really want to do useful work, I recommend something that involves interspecies negotiations. Will you fulfill your end of the bargain?"

"I'll ask Dorothy," Samuel confirmed. "She'll probably do it since she really enjoys a challenge." He watched as Baa carefully worked the sleeve back down over her arm, against the grain of the feathers. "What if you just wrapped something around your arms before dressing? Then you could wear anything you wanted."

"Our feathers aren't just here to enhance our beauty, they're a big part of our natural thermodynamic control system. Any protective wrapping would prevent them from erecting and I would have to shed the heat from my arms elsewhere. It's another reason not to overtax my brain," Baa concluded, and gave her arm a final shake to settle the loose sleeve. "Now, it's time for me to go back to work before somebody notices that I never clocked out."

"You're cheating Jeeves?"

"He leaves office management to his partners," the mage said over her shoulder as she headed for the exit.

Samuel picked up his tab again, and after a final look at the homework assignment, he gave the screen a disgusted swipe and navigated to the Open University catalog, where he was soon immersed in reading descriptions of course concentrations on offer.

Jeeves was waiting for Baa in the lift-tube capsule.

"You owe me a favor, Stryx," the Terragram mage said. "I'm not volunteering to participate in all of your little schemes just because you increased my cut of the profits. You and your Humans are making a good business out of my enchantments."

"I'll add you to my favors-owed list," Jeeves said, affecting a tired voice. "And don't forget you promised to behave yourself this evening. My reputation is on the line here."

Thirteen

"Come in, come in," Kelly greeted the guests from Flower. "Joe set up for the game earlier and he'll be back in a minute. Grab a seat on the couch and I'll show you my photo album."

"I took those wedding pictures, Kelly," Lynx reminded her. "Woojin and I have seen them all before, unless you've added stills from the Grenouthian crew who shot the SBJ Fashions commercial or from the station's security imaging."

"This is a new album I started for our embassy renovation," Kelly explained, fetching it from the top of the bookshelf as her friends from the Eccentric Enterprises circuit ship took their seats. "I asked Libby to capture a single security image every day and then I got Donna to print them. If you flip through the pages, it's like watching a movie," she added as she handed the album to Woojin.

"Nothing's happening," he said as he slowly flipped through the pages. "Wait, somebody cleaned up the garbage. Okay, and now they're tearing the place apart." Then he came to the end of the images. "That's it?"

"I had some trouble finding a contractor at the start but now everything is full steam ahead," Kelly told them enthusiastically. "The construction crew from one of Daniel's sovereign human communities is going to start installing the finish panels and the millwork tomorrow."

"Then we'll have something to look forward to when we return next time," Lynx said, waving off the proffered photo album. "By the way, I can report that our push to get everybody to refer to the Conference of Sovereign Human Communities by the original acronym is succeeding. CoSHC is just easier to say, even for the aliens."

"The big test will come at the next major conference Daniel is hosting, but that's not for another four or five cycles. So what's new with Flower?"

"She's begun substitute teaching in some of our schools," Lynx informed the ambassador. "Flower has always been partial to children, and I know she discusses the lesson plans ahead of time with Libby."

"The biggest change is adding Union Station to the midpoint of our circuit," Woojin said. "The Dollnick distributors were getting antsy about running down their stock of parts, but they didn't want to pay just to have a few hundred crates of this and that delivered because it's a low-margin business. Plus, the extra stop gives the aliens who signed on a break from being surrounded by humans all the time."

"And our police deployments?"

"No issues on the open worlds, but things on some of the habitats and human mining outposts were getting out of hand, and they've had to use force in some instances. That's why we recruit from ex-mercenaries."

"How about cooperation with the other species on crooked labor contractors?"

Woojin nodded. "Going well, especially with the Dollnicks. Your sabbatical replacement put us in touch with the middle managers for several Dolly princes and they've agreed to do business with the bad actors in order to gather evidence. It's almost surprising how many people there are left on Earth who will sign up with an illegal labor contractor, but the recruiters play the affinity card in poor areas and go after the young. With the help of the

Dollnicks, I think we're beginning to see a light at the end of the tunnel."

"Turning poetic in your old age, Wooj?" Joe asked, taking a seat in the living room area. "And where's the heiress to the Pyun fortune?"

"Em is sleeping," Lynx told him. "InstaSitter extended their services to Flower while she's in the parking area. I'd forgotten how easy it was to get a sitter on no notice."

"That reminds me," Woojin said. "I should call in and make sure that—"

"Stop," his wife ordered, rolling her eyes. "Men."

"Where's the beetle doctor?" Joe asked. "I set out a special leaning chair for him. My son-in-law took it in barter from some crazy trader who actually does business in Farling space."

"Probably rushing around and seeing all of his former patients," Lynx replied. "Gryph gave Flower permission to send one of her bots aboard with him, and I'm sure they'll be along any minute."

"Why would Flower send a bot to Union Station?" Kelly asked.

"She wants to play," Woojin explained. "Lynx and I made the mistake of teaching her poker and she can't get enough of it."

"I was only planning on eight players," Joe said. "I better set up a second table and see who else I can hunt up. It's a weird night because Libby scheduled some last-minute school thing for parents and the Grenouthian Network is giving Chastity an award for the best primitive news service, so that tied up Blythe and Clive as well."

"We're not playing," Lynx told him.

"Flower has sort of ruined us for cards," Woojin confirmed. "At first it was funny watching a twenty-thousand-

156

year-old Dollnick AI become addicted to a simple game, but she got so obsessive about winning that playing turned into a chore. She's even started waiving morning calisthenics for humans who will play poker with her."

"Did she hook in the Farling?" Joe asked. "He's a pretty good card player."

"M793qK always says he's too busy," Lynx said. "What with sports injuries from the mandatory team competitions Flower insists on, and a backlog of underserved patients at every habitat and mining outpost we visit, we could do with two more of him." She glanced around to make sure the beetle hadn't arrived yet, and added, "You should see the doctor with the poor people. It's not like he ever charged anybody more than a handful of creds, but he always makes sure to get something from them so they don't feel like charity cases. I once saw him accept a shiny rock from a little boy, and he keeps it on top of his DNA analyzer as if it's a treasure."

"Well, the two of you are missing out on an opportunity to win some money," Joe told them. "We have a couple of newbies coming tonight."

"Who?" Kelly asked.

"The Vergallian ambassador, for one. I thought I told you."

"I didn't realize you were on such close terms," his wife replied, letting a slight edge creep into her voice.

"We talked during the dinner at the fundraiser and she mentioned that she always wanted to see Dring at work. You remember how she bid against herself for Affie's crazy sculpture so she has to be a genuine art lover. I brought her over to Dring's a few days ago, and the next thing I knew, he asked if we had room for her at the game."

"So who else is coming?"

"Dring and Aainda," Joe counted off on his fingers, "Jeeves, with a guest who he said has never played before makes four. Herl, Doc, and we just found out that Flower is sending a bot, so that's seven, plus me," he concluded, folding down an eighth finger and standing up to welcome the Maker. "And here's Dring."

"Woojin, Lynx," the chubby reptilian shape-shifter greeted the Pyuns. "I hope your second circuit with Flower is meeting with resounding success."

"I'm not sure I'd put it in such strong terms, but we're doing alright," Lynx replied.

Woojin leaned in close to the Maker and muttered, "Watch out for Flower bluffing when she starts speculating about everybody else's hands out loud."

A giant beetle strode into the ice-harvester, and then there was a minor scuffle at the top of the ramp behind him as Jeeves and an unfamiliar bot tried to enter at the same time. Baa pushed between them, looked around suspiciously for any dogs, and then reached into her fashionable purse and ostentatiously tied a gauze surgical mask over the lower part of her face.

"M793qK, Baa, Jeeves," Kelly greeted them in order. "And you must be Flower's bot."

"For all intents and purposes, I am Flower," the Dollnick maintenance bot responded. "My Stryx mentor is providing me with additional data from the station security system to enhance the limited sensor suite of this crude extension of my presence. What's the buy-in?"

"Twenty creds," Joe replied without batting an eye.

Flower's maintenance bot popped open a side panel, revealing a mechanical counter of the type used by Dollnick merchants to make change. The bot depressed a lever, allowing a twenty-cred coin to fall from the bottom of the fattest tube, and handed the coin to Joe, who began counting out poker chips.

The Drazen spymaster and the Vergallian ambassador entered together, so deep in conversation that Herl almost walked right into Baa before he noticed her presence. His tentacle immediately stood on end and he stuttered an apology.

"Oh, don't be a baby," the Terragram mage said. "I'm not going to turn you into anything, at least not with all these people watching."

"Joe told me that we might be short a few players tonight so I invited Baa as my guest," Jeeves announced. "She's never played poker before."

"Neither have I," Aainda said, "but Vergallians play a similar game, so I hope I don't slow you down."

"You'll catch on in a hand or two," Joe told her. "I used to play some of your games in the barracks when I was stationed on Empire worlds. The main difference is we have more numbered cards and a smaller royal family, but it's backwards."

"Enough chit-chat," M793qK rubbed out on his speaking legs, and then his multi-faceted eye fell on the Farling chair Joe had put out for him. "You rented me a recliner?"

"Kevin traded for it," Joe told the alien doctor. "He wanted you to know how much he appreciates your fixing up his radiation poisoning when he first came to the station."

The beetle eased himself down on the belly of his carapace and checked the distance to the table for his uppermost set of legs, which he used for card handling. "I will have to drop in and express my surprise that a human is capable of higher emotions such as gratitude."

"I wish I had your way with words," Baa said, settling in two chairs to the Farling's left. "Where are my chips?"

"Twenty-cred buy-in," Joe said.

"I'll pay you after the game," the mage offered.

"I'll get it from her," Jeeves said, sliding the banker forty creds. "I can always dock her pay."

"Here's your vegetable smoothie," Kelly told Dring, setting the tall glass in front of him at the table. "You'll have to mix your own Divverflip, Herl. I'm not touching that stuff."

"What will you have, Aainda?" the Drazen spymaster asked as he began mixing a drink at the McAllister's bar cart.

"The ambassador's husband mentioned something about a home brew I'd like to try," the Vergallian replied.

"One for me as well," the Farling said, raising a leg. "And some of those twisted flour things with salt."

"Pretzels." Joe put the box of poker chips aside and retrieved the large bowl of pretzels he'd put out on the sideboard. Beowulf materialized out of thin air to demand his tithe and Baa tightened her surgical mask.

"Why don't you ask the doc if he's got something for your allergy?" Joe suggested to the feathered mage.

"My body may display a superficial resemblance to humanoids, but my species has been around for longer than the Farlings and our biology is too complex for them to decipher."

"The allergy is psychosomatic," M793qK retorted. "Likely brought on by feelings of guilt associated with playing god to primitive species."

"If nobody else is going to deal, I will," Flower said sharply, and her bot extended a custom-made appendage that looked like it was engineered specially for playing cards. "If you've overlooked the obvious in preparing for this party, I brought my own deck."

Joe broke open a fresh pack of cards and passed them to Dring, who gave them in turn to Aainda, who placed them in the bot's deck-sized holder. Flower immediately performed a number of high-speed shuffles that would likely have resulted in a lost finger for a biological, if any were capable of moving so quickly, and then held the deck out for the Vergallian to cut.

"What do I do?" Aainda asked.

"Just tap the top card to show that you trusted the shuffle," the Maker advised her.

Aainda tapped the deck, and then a manipulator tipped with a suction cup began lifting off cards and shooting them smoothly around the table so they stopped exactly front-and-center for each player.

"Five-card stud," Flower announced. "I find it's a good game for beginners. What's your traditional ante?"

"Twenty millicreds," Joe told her. "Two yellows."

"Hardly worth playing," Flower replied, using a different attachment to push two yellows into the pot. "We bet after each up-card," the Dollnick AI continued for the sake of the newbies. "High card showing controls the bet, and then we proceed clockwise. Do you play a bring-in?"

"Not usually. It's up to the dealer," Joe replied, somewhat impressed with Flower's level of knowledge about one of the less popular poker variations.

"Then I'll keep it simple. The bid goes to our fine feathered friend with the king showing."

"But the Farling has a queen showing," Aainda said.

"That's what I meant about the face cards being backwards," Joe told her. "And there's a single prince character called a jack instead of eldest and youngest princesses."

161

"Ah, that explains why your people never figured out how to govern themselves."

"I'll go a red one," Baa said, moving a chip into the pot.

"You're allowed to look at your hole card," Jeeves told her.

"I know what it is," the mage replied irritably. "And yours is a seven of diamonds and Joe has an ace of clubs."

"Are we allowed to use our abilities?" Flower asked eagerly. "I've been playing the humans on their level."

"No, we are not allowed to cheat," Jeeves said. "Baa, you gave me your word not to use any of your powers. I'm very disappointed."

"I can't even use my eyes? I saw your seven because you practically shoved it in my face, and Joe would do well to place his beer mug forward of his hole card, rather than behind it where the reflection is clear as glass."

"You were a little sloppy looking at your card," the Farling told Jeeves. "I also saw it out of the corner of my eye and I wasn't even trying to look."

"That's because those multi-faceted eyes of yours have a thousand corners," the Stryx grumbled.

"Does the Drazen bid?" Flower asked impatiently.

"Fold," Herl said, turning over his up-card.

"Ace-queen raises," Joe said, throwing in a red and a blue.

Dring pushed his cards in. "I'll sit this hand out. So you believe that Humans would be better governed by queens, Aainda?"

The Vergallian showed the Maker her hole card, and then mucked the hand when he shook his head in the negative. "It took hundreds of thousands of years for our hereditary ruling families to establish their bloodlines. I'm afraid the Humans don't have anybody biologically qualified for the task."

The bot Flower was operating flipped over its up-card rather than staying in. "Doctor?"

"It's a pity that EarthCent hasn't grown into a true government," M793qK commented as he folded his hand. "CoSHC comes closer to the classical definition, though the member communities seem surprisingly reluctant to take the lead."

"EarthCent is coming along just fine, thank you," Jeeves said, pushing away his cards. "It's only that their representatives lack credibility with the other species because their selection process is opaque."

"Your selection process," Baa corrected the Stryx. "Oh, take it," she said to Joe, who pumped his fist in the air and raked in the antes plus the mage's red. "The Stryx just need to make the criteria for choosing EarthCent employees public and then manipulate the process to reach a desirable outcome."

"Five-card draw," the Farling announced, accepting the deck from Flower's bot. "Who hasn't paid the ante? Baa?"

The mage made a shrill buzzing sound at the beetle, who merely clicked his mandibles in amusement as he began shooting cards around the table.

"We been looking into tests," Jeeves said, carefully bending up the edges of his cards to check what he'd drawn.

"Nearly two years of watching the schools onboard my ship has taught me that Humans love tests," Flower informed the Stryx. "They also seem to embrace failure."

"Are we supposed to turn any of these over?" Aainda asked.

"The goal in draw is to make the best five-card hand," Joe told her. "You can request up to three new cards from the dealer after the first round of betting."

"So it's the best five-card hand out of eight?"

"No, you have to give up the cards you don't want to keep before getting the new ones."

"I'm in for a red," Jeeves said, flipping a chip into the pot. "The problem with tests the way you mean them is that they only provide a glimpse of how a person responds at a particular time."

"Are five red cards a flush?" Baa asked.

"Only if they're all diamonds or hearts," Joe told her.

"So three of one and two of the other is a poor hand?"

"Unless they're all in order. That would be a straight."

"Then I guess I'll call," the mage said, throwing in a red. "So how have the Stryx been selecting candidates to date? Are all of those little teacher bots spying on the Humans?"

Herl silently pushed in a red.

"I forgot to put out peanuts," Joe said, tossing in his hand. Beowulf left his begging stand next to the Farling to go supervise the transfer of cocktail peanuts from a can to a glass dish.

Dring lifted a single red off his stack and carefully placed it in the pot. "I've studied the teacher bots to satisfy my own curiosity on a few points and I don't think it would be fair to characterize their data-gathering function as spying. Retaining some information is necessary for tailoring lesson plans, especially as the student advances."

"How convenient," Baa said, affecting a sniff that turned into a sneeze.

"Psychosomatic," the beetle repeated.

"I'm only staying in with these cards because it's inexpensive to do so," Aainda announced, contributing a chip. "My daughter used to play with the children of the mercenaries serving in our household guards. We allowed them to bring their teacher bots to the planet despite the tech-ban since they were so attached—"

"Call," Flower interrupted. "I would have raised, but at the rate you people play it would have turned into the last hand of the night."

"My own cards are acceptable," M793qK said. "Now who wants what?"

After the Dollnick AI's complaint, the rest of the betting went smoothly, with Baa eventually taking down the pot, thanks to drawing an outside straight. After an uneventful hand of seven-card stud dealt by Jeeves and won by Flower, Baa chose to revisit five-card draw, which had been established as her lucky game. She dealt slowly, as if she regretted the loss of each card from the deck.

"If the Stryx don't want to pick EarthCent employees anymore, I could do it," Flower volunteered, her winnings from the last hand having produced a marked improvement in attitude. The bot she controlled finally stopped fidgeting and executing empty shuffles, much to the relief of Aainda, who hadn't wanted to call out the testy AI on its unconscious behavior. "Just send me the criteria and I'll start harvesting candidates from my schools."

"Aren't they a bit young?" Herl pointed out.

"You have to start young if you want to train them up right," Baa said. "In my experience, good diplomats are made, not born."

"I beg to differ," the Vergallian ambassador objected. "The best diplomats are made in equal parts from professional training, vocation, and family. Of the three, only the professional training can be taught."

"Discovering their true vocation is as difficult for some Humans as finding suitable mates," Herl observed.

"It's biological," the Farling contributed, taking a sip from his beer. "Their reproductive systems are built for speed rather than endurance."

"Hey, just because I folded my hand doesn't mean I'm not here," Joe reminded them.

"There's something to be said for rapid reproduction," Jeeves ventured, peering at his cards as if he expected them to morph like a Horten rainbow deck. "Especially if somebody's daughter starts designing baby clothes."

"To go with her new line of maternity clothes?" Dring asked. "Dorothy stopped in just a few days ago to seek my opinion about hand-stitching decorative hems on ponchos and incorporating precious stones. I don't claim to have a head for business, but it seemed to me they would be too pricey for expectant mothers with other priorities."

"I've played with second-graders who were less chatty than you aliens," Flower said, her patience exhausted. "Are we going to gamble or talk about what's wrong with humanity all night?"

"You've been teaching your second-grade class how to play poker?" Lynx called over from the living room area.

"It's just an expression," Flower's bot replied after an uncharacteristic hesitation. "Or a glitch. Forget I said anything."

Fourteen

"Are you working on a poncho for a Dollnick expecting septuplets?" Flazint asked. "That thing will be dragging on the floor."

"This is a special order for my mom," Dorothy said, taking a break from the sewing machine. "She wants curtains for the new embassy conference room and the only human draper on the station has a three-month backlog."

"But the EarthCent embassy isn't anywhere near the ends of the station. It can't have any windows."

"Mom got a deal on some defective corridor display panels that are stuck showing exterior views, like the traffic coming in and out of the station core."

"But all of the corridor display panels show exterior views."

"And advertising," Dorothy reminded her. "These displays stopped accepting the advertising feed. I asked Jeeves why they don't just fix the interface, but he said the panels are too close to the end of their design life."

"Then why even bother installing them in the conference room?"

"Because the design life of the panels is a lot longer than ours."

"Oh, right. Did he say anything about, you know, using our fabric and equipment and stuff?"

"I'm sewing the SBJ Fashions logo into the corner of each drape so it counts as advertising. Besides, Jeeves would rather see me working on anything other than developing my Pregnancy Ponchos idea." Dorothy glanced at the Frunge girl out of the corner of her eye to check her reaction to the statement, but Flazint maintained a poker face. "Going by that elaborate trellis you've got on your head, I'll assume you know that Jeeves asked Tzachan to come in and talk to me about trademark issues."

"This old thing?" the Frunge girl said, touching the hair vines that must have taken an hour to weave in place through the intricate structure. "You've seen me wear it before."

"You're a lousy liar. Zach will be here at noon on our clock so I ordered crustless pizza for lunch."

"What time is it now?" Flazint asked innocently.

Dorothy glanced at her new watch. "Four months, two days, and—you tricked me!"

"I knew that Flower was here taking on supplies and I bet Affie you would go straight to the Farling doctor and get one of those countdown-to-delivery watches."

"I did not go to the Farling doctor. He stopped by our cargo container when he came to Mac's Bones to play poker."

A soft bell informed them that somebody was at the door, and Dorothy began to extract herself from the pile of fabric she was hemming.

"I'll get that," Flazint said. "You shouldn't do anything in a hurry, you know. You're balancing for two now."

"And you're worse than the beetle who warned me not to run with scissors," Dorothy grumbled. She reached for her purse to pay for the pizza but her friend had already left the room.

Flazint returned a minute later. "It was just the food so I put it in the meeting room. Then I asked the station librarian and she said it's five minutes before noon on your clock. Let me help you fold that up and we can get ready."

"I don't need to get—" Dorothy began, but the doorbell chimed again and Flazint dropped the folds of drapery she had gathered and practically ran out of the room. The ambassador's daughter finished folding the drapes herself, marveling over the liquid-like nature of the fabric that was guaranteed never to wrinkle or need washing. Then she pushed herself up from her customized seamstress workstation and made her way down the hall to the meeting room.

"Mrs. Crick," the Frunge attorney greeted Dorothy formally. "Stryx Jeeves requested that I speak with you about trademark issues surrounding your latest endeavor."

"He wants you to talk me out of it," Dorothy replied bluntly, stopping at the little kitchenette corner to retrieve metal plates and forks.

"I don't think it will take more than a few minutes to explain the legal principles involved. Would you rather eat before or after?"

Dorothy opened the pizza box and steam billowed up from the mound of melted cheese and toppings. "This is going to take at least ten minutes to cool down to the point that I don't get blisters in my mouth. Would you guys be offended if I had a few digestive crackers with mine? I'm supposed to eat plenty of fiber."

"Not at all," Tzachan told her. "I work in a multi-species firm and I'm perfectly comfortable with grains and paper as long as nobody expects me to handle them myself.

"So why is Jeeves so opposed to my Pregnancy Ponchos? I think they're a great idea."

"I can't speak to the business or marketing aspects, but from the standpoint of trademarks, it would be a weak one at best. It would have no value at all on the Stryx stations, which make up the majority of your market."

"Why not?"

"Both are common words being used in a natural manner. Some species with easy-going registrars might initially allow Pregnancy Ponchos as a trademark for a phrase that acquires secondary meaning, but that meaning is so literal that any attempt to litigate on our part would be doomed to failure."

"But all of you loved Baa's Bags. What could be more literal?"

"Baa's Bags is a strong trademark," the attorney explained. "The word 'Baa' is a personal name, and 'bags' can refer to any number of things in your language, from bags under your eyes, to—" here he cast an apologetic glance at Flazint, "—paper bags, to women's purses. The phrase 'Baa's Bags' therefore has a unique and distinctive meaning as the enchanted bags-of-holding being created and marketed by SBJ Fashions."

"But nobody else is selling Pregnancy Ponchos. They'd be unique, too."

"The product may be unique but the name is simply descriptive of the function. It's the same as if you tried to trademark 'High Heels' or 'Wedding Gown.'"

The ambassador's daughter looked to Flazint for support, but the Frunge girl was staring at Tzachan as if the attorney had just delivered a Galaxy Prize-worthy lecture. "What if we called them 'Dorothy's Pregnancy Ponchos.'"

"That would be acceptable from a legal standpoint," Tzachan allowed.

"Nobody would buy them," Flazint said, snapping out of her reverie. "And if for some crazy reason somebody did buy them, the rest of our lines would suffer."

"Why do you say that?" Dorothy asked.

"We sell fashions to make women look beautiful. No offence, but your ponchos make women look like tents. And if you've been reading Brinda's marketing reports, you'll know that more than forty percent of our unit sales are to girls who are just starting to date. How many of them do you think want to associate themselves with a pregnancy brand?"

Dorothy transferred some of the cheesy mound of pizza toppings to her plate and used her fork to spread a little on one of the biscuits that Ian imported specially from Scotland for Pub Haggis. "Well, Jeeves can choose between the ponchos and my fashion show idea," she said finally. "I'm not giving up both."

The two Frunge let out sighs of relief and turned their attention to the crustless pizza, which disappeared rapidly. The alien lovebirds soon made themselves equally scarce, and in an instant, Dorothy went from feeling like a third wheel to feeling like a unicycle. The doorbell chimed again.

"Whose idea was that bell anyway?" she asked out loud as she rose from the table.

"Affie's," the station librarian answered immediately. "The Vergallians have a superstition that expectant mothers who are startled by unexpected visitors eventually give birth to nervous children. The bell is just so you know somebody has entered the office."

"I wish everybody would stop trying to protect me," Dorothy grumbled, settling back down in her seat to finish her fruit juice in peace. "Who's here anyway?"

"Me," answered Judith as she entered the meeting room wearing her usual black combat fatigues. "I need to talk to you."

"Did I do something?" Dorothy asked the EarthCent Intelligence trainer who had replaced her father at the Mac's Bones training camp. "What is it?"

"You didn't do anything, but you're kind of my only female friend, other than Chance, and she's an artificial person. I need to talk to another woman."

"Talk about what?"

Judith slumped into a chair and rolled up her sleeve, revealing a watch that was the twin of Dorothy's. "How could this happen to me?"

"Do you mean, like, technically?"

"No I don't mean technically, though Bob has some explaining to do. He told me he couldn't have children."

"Are you sure he didn't say that he couldn't have children without you? I kind of remember both of you being tipsy when I recruited you for my wedding party and him saying that he wouldn't have children with anybody else."

"Bob's a goof. But we've been living together for years and nothing. Then you talk me into getting married at your wedding, and the next thing you know I'm gaining weight like—is there any pizza left?" Judith interrupted herself.

"Just what you see. I ordered crustless for Flazint and her boyfriend."

Judith took one of Dorothy's crackers and attempted to scrape a little bit of tomato sauce with a half a mushroom from the empty box before giving up. "What am I going to do?" the normally unflappable intelligence agent practically wailed.

"I'll order another pizza, with crust this time. I'm still hungry."

"That's not what I meant—but get pepperoni and sausage. There, do you see what I mean? I never cared about food."

"That's because—"

"Don't you dare tell me I'm eating for two. And that stupid beetle doctor told me I should stop fencing."

"That does seem like a reasonable idea. I had to give up running with scissors."

"You're not helping anymore than Chance did," Judith complained.

"You went to Chance first?"

"I don't discriminate against AI. Besides, she's the one who has to start taking over my unarmed combat classes."

"Come on, this is great," Dorothy said. "Didn't you always want children?"

"No! Did you?"

"Sure, I guess. Children are awfully cute and they outgrow their clothes so fast they're like a designer's dream come true. Even Jeeves won't be able to complain when he sees how little fabric it takes to cover a baby."

"You're working on baby clothes already? All I have for clothes are mercenary fatigues and the bridesmaid dress you gave me. Can you let it out?"

"Not enough to make a difference, but I can let you have a poncho," Dorothy offered eagerly.

"Is it waterproof?"

"No, it's fashionable."

"Somehow I doubt that. What am I going to do for the next six months?"

"The same things you did for the last six months, only slower."

The doorbell chimed again, and this time Dorothy didn't even start to get up.

"What if that's our pizza?" Judith asked.

"I haven't even ordered yet."

"Smells like pizza to me."

"Knock, knock?" Vivian asked from the doorway. "Are you guys busy?"

"We're just sitting around expecting," Judith said.

"Hey, Viv. Is that for us?" Dorothy eyed the box hungrily.

"I was hoping to have a slice or two, but yes. It's a bribe," the teen said, setting the box from the Little Apple on the table.

"Wow, you really need to go through our holo-training for paying off alien customs agents," Judith said. "You're not supposed to tell the people who you're bribing that it's a bribe."

"I just came from signing up," Vivian told her. "I'm going to start going through all the training camp courses as my Open University schedule allows. I'm thinking of a career change."

"From what?" Dorothy asked, cracking the lid of the pizza box and pulling back sharply from the steam. "How come they're always so hot?"

"It's the Drazen box technology," Judith said. "Herl explained it to me. That's why the pizza places always ask you to estimate when you'll get home if you pick it up yourself rather than getting delivery. They take it out of the oven early and it finishes cooking in the box. That cardboard looking circle that the pizza sits on is actually a one-shot exothermic pulp that stays as hot as a pizza oven on the top side as it solidifies while the bottom side remains cool."

"You discuss pizza box technology with the head of Drazen Intelligence?" Vivian asked.

"He likes food."

"You've never come to see me before, have you, Viv?" Dorothy observed. "Are you and Samuel having problems?"

"Never," the girl said firmly. "I mean, yes, but not with each other. It's school, and I don't want to ask any of my alien friends because they'd just laugh. Somehow they all knew what they wanted to do long before they start at the Open University."

"You're what, now? Sixteen? Seventeen? You must have been the youngest university student on the station when you began there and you're hardly getting old. What's the problem?"

"My mom and Chastity had already started InstaSitter by the time they were my age and it wasn't even their first business. My brother fills in for Tinka when she goes on vacation, and she put him in charge of our employee LARPing league. Me? I've spent the last couple years taking classes about running a dynasty because I wanted to prove that my family is as good as any of those alien clans that have been around for hundreds of thousands of years. I'm beginning to think it was a mistake."

"So what do you want to do, then?" Dorothy asked. "Aside from marrying my brother, I mean."

"I'm going to try EarthCent Intelligence. The students in my seminar suggested it because they think it belongs to my parents, and that with Samuel inheriting the ambassador job, we could combine to take over humanity."

"But Samuel can't inherit mom's job."

"Try telling that to the aliens. And it's not like either of us wants to take over humanity either. What are you

175

doing?" Vivian stopped and asked Judith, who was poking at different pizza slices with her index finger.

"Trying to find one cool enough to eat. Hey, did the beetle warn you about eating pizza?" she asked Dorothy.

"Only to avoid onions and anchovies when nursing. It's fine before that as long as it's well cooked, and we won't have any problems on that score."

"So what should I tell Samuel?" Vivian continued. "I don't want him to think that I'm a quitter."

"It's not like you're dropping out of school altogether," Judith said, and then a thought struck her. "If you do quit, you could take over my fencing class at the training camp."

"I'm going to switch over to taking intelligence courses at the Open University. I was kind of surprised, but it turns out to be a pretty popular subject."

"So what's the problem?" Dorothy asked. "Samuel isn't going to give you a hard time about changing your major. He's pretty confused about what he wants to study himself."

"That's why I don't want to just drop it on him, like I'm all set and he's still struggling. I know he's getting frustrated with Space Engineering, but he can't decide what else to take."

"Don't they have any diplomacy courses?" Judith asked. "He'd be good at that." Then she picked up a slice of pizza and began blowing on it so vigorously that a slice of pepperoni broke free and forced Vivian to duck. "Sorry."

"You know, this has never happened to me before," Dorothy remarked suddenly.

"Being pregnant?" Vivian asked.

"Being the person who other people come to with questions about life," the ambassador's daughter replied seriously. "It's kind of neat."

"Thanks for making me feel worse," Judith said.

"So how are the ponchos going?" Vivian asked.

Dorothy looked around and motioned to the two women to draw in closer before whispering, "I gave up on them as soon as I saw myself in the mirror, but don't tell anybody. I've kept it alive as a bargaining chip to get Jeeves to accept my fashion show idea. You two are modeling, by the way."

"Is this part of your sponsorship deal for the LARPing league?"

"It's an add-on. I got the idea when Baa, Affie and Flazint went to hand out our bags-of-holding at the first LARP of the season. Then I caught Baa randomly enchanting some of our other bespoke fashions just because she thinks it's funny, so now we have travel cloaks that will stop a fireball and hats that will stand up to a spiked mace. It's all based on armor percentages that I don't really understand, but it's a great way to get exposure for our brand."

"I remember when I asked you to build offensive capabilities into the command-and-control interface for your heels you refused," Judith rebuked the ambassador's daughter.

"Enchantments for LARPing are different, and Jeeves only agreed to one-offs for marketing. The problem is that role-players dress in character, so while we can work in a cloak or a hat, who wears a halter top into combat?"

"An Elf dancer," Vivian said. "I've been reading through the guides that Jonah brings home, and there's a dancer class that can buff the whole group with morale and health by doing certain dances."

"Really? That's great. Now all we need is a character who wears heels."

"Plenty of female players equip high heels, though there's a lot of controversy about it. It's not out of the question for magic wielders, who are glass cannons in any case, to go for a fashion statement. I also remember seeing one assassin-specific class whose high heels have built-in spring technology that increases jumping ability by a factor of five, both taking off and landing. I guess if you spend a lot of time ambushing targets in dark alleys or forests, jumping can be pretty important."

"Our heels can practically do that without enchantments," Dorothy said excitedly.

"Assassin doesn't sound that bad," Judith said, snagging another piece of pizza from the box. "Maybe I can do that in your fashion show."

"Check with the beetle before Flower leaves the station," Dorothy ordered. "You're not showing much yet, but that doesn't mean it's safe for you to be jumping off roofs."

Fifteen

"Everybody please be on their best behavior," Aisha addressed the group of excited nine-year-old Junior Station Scouts. "We're about to enter the EarthCent Embassy where Mike's father is the associate ambassador. They do very important work here, so we need to remain quiet and respectful, as if we were in a library."

"What's a library?" one of the children asked.

"Grandma Kelly's house," Fenna piped up. "And she's the ambassador too."

"But we're here to see my dad," Mike said. "I'm going to earn my 'Visit a parent at work' merit badge today."

"Just keep your hands in your pockets and don't run around inside making a mess," Aisha pleaded with the children, some of whom still had an excessive number of sparkles in their hair from an eventful visit to the workplace of a parent who operated a hair salon and hadn't realized one of the children would be tall enough to reach that shelf. "I'll just ping Mike's father and let him know we're here."

The embassy door slid open and the scouts were met with the high-pitched whine of power tools. There were scraps of metal paneling everywhere, along with several sets of saw-horses set up in the reception area, which was littered with packing materials. Daniel almost tripped on his way to meet the visitors after getting his foot stuck in a loop of discarded strapping from a crate.

"Sorry about the noise and the mess," he yelled. "Just give me a minute and I'll ask the crew to go on break."

"This is so cool," a boy with straw-colored hair said to Mike. "I thought you said your dad had one of those boring talking jobs."

The construction crew put down their cutting tools, making sure that the biometric safeties were engaged so the children couldn't accidentally trigger them, and then moved through the open wall into the old travel agency to work on panel installation.

"What's going on, Daniel?" Aisha asked. "I thought the job was supposed to be finished today."

The associate ambassador grimaced. "Somebody messed up on the measurements for all of the custom fit panels we ordered. They're too short and too narrow."

"How does cutting them help?"

"That's the lucky part. The distributor accidentally shipped twice as many as we needed so the crew is custom fitting them horizontally rather than vertically. It means a few more seams, but it should work out fine."

"Didn't you measure?" asked a little girl.

"Measure twice, cut once," a boy recited, having just earned a merit badge in measuring.

"The original contractor did measure, and they used a Dollnick laser system that's accurate to the wavelength of—smaller than a human hair," Daniel substituted at the last second. "The problem is that the room changed."

"How can the room change?" Mike asked his father. "It's all metal and stuff."

"It has to do with the lease. Does anybody know what a lease is?"

One of the scouts tentatively replied, "Like for dogs?"

"That's a leash," Daniel corrected her. "A lease is a contract, an agreement between two parties, I mean, people, where the owner transfers the rights to use something like an office in return for a periodic payment."

The children stared at the associate ambassador like he'd been speaking an alien language, so Aisha interpreted for them, "It's like renting."

"Oh," the children chorused, and then Mike followed up with, "But how does renting change the size of the room?"

"In the lease, in the rental agreement that we made with the Stryx, there are conditions, rules about what we can do with the office," Daniel explained. "One of the rules is that anybody who wants to remodel the inside of the office has to remove any previous construction first. That's what the main part of the job has been, taking out the false walls and ceiling from the last renovation."

"But why?" Fenna asked.

"It's because Union Station was built a long, long time ago and it will be here for a long time to come," Daniel said. "If the Stryx let every tenant add new walls, ceilings, and floors inside their space without taking out the old ones, pretty soon every home and office would be a tiny little box that nobody could fit in."

The children didn't appear to be very convinced by this argument, so Aisha elaborated with, "Think of an office like a lift tube capsule. Every time somebody enters, there's room for one person less. Remember how we had to squeeze to all fit in at the same time?"

"That's because Greg brought his backpack," Mike said.

"I was the only one who came prepared," the scout defended himself stoutly. "It's in the manual."

"We're only Junior Station Scouts," Fenna reminded him. "The manual is for older kids."

"I want to be ready early," Greg retorted. "Early is on time."

"So who wants to see my office," Daniel asked, clapping his hands to get the children's attention. "It's where I have holo-conferences with humans from all over the tunnel network."

"Why?" a girl asked.

"We have an organization, the Conference of Sovereign Human Communities, and my job is to make sure that everybody knows what everybody else is doing so we can work together smoothly."

"So it's just talking after all," the boy with the straw-colored hair said in disappointment. "I thought you got to cut metal panels and make lots of noise."

"No, but the people I talk to ship millions of tons of metal panels a year," Daniel told them. "And floaters for ground transportation, and machines, clothing, and furniture. We're expecting the table and chairs for our new conference room to arrive from one of the CoSHC worlds today."

"What's a conference room?" another scout asked.

"It's where they talk," Mike supplied the answer, "and eat Gem catering."

"I'm hungry now," Fenna said.

"That's because we've been walking all morning visiting parents and now it's time for lunch," Aisha said brightly. "Does everybody know where we're going next?"

"The Little Apple!" the scouts shouted.

"My dad's pizza place," the straw-haired boy said, and the other children all looked at him enviously.

"I guess diplomacy can't compete with pizza," Daniel commented to Kelly, who emerged from her office just in time to see the children leaving. "When did Aisha become the troop master for the Junior Scouts?"

"The Grenouthians are major supporters of scouting so they let her skip studio prep if the troop needs her," she told him. "And with two kids of your own, you should know that nothing trumps pizza, except maybe dogs. What happened to our construction crew?"

"They're all next door installing the re-cut panels. Going by the stack, I think they only have a few left and then the walls will be done."

"I almost wish we had just washed the old walls and lived with the weird shelving and cabinets," Kelly admitted. "Who would have thought that one little construction project could be so much work?"

"Just concentrate on the benefits when the conference room is finished. You'll finally be able to start paying back the other ambassadors for their hospitality over the years."

"I know," Kelly said with a groan. "Ortha and Crute already sent me lists and I have the feeling that the Grenouthian ambassador won't be far behind."

"Lists of meetings they want you to host?"

"Worse. Lists of all the meetings I've attended at their embassies over the last twenty-seven years, plus the meetings of the two previous EarthCent consuls who served here before the consulate was upgraded to an embassy. I didn't think anybody kept track."

"They all keep track of everything, or at least their intelligence services do. And now that you know, you can start keeping track of how many meetings they attend here, right from the beginning." Daniel escorted Kelly back towards her office as a woman with a claw hammer hanging from a loop on her tool belt appeared with a recycling cart and began gathering another load of debris. "So how many meetings do we owe them?"

"I remember Ortha's number because it was low, exactly a hundred and one. The Hortens don't host many meetings, and the ambassadors from the other species don't like going there because of all the decontamination procedures. Crute's number was over five hundred, and that might be the highest of any of the species. The Dollnicks are always willing to host because they see it as an opportunity to control the agenda."

The heavy plastic curtains that the workers had installed to prevent dust from invading Donna's space parted, and the embassy manger slipped through the gap.

"We just received a live address alert from the president's office," she informed them. "Starting in five minutes."

"A live address as in a speech?" Kelly marveled. "He's never done that before."

"I pinged Blythe and asked if she knew what's going on. She said it's nothing to worry about, but the president specifically asked EarthCent Intelligence not to spoil the surprise. She and Clive are on their way here to discuss it with you after the broadcast."

"I bet it means that the Stryx have approved a new recruitment system for EarthCent," Kelly speculated. "Either that or the president is going to publicly congratulate me for finally turning in my sabbatical report. Let's go in my office and watch."

"I'll grab an extra chair," Daniel said. "Just think. Another week or so and we'll be doing this in the conference room. No more carrying chairs around."

Donna followed Kelly into her office, where the ambassador asked the station librarian to bring up the president's feed as soon as it was live.

"I wonder how many of the aliens will be tapping in?" Donna asked.

"And I wonder how many humans will be watching," Kelly replied. "After all, we just found out about it three minutes ago."

"For humans on the tunnel network, it will be the only show playing," Libby informed them. "President Beyer invoked the preemption clause in your Stryxnet contract."

"Wow," Daniel said, setting down the spare chair from Donna's desk and taking a seat. "That's going to make a lot of people angry."

"It's a short speech and we're going to try to fit it into the first commercial break on the hour, before viewers get up for snacks or to use their facilities."

"Do you mean that everybody in the galaxy who's getting live broadcasts over the Stryxnet sees commercials at the same time?"

"Of course, it's the only way to run a fair auction system for ads," the station librarian responded. "Starting in five, four, three, two, one—"

"I'm President Stephen Beyer of EarthCent and I'm interrupting this commercial broadcast to bring you a special announcement. As of next month, EarthCent will begin conducting regular civil service exams for all new job openings. Details will soon be available through your local embassy or our official information site accessible through any teacher bot. We believe that competitive exams will help us build a stronger and more independent diplomatic service moving forward towards the day when we achieve true self-government." He glanced at somebody off camera and added, "Thirty seconds, not bad."

"Does he know he's still live?" Kelly asked.

"You're getting a direct feed now, like a regular holo-conference," Libby said. "We released the main broadcast channels to their regularly scheduled programming as soon as he finished."

"So the Stryx inform me that I'm only speaking to embassy staff at this point," the president started in again. "I'm sure this announcement comes as a surprise to all of you, but Hildy and I have felt for some time that the only way to increase our credibility with alien governments is to show that we are moving away from total dependency on our benefactors. I know, I know," he said, holding up his hands as if he could hear the objections, "many of you have the respect of the local alien ambassadors and participate in important multi-species initiatives on the tunnel network. But there's a difference between making a positive impression on one diplomat serving far from home and gaining credibility with a whole species."

"What kind of civil service exam are we talking—" Kelly began, but the president started speaking again.

"I'm sorry if I cut a number of you off, but I was just inserting a significant pause," he continued. "This is actually a one-to-many communication so I can't hear what any of you are saying, but Hildy projected that eighty-three percent of you would want to know further details about the exams. The baseline test criteria have been provided by the Stryx in accordance with the methodology that was used to choose all of us, myself included. We will be establishing working committees of diplomatic personnel and support staff to supplement the basic exams with questions from your work areas. We're currently accepting volunteers for these committees, and if we fall short, I'll cast lots. That's it for today. Everybody remember to do your best for humanity and the rest is commentary."

The hologram flickered out and the embassy staff all took a moment to digest what they'd heard. Kelly spoke first.

"I can't believe how quickly Jeeves reached an agreement on a new system with EarthCent human resources."

"The president did say that they're still working out the details," Donna said.

"Sounded to me like they're just intending to add a vocational gloss to the new tests," Daniel said.

"Blythe and Clive are here," Libby announced.

Daniel went over and swiped open the security lock, allowing the director of EarthCent Intelligence and his wife to enter.

"So you two knew what the president was going to say ahead of time?" Kelly demanded. "I'm the Minister of Intelligence!"

"The president swore us to secrecy, and the only reason we were in the loop was because he needed Blythe," Clive said. "I was as much on the sidelines as you were."

"Blythe?" Kelly addressed Donna's elder daughter. "How were you involved in this?"

"Jeeves dragged me in. Chastity too."

"The president wanted to keep this a secret so he and Jeeves brought in the publisher of the Galactic Free Press?"

"Chas promised to keep quiet in return for an exclusive. She published it as soon as the president began his speech."

"But why the two of you?" Daniel asked.

"InstaSitter," Donna guessed immediately.

"Right," Blythe acknowledged. "The recruitment process the Stryx have used to date for EarthCent candidates wouldn't really transfer to an exam because they take everything into account."

"Everything?" Kelly asked.

"Everything about everything. When you add up all of their sources of information, they may as well be omniscient. That doesn't translate well to multiple choice tests, but Jeeves didn't want to start from scratch so he asked Chastity and I to let him use the questions we ask kids who apply for jobs at InstaSitter."

"But most of your babysitters are aliens," Kelly pointed out.

"We've still hired millions of humans over the years," Blythe said. "And since we track every single babysitting assignment, we've been able to continuously tweak the test questions for the best outcome, which happens to be more or less the same as what you'd look for in a diplomat. If you were in charge of hiring EarthCent employees, what qualities would you insist on?"

"Wait a second," Kelly said. "I remember the president once telling us in an intelligence steering committee meeting that he'd hired a Thark consulting firm to analyze EarthCent's personnel files in order to determine how the Stryx were selecting us. The first thing was," she paused trying to recall, "no megalomaniacs."

"Right," Blythe said. "The last thing we want in a babysitter is a girl who thinks her job is telling our clients what to do."

"And the other thing was that diplomats have to display empathy for what aliens and AI are feeling."

"Exactly. We need sitters who can empathize with all sentients."

"Not to mention maintaining a professional appearance and showing up on time," Clive added.

"But how do you test for megalomania and empathy?" Kelly asked.

"It takes a lot of questions and they get repeated in tricky ways to try to catch people who are faking," Blythe said. "Back when we started, Chastity and I explained what we were looking for and Libby helped create the tests."

"And they're really just multiple choice?" Daniel asked.

"Yes." The co-founder of InstaSitter hesitated for a moment, then added, "Of course, the station librarian grades the tests for us."

"Based on the answers or something else?" Kelly inquired suspiciously. "Libby?"

"I would never invade the privacy of station residents to compliment the results of a test. Ethical considerations aside, doing so would be the same as granting a competitive advantage to InstaSitter. Our neutrality on business matters is the glue that holds the tunnel network together."

"That and the tunnels," Clive commented cheerfully. "And the Stryxnet."

"Ship controllers," Daniel contributed.

"Not to mention the peace dividend for members," Kelly said, "but I accept your explanation."

"Thank you for your trust and for finally turning in your sabbatical report," Libby replied mischievously. "I especially enjoyed your account of the great Union Station chocolate war."

"Chocolate war?" Blythe asked.

"You had to be there," Donna said. "It was tasty."

Sixteen

"Next, please," the Dollnick clerk behind the add/drop counter called out.

"Hi. I'm Samuel McAllister and—"

"I have a quota and you're wasting time," the towering alien cut off the ambassador's son. "Just hold up your student tab until it syncs with my interface. Good. Now are you adding or dropping?"

"Both. I'm actually—"

"What are you dropping?" the Dollnick interrupted again as he brought up a holographic display of the teen's academic records.

"Structural Engineering 202, Materials Engineering, Field Theory 100, and Beginning Concepts in Containment."

"You aren't registered for Beginning Concepts in Containment."

"I'm auditing."

"So it doesn't matter if you show up or not," the alien said, casually wiping out several lines of Samuel's records with a wave. "What are you adding?"

"That's the thing. When I changed my study track at admin, they—"

"What are you adding?" the Dollnick repeated in a bored tone.

"Diplomacy 302, Interstellar Resource Economics, Advanced Conflict Resolution and, uh, Public Toasting," he added in an undertone.

"Good course, Public Toasting. Never know when you'll be called upon at a meal to stand up and say nice things about somebody you despise. Is that it?"

"But I don't know how I got approved for all the advanced courses," Samuel protested. "I don't want special treatment just because—"

"Next," the Dollnick called loudly, and as the teen stepped aside to make room for a burly Grenouthian, he overheard the clerk saying to the bunny, "How was that for conflict resolution?"

Samuel shook his head and jogged down the corridor to the cafeteria, where he was already late for lunch with Vivian and their friends. After he went through the serving line and paid for his food, he couldn't see his girlfriend anywhere. Spotting Marilla eating with Jorb and Grude, he headed over and took a seat next to the Drazen.

"What's wrong with you?" the Horten girl asked, studying the ambassador's son from across the table. "You look different."

"He was expecting to see Vivian and got stuck looking at you," the Drazen said.

"I dropped out of Space Engineering," Samuel told them in a rush, in part to get it over with, and in part to head off another silly name-calling contest between Marilla and Jorb. "And I did think Vivian would be here."

The Dollnick leaned forward, extended both of his upper arms, and placing his hands on Samuel's shoulders, gave a solemn squeeze. "You did the right thing," Grude said. "Your lifespan is too short to waste your university time studying a subject that isn't your passion."

"He can't do the math either," Jorb added. "It would be like me trying to learn musical notation at my age."

"You didn't do something really stupid and drop out of the university altogether, did you?" Marilla demanded.

"I swapped into Diplomatic Studies," Samuel admitted sheepishly, given that his friends had all recommended exactly that course of action on multiple occasions. "But they gave me credit for a bunch of courses I never took."

"That's a good thing," Grude said as the others returned to eating. "It wouldn't make any sense for you to start with intro courses. You're practically a diplomat already."

"I don't mean they just put me in advanced courses, I mean they gave me full credit for the earlier ones based on life experience. It feels like I'm cheating."

Jorb started to talk and choked on something, which he promptly spat out in his hand after pounding his own back with his tentacle.

"Gross," the Horten girl said, turning her chair ninety degrees so she was facing Grude rather than the Drazen, whose eating habits she was always complaining about.

"You Humans crack me up," Jorb said when he recovered his breath. "Who complains about getting credit for life experience?"

"It's just that I think they gave it to me for being our ambassador's son," Samuel said. "You know that the station librarian makes all the decisions about this stuff."

"Of course they gave it to you for being who you are, that's what life experience means," the Drazen cried in frustration. "Look. What's our ambassador's name?"

"Bork. Half the students in the university probably know that."

"What are his hobbies?"

"He does historical reenactments. But what does that have to do with anything?"

"If you offered him a bribe, would he take it?"

"Sure. Most of the ambassadors take bribes, but it doesn't mean you'll get any special consideration in return. It's just a perk to them."

"And who's our ambassador," Marilla asked, catching on to Jorb's game.

"Ortha," Samuel replied, frowning. "I could have gotten the names of all the ambassadors out of a single story in the Galactic Free Press."

"What's his biggest fear?"

"That the Horten pirates will do something so outrageous that your navy will be forced to go after them for real," Samuel said. "It would practically cause a civil war, given all of the family ties involved, not to mention the hundreds of thousands of years of tacitly accepting piracy on your frontier as a buffer zone between the tunnel network and Sharf space. And there's a rumor that your people use the pirates as a dumping ground for nonconformists and criminal elements from your worlds."

"If you really needed something from our ambassador, I mean, if it was life and death for your people, how would you go about it?" Crute asked.

Samuel turned to the Dollnick as the lesson that his friends were trying to teach him began to sink in. "I'd start with an assessment from EarthCent Intelligence, but I think the main thing would be to offer him enough in return that he wouldn't be insulted, even if it meant promising more than I could actually deliver."

"How many of the students in Diplomatic Studies do you think could have answered those questions off the tops of their heads?" Jorb demanded. "And that doesn't even take into account how you ran our committee for outfitting Flower. You're a natural at this. Denying it is like saying that I'm cheating at life by being so good-looking."

Orsilla began to choke on something and Grude reached over and thumped her on the back with one of his giant hands. A round Picaf bean shot out of her mouth and landed in the Drazen's soup, where he quickly mashed it in with the other vegetables before she could reclaim it.

"Hey, guys," Vivian said, setting her tray down next to Samuel. "What did I miss?"

"Samuel changed into Diplomatic Studies and Jorb's lost what little was left of his mind," Marilla said. "You're running late."

"I had to go by admin."

"Did you drop out of Dynastic Studies?" Samuel guessed immediately.

"I just don't see the point anymore," Vivian confirmed with a sigh. "I signed up for Inter-Species Intelligence. And guess what?"

"You got advanced placement for being who you are?"

"They waived my physical education requirement entirely," the girl reported proudly.

"You're a good fencer," Jorb said. "I'll bet you could beat all the Hortens in our dojo."

Marilla glared across the table at the Drazen.

"Actually, they gave it to me for the years of Vergallian ballroom competitions I entered with Samuel when we were kids," Vivian said. "Apparently dancing is a more important skill for spies than combat. I'm going for the femme fatale track."

"You're what?" Samuel sputtered.

"I'm kidding," the girl said. "I couldn't believe how many Intelligence courses there are to choose from, includ-

194

ing Advanced Seduction. I checked with Libby, and it turns out that students studying business and industrial engineering have intelligence and counterintelligence courses in their core requirements."

"So Grude and I won't see you in our Dynastic Studies courses anymore," Jorb said to Vivian. "I'm going to miss you calling out that princeling on all the mistakes he makes."

"You're still taking Dynastic Studies courses?" Samuel asked Grude. "But you're doing Space Engineering and you don't want to take over the family bakery."

"My father made me promise to audit the Dynastic Studies courses in case I changed my mind and decide to take over the bakery chain," the Dollnick replied.

"And I won't see you in my courses anymore," Marilla said to Samuel. "You were our only Human."

A beautiful Vergallian student glided up to the table and stood behind the Horten girl, her eyes on the ambassador's son.

"Aabina?" he asked, recognizing the Vergallian ambassador's daughter from the Dynastic Studies seminar he'd attended as Vivian's minion.

"May I have a word in private?" Aabina favored Samuel with a dazzling smile that made Vivian grit her teeth.

"Uh, sure," the ambassador's son said, grabbing the apple from his tray as he stood. "I'll be back in a minute, guys."

Aabina led Samuel to the cafeteria's dead zone, an area set aside for students who wanted to study without distractions while they ate. The overlapping acoustic suppression fields at the dead-zone tables made it impossible for sounds to travel more than an arm's length. The Vergallian girl waited for Samuel to pull out a chair for her, took a seat, and then leaned in close when he sat down next to her.

"Am I the first to find you?" she asked. "I just saw the notice that you switched to diplomacy and I asked the station librarian for your location."

"The courses we sign up for are posted publicly?"

"You didn't know that? How else do you find students to borrow notes from when the class schedule is so far off your biorhythm that you'd be attending in your sleep?"

"I always set an alarm and drank a lot of coffee," Samuel admitted. "But I just changed those courses fifteen minutes ago. How did you happen to notice so quickly?"

"We track all of the offspring of senior diplomats on the tunnel network."

"You're in Vergallian Intelligence?"

Aabina pulled back as if he'd slapped her, but she shook it off quickly and leaned in closely again. "No. My family is on the other side of that particular fight. I'm here about the student secret society for the diplomatic track."

"I've never even heard of any student secret societies," Samuel said, then blushed as the Vergallian girl giggled prettily. "Okay, that was a dumb thing to say. But I'm really not a cloak-and-dagger type. I believe in open communications and information sharing."

"Your naiveté is charming. I can see why my mother is so taken by your species."

"I appreciate the invitation but my friends are waiting," Samuel said, rising from the table. The Vergallian girl captured his wrist in a surprisingly strong grip and pulled him back down, again bringing her head close to his.

"This would have gone much smoother if I was forty years older and my pheromone glands were functioning," she said in frustration. "As the son of a tunnel network ambassador taking Diplomatic Studies, you're going to be pestered about this by every member in our secret society looking to score points. Let me be your sponsor for the initiation and you can always decide to quit if you don't like the way we do business."

"But why does a student club for diplomacy need to be secret?" Samuel persisted.

"It's a compromise. Half of the members are just as eager to do everything in public as you are, but history has shown that it creates too many hard feelings with the students who are left out."

"I don't get it. Why should anybody be left out?"

"Come on, I know you've been on committees. Can you hold an intelligent discussion with a thousand people in the room? How about a hundred? Does everybody get to speak or do you just have a self-selected group do all the talking? Secret societies at the Open University don't exist to keep secrets, they exist to limit the membership to groups of sympathetic students who can work together. For all I know there could be a dozen other secret societies for diplomacy students that I'm not even aware of. Do you remember the Dollnick princeling from the Dynastic Studies seminar you attended?"

"Is he in your secret society?"

"No, and that's the point. When his name came up for consideration, the bowl practically overflowed. I swear there were more black balls than there were members at the meeting."

"So, wait. You mean you already voted on me?"

"Back when you ran your student committee, but the invitation was deferred until you publicly manifested a career interest in diplomacy. We aren't a social group for the offspring of politicians."

"I don't know," Samuel said. "Can I have a little time to think about it?"

"Sure, but it's not like you're that long-lived. You'll see an official invitation from me on your student tab next time you look. All student secret societies are chartered by the Open University, and they give us group messaging capabilities and free access to meeting rooms. Oh, and there's dues."

"How much?"

"It's just ten creds a year for record keeping, but there's a fifteen-cred charge for every meeting you attend, and you should always reserve your space in advance so we can tell the caterers to have something for your species. Cash bar."

"We drink at meetings?"

"It's good training for diplomats."

"I'll let you know soon," he promised, and headed back to the table. Jorb, Marilla and Grude were still there, but Vivian was nowhere to be seen.

"Where'd she go?" Samuel asked.

"Some Verlock dragged her off," the Drazen said casually. "He's probably recruiting her for a secret society."

"That was the Vergallian ambassador's daughter, right?" Marilla inquired. "If she offered to be your sponsor for a diplomatic secret society, it's an honor."

"You guys know about the secret societies?"

"Of course," Grude said. "I'm in two of them."

"Why didn't anybody ever tell me?"

"Because they're secret?" Jorb suggested, sneaking a celery stalk from Vivian's abandoned plate. "You know how slow the Verlocks talk," he said apologetically. "Her food will all be spoiled by the time she gets back."

"Is everybody playing with me or something? I never heard of student secret societies until five minutes ago, and now I find out that all of my friends not only know about them but are in them."

"It's awkward," Marilla said. "Nobody wants to tell a friend about the existence of secret societies unless they can extend an invitation at the same time. If you had known there was a secret society for spaceship engineering, would you have been offended that you weren't invited?"

"I'm offended now. You're a member?"

"I would have put your name up if I thought you'd be approved, but most of the other students were skeptical you'd make it through any of the advanced courses. It doesn't mean you couldn't have done interesting things with spaceship design," she hastened to add. "It's just that you wouldn't have been able to follow so much of what our alumni speakers talk about at the meetings that it would have been uncomfortable for everybody."

"But what about that princeling who's always giving you a hard time, Grude. Aabina told me that—"

"Shshhh," all three aliens interrupted him, and the Dollnick actually reached over and clamped a hand over Samuel's mouth.

"Think," Grude instructed in a low whistle that translated to a whisper. "Is it likely that a princeling would be aware of the existence of secret societies for students?"

"Yes," Samuel said in a soft tone when the Dollnick removed his hand. "So why would it matter?"

"Let's have a hypothetical discussion," Jorb said. "Suppose there was a proud species whose leadership was concentrated in the hands of certain families of great wealth and power."

"With four arms," Marilla put in.

"And say the scion of one of those powerful families was taking courses on a multi-species university campus."

"Like this one," Grude contributed.

"Now, say there were such things as secret societies," Jorb continued, making Drazen air-quotes around his last two words with both thumbs on each hand, "and say our hypothetical jerk wasn't welcome in a society that he would claim as his natural right, if he was made publicly aware that it existed."

"He'd be furious, and nobody wins by making a wealthy and powerful hypothetical jerk angry," Samuel said, nodding. "By keeping everything secret, you save face for the students who aren't welcome for one reason or another. But isn't it good training for diplomats to have to deal with difficult sentients?"

"We're not all diplomats," Marilla said, "and you don't have to come to the Open University to experience a bad working environment. The main function of the secret societies, other than sharing old competency test questions, is connecting with alumni and establishing cross-species channels of communication. Humans don't care who they associate with, but most Hortens wouldn't be caught dead sitting with a Drazen in public. The secret societies allow those interactions to take place."

"But you're friends with Jorb," Samuel objected.

"We're both friends with you and Vivian," the Drazen corrected him. "We tolerate each other's company because you're here."

"And my little sister, Orsilla, was on 'Let's Make Friends' with a Drazen," Marilla reminded the ambassador's son. "Hortens who want a reason to look down on my family already have one, so it gives me a sort of freedom of association."

"Well, that was weird," Vivian said, taking her seat and swatting away the Drazen's tentacle, which was reaching for her half-eaten brownie.

"Secret society?" Samuel asked.

"I'm not allowed to say."

"The Verlocks are really strict, and if it's a secret society for spies, they probably have all sorts of extra rules," Grude said. "Is there a handshake?"

"Not until I pass the initiation," Vivian replied, then realizing she had been tricked, hastened to change the subject. "Do you guys want to make some easy creds?"

"Doing what?" Marilla asked.

"My sister-in-law, I mean, Sam's sister, is putting on a LARP fashion show. She's looking for alien models for enchanted fashions, and since you guys have already met Baa, you aren't terrified of her."

"I am," Grude said, hastily taking his tray and standing up. "I'll see you guys later."

"Would I have to walk like there's something wrong with my hips or undress in front of the other models?" Marilla asked.

"I don't think so," Vivian replied. "Dorothy said they're shooting it in a holo-studio with staged combat. It won't exactly be a LARP, but it won't be a catwalk either."

"I can't say I'm crazy about working with Baa, but it wouldn't be fair to deprive the galaxy of this," Jorb said, framing his face with his hands. The Horten girl made a gagging sound.

Seventeen

"This is definitely not in my contract," the enraged Horten commentator shouted, his skin color shifting to a deep blue. "I won't do it."

"In the absence of Stryx Jeeves, the management of SBJ Fashions has authorized me to represent their legal position," Tzachan informed the pair of network employees. "Although I specialize in intellectual property, it's plain to me that the sponsorship agreement commits you both to announcing any pre-LARP action featuring Baa's Bags."

"In case my chameleon friend Poga isn't getting the point across, we categorically refuse," snarled the Drazen half of the duo. "And going by the way you're dressed, I'd guess your legal specialty is skulking around in the woods and shooting arrows at innocent passersby."

The Frunge attorney's close-cropped hair vines paled under his forest ranger hat, but he maintained his composure and shook his head sadly at the live broadcast team. "I'd hoped to settle this matter with you like gentlemen, but if you insist on ignoring your contractual obligations, I'll have to let our design team deal with you."

"Getting scared yet, Bunk?" the Horten joked with his co-host. "Do you think they'll hit us with their purses?"

Tzachan gave the commentators a wooden smile and turned to Flazint, who was also dressed as a forest ranger. "Get Baa," he instructed her.

"Wait!" the Drazen cried, jumping up from his folding canvas chair. "Let's not be so hasty."

"There's no need to involve the T – T – Terr – Terragram," Poga stuttered. "Let me see the script."

"I sent it to both of you two hours ago as stipulated by the agreement," Tzachan said. "But if you accidentally removed it from the queue for your heads-up teleprompter, I'm sure Baa has—"

"Found it," Bunk declared, his eyes rapidly scanning a text that only he could see. "I, uh, I must have been looking at something else before. We can definitely do this."

"What's a gaiter?" the Frunge inquired.

"It's ankle protection that fits over the shoe," Flazint spoke up when Tzachan nudged her.

"Iridescent?" the Drazen asked.

"Something that changes color when the light catches it, like the inside of a seashell," the girl told them.

"Raglan?" Bunk squinted and scratched his head with his tentacle.

"It's when the sleeve goes all the way to the shoulder without a seam," Flazint told them, basking in the admiring gaze of her fellow Frunge.

"And a knife pleat is a kind of hidden scabbard," the Horten bluffed.

"No, it's a sharp fold, usually when there's a bunch of them together, like a fan."

"So why don't you call it a fan-fold?"

"Knife pleat sells better."

"We'll be fine," the Drazen asserted, though his expression failed to confirm his words. "We've got five minutes to nail this down, Poga. It'll be just like the old days when they were adding all of those Human-derived monsters nobody ever heard of to the LARPs and we had to wing it."

"I don't think I can read this line without getting in trouble at home," Poga objected. "What kind of woman would consent to wearing a yoke?"

"It's not a plow yoke," Flazint said, suppressing her laughter at the Horten's skin color shift to bright yellow, which showed how nervous he was at the thought of getting on the wrong side of the females in his family. "It's what we call the neckline of a dress, front and back. Baa likes to wear a usekh broad collar. I make them out of precious metals."

The two commentators exchanged a quick look. "Anything that's fine by Baa is fine by us," Bunk said. "You just make sure that your models are ready to go because we can't delay the actual starting time of the LARP broadcast for a fashion show."

"Unless Baa wants us to," Poga added.

"Right," the Drazen confirmed. "Uh, when is Stryx Jeeves getting back to the station?"

"He doesn't keep me informed of his plans," Tzachan replied. "Oh, and our band didn't bring an engineer so I hope your guys can mix them."

Bunk opened his mouth to protest, but the Horten was faster, saying, "Absolutely. No problem. Tell Baa we're happy to cooperate."

"I think that went well," Tzachan murmured to Flazint as the Frunge couple made their way back to the dressing room. "I wonder if Baa would be available to sit with me in court next time I have a tricky case."

"Jeeves made her promise not to intimidate anybody on the station," Flazint said. "Of course, if she doesn't know…"

"I'm glad you're adjusting to her presence. I remember how uncomfortable you used to be sharing an office with her."

"Seeing Baa struggle to open some of the puzzle clasps I use on our bespoke bags made her a little less scary. And she's kind of pathetic about a mage guy," the Frunge girl concluded in a whisper as they entered the backstage area.

"Final inspection," Dorothy shouted, waving the tab with her checklist. "Everybody line up in the order you're going out. We only have five minutes from when Mornich and his band start playing the accompaniment to get through this."

"How am I supposed to slay a troll by myself in under twenty seconds?" Affie's boyfriend complained. "Last time we went after one, I was with a half-dozen barbarian warriors and I still got killed."

"Just duck under his club and lunge," Dorothy told the Vergallian. "Chance and Thomas choreographed all of the action and your opponents are going to crumple up and die even if you barely touch them. It's a fashion show, not combat."

"Are these slits supposed to come up this high?" Marilla asked.

"They're vents, and it's a pencil skirt. You wouldn't be able to move without them," the ambassador's daughter informed her. "You. The handsome Drazen who hangs out with my brother. What's your name?"

"Jorb."

"The strap goes over your shoulder, not around your waist."

"But it will look like a purse!"

"It's a man's bag-of-holding. Trust me. If you wear it around your waist, it makes you look like a Horten message carrier."

Jorb almost broke the buckle in his haste to get the purse off his waist and sling it around his neck.

A large bunny leaned in through the passageway from the holo-stage and shouted, "Two minutes."

"You guys ready?" Dorothy asked Samuel and Vivian as she reached the front of the line. "I'm counting on a big opening."

"Block, twirl and stalk," her brother said. "Piece of cake."

"I still think I should go out first," Baa called from the final spot in the single file of models. "I'm the one who enchanted everything."

"The auteur always goes on last," Dorothy told her for the fourth time that day. "It's an honor. If you went first, everybody would think you were just a model. No offense, models."

"One minute," the Grenouthian shouted, and from the stage area, a bass line began thumping.

"Remember. Don't look at the immersive cameras and try to act like it's all a great big bore. I want the watchers to think you've been killing monsters since you left the cradle, and whatever you do, don't forget to put any dropped loot in your bags. Why are we here?"

"Baa's Bags," the models replied dutifully.

"I can't hear you," Dorothy shouted back, and she really couldn't hear them with Mornich's band cranking up their instrumental. "Who's paying you?"

"BAA'S BAGS," the models all shouted.

"Now get out there and kill them," Dorothy instructed. She pointed dramatically at the entry to the holo-stage just as the bunny leaned back in and began a five-second countdown.

Vivian reached with her left hand and took Samuel's right hand, and as the bunny folded down his last finger at zero, the couple strode out into the bright lights.

"I don't know about you, Poga, but there's nothing I hate worse than getting pin-cushioned by pesky projectiles fired out of concealment," the Drazen commentator read from his script as the sound engineer frantically sought the right mic level to mix over the loud music for the home audience.

Right on cue, a cloud of arrows streaked towards the young couple. Samuel and Vivian raised their travel cloaks to deflect the projectiles, then twirled to show off the full expanse of the fabric, revealing at the same time the matching bags-of-holding worn crossways across their chests. With no loot to gather, they immediately spun about and stalked towards the exit.

"And nothing offers better protection against acid-spitting monsters than an enchanted unitard," Poga read from the script as Chance strode onto the stage in a skin-tight garment that covered her whole body, from the ankles to the wrists.

An enormous holographic toad suddenly appeared and spat a stream of bright green fluid at the artificial person. Rather than dodging, she launched herself directly into the liquid attack and skewered the giant amphibian with her sword, causing it to disappear in a puff of smoke. Chance scooped up the nugget of gold her vanquished enemy left behind, making sure to flash the Baa's Bags tag at the immersive cameras as she stored the treasure in her purse. Then she moved off stage in time with the beat.

"And the four-feather bag-of-holding sported by our Horten assassin gives her a place to stash the loot," Bunk read, as Marilla came onto the stage and plunged two daggers in the back of an unsuspecting barbarian warrior. She paused to pick up the broadsword her victim had dropped after vanishing, and fed the blade into her tiny evening bag, which swallowed the weapon like a circus performer.

"I don't know about you, Bunk, but I'm not going to be the first one to tell that berserker that he's wearing a purse," Poga said, slipping into his standard color-commentator role before recalling the script. "And those, uh, welt pockets disguise the carrying capacity of his jerkin, and double as holders for throwing knives."

A spider the size of a horse charged Jorb. He started the swing of his battle axe from low behind his back, and rising on his toes, brought it around through a glittering arc and sank the head into the super-sized arachnid's body. The spider vanished with a screech that fit right in with the band's instrumental. Jorb recovered the dropped fangs and poison sack and stuffed them in his purse with a look of disdain, as if the loot was below his notice.

"What LARPing expedition would be complete without a troll?" Bunk read as Stick came on stage and charged the hulking creature, which nearly took the Vergallian's head off with its club. "Nice sword thrust, but it's an even nicer backpack. I'll bet that tree the troll was waving around won't weigh more than a spare water bottle once that three-feather weight reduction hits."

"A really big water bottle," the Horten ad-libbed.

Flazint and Tzachan were out next, and for variety, Dorothy had staged it so that her Frunge friend had the attorney's backpack stashed in her purse. Tzachan only needed one well-placed arrow to bring down a charging beast that looked like somebody's nightmare, and as he gathered the heavy hide dropped by the creature, Flazint pulled his large backpack from her tiny bag and held it open for him while he stuffed in the loot. Spinning the pack to present the four feathers to the front camera, she lifted it easily by the straps while Tzachan slid into them. Then the couple walked off stage hip-to-hip, appreciably closer than a trained Frunge chaperone would have allowed.

"Raglan sleeves and an iridescent buckler complement the no-nonsense bag of our duelist," Poga read as Judith marched out, her rapier held loosely in one hand as she scanned the studio area for her opponent. A spherical creature displaying no teeth or claws rolled up to her and waited for its death blow.

"Looks like we have a new monster as well," the Drazen commentator said. "I'll bet it's one of those magical creatures that drains your life force if you let it come too close."

"Maybe it's iridescent too," the Horten suggested.

Judith sighed when she realized her supposed opponent wasn't going to fight, so she took out her frustration on the fur ball, running it through with her sword. When the puff of holographic smoke cleared, a jeweled tiara was left floating conveniently at waist height, no doubt to save her the effort of bending over to pick it up. She stuffed the loot in an oversized bag that could easily hold a day's supply of diapers, and strode off the stage with a look of disgust.

The Drazen commentator stumbled over the cap sleeves on Affie's tunic, and Poga, who like most Horten males had an eye for high-caste Vergallians, got the color of her purse wrong because he was staring at something else. The wasp-waisted designer let her royal training show when she sliced and diced a holographic cobra into snake sushi. The departed serpent left behind a ring of dexterity, which Affie scooped up on the point of her thin blade and deposited in her fashionable handbag.

"Amateurs," Thomas grumbled to himself as the announcers missed his entry because their eyes were following Affie as she strutted off. He twirled his halberd like a baton, and then dispatched the diving wyvern, which impaled itself on the spear tip.

"Uh, jouy print," Poga said, having lost his place in the script. "I mean, a dismounted dragon-rider is always a target for lesser flying critters, but check out those saddlebags he's carrying."

"And enchanted gaiters to reduce chafing from that tough dragon hide," the Drazen contributed.

Thomas recovered a large golden chain dropped by his departed adversary and fed it into the enchanted saddlebag that fell across his chest. Then he moved off towards the exit, but stopped on his designated mark as Baa strode onto the stage.

"And here's the enchanter of Baa's Bags, the Terragram mage who has honored us with her presence," the Drazen concluded dramatically.

"She's wearing a jouy print that details scenes from her prior conquests, and that's a five feather bag she's carrying. I'll bet she could fit a whole Stryx station in there," the Horten said, going off-script again in his eagerness to please.

"A planet," Bunk upped the ante.

"A star system," Poga shot back.

Baa raised her arms and lightning flashed from her fingers, the rolling thunder drowning out even the driving beat of the band. It wasn't clear whether she was incinerating an attacker at a distance or just putting on a show, but that didn't stop the Drazen from declaring, "Devastating. Never mess with a mage."

The other models all came back out behind Baa, lining up in a loose arc that ended with Thomas, and they all did their best to stare haughtily at nothing for a full five seconds before spinning on their heels and heading backstage.

"That was great, people," Dorothy told the models as the scene in the holo studio shifted to an underground cavern where a team of adventurers walked into a goblin ambush. "Catered after-party in our offices in fifteen minutes." The ambassador's daughter sidled up to Marilla on the way out and told the Horten girl, "I invited the band, so you better come."

By the time the models arrived, the Gem caterers had already laid out a spread that consisted mainly of desserts for humans, but also included a fruit and cheese platter that the Frunge could enjoy without feeling guilty. Shaina and Brinda stopped in to congratulate the design team and models on the show, but neither of them could stay long since it was almost bedtime and they had stories to read to their children.

"Don't even think of lighting that in here, Stick," Affie hissed at her on-again, off-again boyfriend. "If you have to burn some Kraaken Red, do it in the corridor."

"Why?" he complained. "Everybody is cool with it."

"Dorothy and Judith are wearing watches," the Vergallian girl said significantly. "The kind the Farling doctor hands out."

211

"Oh, sorry." Affie's boyfriend replaced his namesake Kraaken Red stick in an inner pocket and looked around. "Where's the drinks?" he asked Flazint, who was making up a plate of grapes and cantaloupe chunks for herself and Tzachan to share.

"SBJ Fashions has adopted an alcohol-free workplace policy for the length of Dorothy's term," the Frunge girl told him.

"Some party," Stick complained, and then slipped out into the corridor for a quick burn. Jeeves floated into the office past him while the door was open.

"I think we'll get the most out of our sponsorship if we alternate giving enchanted bags and accessories to professional players with more mini-fashion shows," Dorothy was telling Baa as the Stryx came up behind her. "You had a good time, didn't you?"

"I'd have had a better time if I'd gone out first," the Terragram replied, staring over Dorothy's shoulder at Jeeves. "And look who shows up for the party when all the work is done."

"Jeeves," Dorothy greeted the Stryx happily. "Everything went smooth as glass, almost. You'll have to get a copy of the broadcast from Libby."

"My parent brought me up to date the moment I arrived," Jeeves said. "Why did you have Judith attack an animated pillow?"

"Thomas and Chance designed the interactive hologram and that was their way around the Farling's prohibition on Judith's fencing," Dorothy told him.

"I might have suggested employing a different model, but I suppose fashion shows could all use a little comic relief. Baa, please come with me. I have something important to discuss with you."

"I didn't do it," the mage replied flatly. "I've been here slaving away enchanting fashion accessories ever since you left."

"I didn't say you did anything," Jeeves replied patiently. "I have something for you that I think you'd prefer to see in private."

"I've got nothing to be ashamed of," Baa replied stubbornly. "My co-workers are the closest thing I've had to friends in the last ten thousand years. I want them to see how you treat valued employees if you're here delivering court summons from the Stryx in another universe for illegal energy siphoning."

"You're siphoning energy from another universe?" Dorothy asked Baa.

"It has to come from somewhere, doesn't it?" the mage retorted.

Jeeves spread the manipulators on his pincer in a sign of submission and then a panel slid open on his casing. Baa turned white as a sheet as the Stryx reached in and pulled out a brilliant red orb that pulsed with a strange energy that was immediately felt by all of the sentients in the room. Flazint shocked herself and Tzachan by suddenly standing on her tiptoes and kissing the surprised attorney, and Mornich and Marilla flung aside their food and embraced each other.

"What is that?" Dorothy said, hugging her belly and wishing that Kevin were there.

"My heart," Baa croaked, and staggering forward as if her legs were about to collapse, she took the glowing orb from the Stryx and pressed it against her chest with both hands. There was a brief moment of resistance, and then Jeeves released the force field he'd used to contain the energy and it disappeared into the Terragram's body. All around the office, couples suddenly broke apart.

"I trust everything is satisfactory," Jeeves said to the mage. "I'm sure I don't need to tell you that—"

"I know. I owe. It's off to work I go," Baa half-sang, and it seemed to Dorothy that the mage's entire body was leaking light.

"Would you describe Baa as iridescent?" Tzachan whispered to Flazint.

The Frunge girl nodded, sighing in relief because his tone showed that he didn't think the less of her for her momentary loss of control.

"Where are you going, Baa?" Dorothy asked.

"To scrape that lying, cheating, free-loading, double-timing, heart-stealing, good-for-nothing, feather-chested mage off the wall of my workspace," the Terragram replied happily.

Eighteen

"How do they look?" Joe asked, stepping back from the last set of custom cabinets he'd just finished welding into place on the bridge of Baa's ship.

"Like original equipment," Kevin told his father-in-law, the highest compliment he could pay the self-taught spaceship mechanic.

"If Baa can't keep her ship tidy with all of this storage space, she's just a slob," Paul added. "I hope she doesn't try to bargain you down on the price now that the work is finished. She's getting a reputation on the station as a deadbeat, but the small merchants who give her credit are too scared to collect."

"Money's already in the bank," Joe said, patting his pocket. "Baa came by early while Beowulf was dragging me through my morning constitutional. She paid in hard creds, even though the job wasn't quite finished, and added a twenty percent bonus because I didn't charge her for parking."

"Is she sick?"

"I asked her if she was feeling alright, and she said, and I quote, 'It's only money.' Then she hugged Beowulf, sneezed, and ran off."

"That must be what Dorothy was talking about when she got home from the party," Kevin mused. "She was half asleep when she came in, but she said something about

Jeeves returning Baa's heart. I thought she was just exaggerating to make me feel like I missed something."

"Why didn't you go?" Joe asked.

"I was here helping Paul carry in these storage lockers," Kevin reminded his father-in-law. "Besides, it was going to be all fashion people. I don't really fit in."

"Do you think I fit in with diplomats? Does Paul look like he enjoys all of those Grenouthian network events he attends with Aisha? It's part of being married to somebody with a career."

"It was just in their office with employees," Kevin protested. "I did feel bad about it, because if I had been there, I would have gotten her home earlier. I told her I'd go to the next one. Dorothy admitted that even Shaina and Brinda just stuck their heads in and left, and then she asked me to add some pickle slices to her omelet. I stole some pickles out of your keg room, by the way."

"That's why I begged all of those little cucumbers from Dring and put them up," Joe said. "Kelly was always craving pickles when she was expecting."

"Just for the record, I actually enjoy going to Grenouthian dinners," Paul said, shouldering his tool bag. "There are always a few bunnies who think that I'm Aisha's agent, and it's worth the shocked look they get when I turn down their bribes to show her scripts for commercials."

Joe pointed at his ear, listened for a moment, and then said, "No rest for the weary. Good thing you already have the tools together, Paul. They should be exactly what we need."

"What's wrong?"

"Kelly pinged me from the embassy. The furniture final-ly came in, and 'some assembly required' exceeds the capabilities of our diplomatic staff."

"I'll come too," Kevin offered. "Dorothy's taking the whole day off from going into the office and I think she enjoys running the chandlery when I'm not there."

"I never thought of her as a wheeler-dealer," Joe said. "Is she making you any money?"

"She's not losing any, and she takes stuff in trade that I wouldn't think of touching."

"How is that good?"

"It's stuff that she wants. Her latest thing is gathering alien fabric scraps to make baby quilts."

"Then let's get going. The sooner we put that furniture together the sooner Kelly will stop talking in her sleep. I really wish she had just given the renovation contract to the Dollnicks back at the start."

By the time the three men arrived at the embassy, the floor was ankle deep in the Drazen equivalent of packing peanuts. Kelly and Donna were trying to gather the little air-filled spheres in webbed recycling sacks, but the peanuts were so lightweight that the small breeze created by reaching for them tended to drive them away.

"Don't worry about those," Joe told the women. "The shell material is engineered to disintegrate under strong ultra-violet. Libby can just crank up the office lights for a few minutes and there won't be anything left."

"I never knew that," Donna said. "I always thought you had to pop them all individually."

"That's just something kids and dogs like doing for fun," Joe told her. "Some adults, too. So where's all the furniture?"

217

"Daniel just took the last chair into the conference room," his wife told him. "It's the table that's the problem. According to the packing list, it's in those four boxes."

"Makes sense that they'd ship it disassembled," Joe said. "The way you described the seating capacity, it wouldn't have fit in a standard lift tube capsule, and moving it down a corridor wouldn't have been any picnic either."

"Look in the box," Kelly told him. "No, wait. Look at the picture from the catalog first."

The men gathered around Donna's display desk and the embassy manager brought up the full-scale image of the conference table.

"Interesting pattern," Paul commented. "Is it symbolic?"

"Worse," Kelly said. "It's literal. We thought that the table top only looked like puzzle pieces."

"You mean..." Joe trailed off.

"According to the instructions, the average human can assemble the tabletop in less than twelve hours," Donna said. "The manufacturer included an adhesive that's guaranteed to be stronger than the onyx, but it's recommended that we lay all the pieces out dry before applying any glue, just in case. The adhesive's working time is only a few minutes and the warranty specifically excludes misplaced pieces."

"Sounds to me like a job for young eyes," Joe said. "I'll get to work on assembling the substrate and the metal track for the legs."

"Did they ship the black pieces and the white pieces separately?" Paul asked.

"I'm not sure," the ambassador admitted. "I kind of freaked out when I looked in the box and saw all those stacks. Does it matter?"

"The table is all black on one end and all white on the other end, so separating the colors gives us an easy place to start," the former game-master said, studying the hologram. "You know what? A lot of these shapes are repeated, especially on the interior pieces, so that makes it easier as well. Is it possible to blow this up, Donna?"

The embassy manager spread her hands over the display desk and the hologram grew towards the ceiling.

"I'll bet that's the size of the actual table," Kevin said when the 3-D image refused to expand any further. "Hey, are those little squiggles numbers?"

Daniel came up to the group holding a large onyx puzzle piece that covered the palm of his hand and was about as thick as his index finger. "Quality stuff," he declared. "I knew we couldn't go wrong ordering from one of our member worlds."

"Can I see the unpolished side?" Paul requested, and then broke into a wide smile. "That's it. They're all numbered and this one goes—" he scanned the hologram and pointed, "—there. This is going to be a breeze."

"Does that mean we can skip the dry fitting?" Kelly asked.

"No!" Joe called from where he was laying out the track segments.

Kevin continued studying the hologram and announced, "The numbers are sequential. The white corner piece at the start is zero and the black corner piece at the end is six hundred and thirteen. Maybe we should clean a space on the floor and arrange all the pieces face down."

"The stacks are in order as well," Paul said, having pulled a couple more onyx puzzle pieces from the protective sleeve that Daniel had opened. "We can fit all the pieces together like Kevin said, glue them, and then stick the substrate strips on the back."

"These metal tracks have holes for guide pins that are pre-installed on the substrate planks," Joe said. "Let's all step into the corridor for a minute and ask Libby to crank up the ultra-violet and get rid of the packing peanuts."

"I'll take care of it as soon as you're out," the station librarian responded to the indirect request. "It will take just under a minute to break down the material, and another two minutes to filter the atmosphere. While the airborne particles are not harmful to biologicals, they tend to create a messy film on display desks if allowed to settle out."

"Take all the time you need," Donna said, as her display desk was the one at risk in the reception area.

"Dring," Joe greeted the Maker, who was carrying a large box in his short arms as he approached the group waiting in the corridor. "I hope this doesn't mean you're moving out."

"Dorothy told me you'd all be here assembling furniture," the alien shape-shifter replied. "I brought an embassy-expansion gift."

"You didn't have to do that," Kelly said, praying that whatever gift the artistic Maker had created would fit in with the décor because there was no way she could refuse to display it. "Did you bring us a sculpture?"

"A globe," Dring replied, setting down the box and drawing out a perfect facsimile of Earth about the size of a beach ball. "It's lacquer on copper, and there's a permanent magnet embedded at the North Pole to suspend it below a ceiling mount that Jeeves will be bringing. The controller handles the axial tilt and wobble, and the globe rotates once a day so you can use it as a clock if you have a good memory for geography."

"It's beautiful, Dring," the ambassador exclaimed. "I can see it hanging directly over the center of the conference table. I don't know how to thank you."

"All finished," Libby announced, and the embassy doors slid open. Dring replaced his globe in the box and carried it in behind the humans. Kelly led the Maker into the new addition to show off the chairs, wall panels, and kitchen, while Paul and Kevin began laying out the onyx puzzle pieces on the floor. Daniel kept the two kneeling men supplied with pieces from the sequentially ordered stacks.

By the time Jeeves showed up with the ceiling mount and controller for Dring's globe, Donna had ordered take-out from the new vegan place in the Little Apple, and the table top was ready for gluing. Everybody took a break and ate while Joe studied the instructions for the adhesive.

"This is great stuff," he commented. "I'm used to Dollnick epoxy, but these Drazen glue-tubes are designed with a special metering applicator that's guaranteed to lay a perfect bead. All we have to do is squeeze a reasonably straight line all around the edges of the pieces, and when we stick them together, the glue will fill the micro-channels scribed into the onyx without any waste."

"Do we use the same stuff to join the top layer to the substrate planks?" Paul asked.

"Yes, and it's also certified as surgical glue for standard humanoids. Does that include us, Jeeves?"

"It does, but given the engineering that went into your table, I wouldn't count on there being any leftover tubes for you to take home for your medical kit." The Stryx rotated a quarter-turn to address Kelly. "I haven't had a chance to talk with you since the new civil service exams for EarthCent were announced, Ambassador."

"Libby told me that it was your project," Kelly said cautiously. "Are you just trying to convince the aliens that Earth is moving beyond being a Stryx protectorate, or will the exams really result in EarthCent hiring different employees than would have been chosen for us?"

"I worked very closely with the president's office on this," Jeeves replied. "I found Hildy to be an impressive collaborator, and I tried to lure her away to work for SBJ Fashions."

"And you didn't answer my question."

"I never should have written that *For Humans* guide about manipulating sentients for fun and profit. None of you ever fall for changing the subject anymore."

"Which guide was—I'm still waiting," the ambassador caught herself.

Jeeves vented a mechanical sigh. "Then I'll be blunt. The ideal outcome would have been a system that chooses exactly the same people that we would have picked for you, but that also would have defeated the point. The resulting civil service exams represent a large departure from the way we used to do things in two ways. First, we, I mean, EarthCent, will no longer be extending unsolicited job offers to people who don't sign up to take the tests. Second, individuals who score high on the exams will be given the benefit of the doubt, even if we are aware of minor discrepancies between their answers and their characters."

"None of us would have ended up working for EarthCent if it wasn't for being asked out of the blue," Donna said. "It's kind of sad to think about it."

"But if you had known that taking a civil service exam was an option, you might have done that," Daniel pointed out.

"No, I barely finished high school with the help of a teacher bot," the embassy manager replied. "I wouldn't have believed I could pass any tests."

"I'd have waited until I finished college, if at all," Kelly said. "I wasn't really thinking about diplomacy when I got the job offer."

"I think I would have eventually applied, but then I grew up around diplomats," Daniel told them. The associate ambassador, whose parents had been accused of taking a Dollnick bribe while managing the contract bidding for EarthCent's Venus terraforming project, poked around in his salad as if searching for something more substantial before continuing. "But just because we'll be accepting walk-in candidates doesn't mean that the Stryx won't be pushing, or should I say, manipulating them through the door."

"No comment," Jeeves mumbled.

"I haven't been to a Drazen gluing party in ages," Dring broke the uncomfortable silence that followed. "As soon as I polish off these carrots, I'd be honored to join you."

"With over six hundred pieces to glue together, we can use every hand we can get," Joe told him.

"Strange," Jeeves said. "I'd almost forgotten about all of the puzzles we did at school."

"In Libby's experimental school?" Paul asked. "I don't remember them."

"That's because you started later than the other children, when Joe brought you to the station. My first few years in Libby's school were mainly spent learning how to communicate with five and six-year-olds. Most of the children were scared of me, but Blythe could talk non-stop while doing three other things at the same time. We used to solve puzzles together, and I can see those skills now in the way she approaches business."

"I'd forgotten you were Blythe's special friend before Paul came to the station," Donna said. "You were so quiet and shy back then, it's almost as if you were a different sentient."

"I have an open requisition for a new Libbyland attraction and I'm beginning to think that something with a puzzle theme would fit," Jeeves announced.

"Without the glue," Paul suggested.

"Or so many pieces," Kelly added. "You need puzzles that people can solve on the spot unless you're going to sell them for home use."

"I don't mean puzzles like your tabletop," the Stryx said, gesturing at the work in progress with his pincer. "My idea is more along the lines of a life-puzzle, something to help young sentients understand where they're going and what pieces they need to prepare to get there."

"Like a mix-and-match resume?" Donna asked.

"Doesn't sound much like a theme park attraction," Kevin commented. "You should build another rollercoaster instead. It's hard to go wrong with rides."

"I want to create a puzzle that will help kids figure out what they should be studying in school and which life skills they should be acquiring in order to reach their goals," Jeeves explained. "Working with EarthCent to create the new civil service exam reminded me of how haphazard your career choices can be. Most of your people choose their life's work according to the availability of a paying job within commuting distance rather than matching their heart's desire."

"That's very thoughtful of you, Jeeves," the EarthCent ambassador complimented the Stryx. "I'm beginning to think that you're all grown up."

"Hardly," the station librarian interjected softly over Kelly's implant.

"It sounds interesting, but how are we going to make it work?" Paul asked. "Are you thinking about some sort of three-dimensional puzzle where the building blocks for a particular career path only fit in order? It would be easy enough to design a system of pips and detents that allow common building blocks for mathematics or language skills to fit into multiple decision trees. But a six-year-old wouldn't understand what he needs to be studying at sixteen in order to become a scientist at twenty-six."

"It's a problem," Jeeves admitted. "I don't believe that representational puzzle pieces would be useful in this application. We would need a way to get the message across through fun activities that lead a participant to the logical conclusion."

"So you're talking about something that's more of a game than a puzzle."

"A game where the actions fit together like a puzzle."

"Won't your elders be displeased if you reveal their methods?" Kelly inquired slyly.

Dring coughed and thumped his chest. "Sorry, I swallowed a carrot the wrong way."

"I'm not talking about manipulating outcomes for the greater good of the galaxy," Jeeves protested. "My idea is to help your youngsters find their own best path."

"Maybe what we need is Live Action Role Playing for children, but with the quests being related to long-term goals rather than gathering treasure," Paul suggested. "Instead of leveling up their combat skills, the players could get credit for educational achievements and practicing new abilities."

"Same problem you mentioned before," Kevin said. "Are you going to give a six-year-old credit for mastering advanced mathematics and naval architecture and then tell him to design a battleship? It might work in the game scoring sense, but I don't see how it would actually lead to a successful education."

"That's why it would have to be a real-time puzzle, to match the player's progress in life," Jeeves expanded on his idea. "Plus, it would keep them coming back to Libbyland, which is always good for the bottom line."

"So you're really talking about vocational counseling?" Donna asked.

"Self-directed counseling, if you want to call it that."

"My advice is that we finish putting this table together and talk about puzzling out human lives later," Joe said, rising to his feet. "You know, Jeeves, you can't protect us from ourselves. People learn by making mistakes, and one of the toughest jobs for a parent is standing back and letting it happen."

Nineteen

"Hey, Viv. I thought you said you had to be somewhere this evening," Samuel greeted his girlfriend. "My shift is over in ten minutes, and then I'm meeting Aabina in a half an hour."

"So you're going through with the secret society initiation."

"Yeah. I talked to my mom about it and she said that some of the other ambassadors have mentioned belonging to student societies, though she didn't know whether or not they were supposed to be secret. Is that where you're going later?"

"I can't tell you," Vivian replied.

"Well, there's only one place you couldn't tell me you're going so that must be it. I guess it makes sense that a secret society for future spies would take security more seriously than diplomats."

"If I were going to a secret society initiation, I think I'd be a little nervous," the girl admitted. "Do you suppose they blindfold candidates and make them take oaths on daggers?"

"Only in Vergallian dramas, I hope. I'm guessing they'll ask me some obvious questions, like, 'What's the name of the Grenouthian ambassador?' or 'How many Dollnicks does it take to change the pulse-width modulator on a Sharf drive?'"

"Those are easy questions?"

"The Grenouthians never tell aliens their names and a Dollnick wouldn't be caught dead working on a Sharf drive."

"I'm really not comfortable with the idea of taking an oath."

"Then tell them that. We're still on a Stryx station so it's not like they can force you to do anything you don't want to."

"Can we keep a private channel open," Vivian asked, leaning across the counter and covering Samuel's left hand with her own. The new couple's rings they'd bought after sacrificing their first set for Bob and Judith's wedding clicked against each other.

"Sure, if you want," the teen said, though they'd never run an open channel before and he'd heard that sharing at that level was both a distraction and a bad idea on general principal. "Do you know the command?"

"It's buried in a submenu on your heads-up display when you ping somebody. I searched it out earlier," Vivian said. "I'll ping you now and walk you through it."

"Okay, I'm here," Samuel responded to her ping, and the girl heard a slight thickening in his voice as the words he spoke out loud reached her ears a tiny fraction of a second after her implant had already received them. "Now what?"

"Navigate to 'custom options' and select the override," she told him. "You have to eye-scroll through a disclaimer before continuing. It's kind of long and I didn't really read it."

"Nobody reads any of these things," he said. "All right, I got a new menu with a bunch of items I never knew were here. I can see where conferencing in my head could get confusing in a hurry."

"Select 'committed relationship,'" Vivian instructed him, her ears turning pink. "It won't allow you to proceed otherwise."

"There must be thirty submenus listed!"

"Don't even look below the third line," she said. "Some of them are pretty embarrassing."

"The first line is scary enough. Mutual location tracking?"

"My mom says that interface designers feel like they're not doing their jobs unless they take advantage of every feature a piece of hardware offers. Our implants are pretty sophisticated."

"I've got it. Line three is 'hold open'. Wow, there's another disclaimer."

"Just accept it and then choose the option for a temporary channel or we'll be stuck inside each other's heads as long as we keep these implants."

"Temporary," Samuel said, carefully selecting the option with practiced eye movements. "Confirm."

"I've got to run to meet my Verlock sponsor. He asked me to come extra early so he'd have time to explain the ceremony," Vivian added over her shoulder as she headed for the exit.

A minute later, Samuel heard her say, "Testing, one, two, three."

"I hear you," he responded. "What's the difference between this and a regular ping that you never break off?"

"Pings automatically disconnect as soon as the implant goes into translation mode," Vivian said. "You never noticed that you can't talk with aliens and ping simultaneously?"

"I guess it never came up. Good luck."

Five minutes later, Samuel's relief showed up to work the next lost-and-found shift and the ambassador's son headed home for a quick bite. He'd just stepped out of the lift tube when Vivian met up with her sponsor.

"Vivian Oxford," he heard the Verlock greet her formally. "Before I brief you on the initiation, you must solemnly swear never to speak about this with another soul."

This sentence took the slow-spoken alien almost a minute to utter, during which time Samuel covered half the distance to the ice harvester, greeted two hounds, and waved to Fenna and Mikey. The nine-year-olds were dressed in their Junior Station Scout uniforms and were trying to build some type of improvised shelter out of old fishing rods and bed sheets without adult supervision.

"I'm not really comfortable with oaths," Vivian told the Verlock honestly. "I don't want to keep secrets from my boyfriend."

"It's just an Open University secret society," her sponsor replied ponderously. "The oath is only binding in the presence of other students."

"My boyfriend is a student too."

"There's an exception for that."

"Can you modify the oath accordingly, just to be safe?" the girl asked.

Samuel heard the Verlock groan, though perhaps it was really a sigh coming from the deep-chested alien, who went on to ask, "Before I brief you on the initiation, do you solemnly swear never to speak about this with another Open University student, boyfriends excepted?"

"Yes," Vivian replied, by which point Samuel had made a sandwich and was beginning to question whether he'd be able to carry on an intelligent conversation with another

230

person while Vivian and a bunch of student spies were talking in his ear.

"The first step of the initiation is—"

"What?" Vivian interrupted the Verlock. "I'm sorry, could you chew quieter?"

"What?" the Verlock responded.

"Sorry," Samuel said. "There was a lot of leftover celery from somewhere."

"What?" Joe asked, coming into the kitchen. "Who are you talking to?"

"What?" Vivian said.

"What?" the Verlock echoed.

"Just a minute, Dad," Samuel said. "This isn't working, Viv. It sounds like you'll be fine and you're not bound to secrecy so you can fill me in later."

"All right," she agreed reluctantly. "We should have practiced. Can you cancel from your end so I don't walk into something trying to navigate the options?"

"What?" Samuel heard the Verlock say again.

"Trying to keep a private channel open with Vivian?" Joe teased his son.

"What?" Vivian asked.

The teen made record time navigating the heads-up menus to the disconnect option. Fortunately, he didn't have to scan or accept any more disclaimers to do so.

"She was a little nervous about a meeting she's going to and asked me to listen in," Samuel told his father. "It was pretty confusing. Do you and Mom ever do that?"

"I told her my implant doesn't have that menu option."

"Does it?"

"I told her that it doesn't and that's all you need to know. Are you bringing Vivian to the grand opening tomorrow afternoon?"

"I thought Mom was going to break in the table with a nuisance-species conference meeting."

"There's a general reception afterwards since all the local ambassadors will already be there. Just diplomats, family, and maybe a few reporters."

"It's not like the embassy is that big of a space," Samuel said. "How many people do you figure it fits now?"

"They got rid of the little kitchenette in the reception area and moved it to the back of the new conference room. We could probably pack in close to a hundred guests as long as everybody stands and we don't get too many of the larger aliens."

"You make it sound really attractive." Samuel gulped down the rest of his sandwich and chased it with a glass of grapefruit juice. "I've got to go to a student secret society meeting. I'm not sure when I'll be back."

"I remember when Paul was in one of those," Joe said.

"He never mentioned it to me. Oh, right."

On his way out of Mac's Bones, Samuel waved to Mike and Fenna, who had given up on the emergency shelter and were riding on the backs of Beowulf and Alexander, apparently in pursuit of a Cayl hound merit badge. After entering the lift tube, he requested the Vergallian embassy, and a few minutes later the EarthCent ambassador's son found himself getting the grand tour from Aabina and her mother, Ambassador Aainda.

"My predecessors had a habit of remodeling the entire embassy complex as soon as they took over, but other than a few minor alterations to the ballroom, I haven't made any changes other than hanging my own family portraits," Aainda told Samuel. "What do you think of them?"

"It would be impossible to judge the paintings as art given the beauty of the subjects," the teen replied without exaggeration.

"How nice of you to say. You seem to be rather taken by that one."

Samuel stared at the handsome Vergallian man and his stunning bride, both decked out in the traditional wedding finery of royalty. "I'm sure I've seen them somewhere before," he replied, tilting his head on his neck as if a different perspective was required to make the connection.

"Take a minute and think."

"It can't be. Is that Queen Avidya?"

"You have an excellent eye to recognize the portrait of a woman you've never met based on knowing her little daughter twelve years ago."

"You're related to Ailia?" Samuel asked, not seeing any reason to correct Aainda about the last time he'd seen the princess.

"Through the male bloodline," the ambassador replied in Vergallian, which allowed her to convey through the tonal richness of the language that she didn't mean to dismiss the relationship as unimportant. "Queen Avidya's husband was my cousin."

"So you're related to Baylit as well."

"Yes. We maintain a closer relationship than—" Aainda paused a moment to choose the correct wording, "— required by tradition."

"Thank you for showing me this," Samuel said, realizing that the Vergallian mother and daughter could have as easily hidden the information and tried to use it to gain some future advantage. "Have either of you met Ailia?"

"Once, when her father was still alive," the ambassador said sadly. "It would be inappropriate for her to travel before she comes of age and assumes her throne, and from a strategic standpoint, it's better that our mutual enemies see no evidence of an ongoing connection between our families."

"Sam and I have to get going or we'll be late for the initiation, Mother," Aabina spoke up.

"You are welcome to visit the embassy anytime, Samuel McAllister," the ambassador stated, reverting again to Vergallian for the formal declaration. "And please don't keep my daughter out too late."

"She always does that," the Vergallian girl complained to Samuel as soon as they were out of earshot. "As if I wasn't aware of my own schedule."

"Are you able to continue your royal training on the station?" Samuel asked. "I've heard it's really specialized with tutors all day long, not to mention the social requirements."

Aabina glanced at the ambassador's son shrewdly. "They taught you about royal training in Vergallian Studies?"

"Maybe I heard about it from my sister's friend Affie," Samuel replied evasively. He could hardly tell her about all of the time he'd spent visiting with Ailia through the agency of the quantum-coupled bots provided by Jeeves. "Am I going to have to wear a blindfold and swear on a dagger?"

"Like in a drama? Oh, you're trying to change the subject. Don't worry, I won't pry into your secrets, and we're on the same side in any case." The lift tube doors opened at their approach and Aabina instructed the capsule, "Secret society meeting for student diplomats."

"The lift tubes are in on it?" Samuel couldn't help asking.

"Nobody would ever find the meetings otherwise. We move them around to foil surveillance."

"Who would target a student meeting for intelligence gathering?"

"The secret society for student spies," Aabina told him. "You know, you speak Vergallian better than any Human I've ever met," she continued. "Did you spend all your time watching dramas when you were young?"

"I guess I just have an ear for languages," Samuel said, flinching internally at how lame that sounded. "I started on 'Let's Make Friends' when I was only five, and the in-ear translators the Grenouthians provided were only on one side and lagged a little. How long have you been in the secret society?"

"Since I started at the Open University. Being an ambassador's daughter and the oldest princess in my family meant I was marked out for diplomacy from birth. We would have invited you earlier but you seemed to be a little lost, career-wise."

Aabina pulled the cowl of her travel cloak over her head and cinched it around her face, concealing her features from anybody who wasn't standing right in front of her with a flashlight. The capsule doors slid open and the students stepped out onto a busy corridor that seemed to consist exclusively of bars and hotels renting rooms for incredibly cheap prices.

"I've never been to this section of the station before," Samuel said. "I'll have to remember it next time somebody comes into the lost-and-found and asks if I know where they can rent a room for a handful of creds."

"And stay for a handful of minutes. I believe we're in the red light district."

"Your mother is going to kill me," the ambassador's son yelped. "Then my father is going to kill me. Let's get out of here."

"The meeting is that way," Aabina told him, brandishing her student tab like a compass and starting off towards the right at a pace that forced Samuel to lengthen his stride to keep up. "The signal is only detectible at short range — it's the final level of security."

"I thought you said that the Open University provides meeting spaces for the secret societies."

"Diplomatic alumni are known for their sense of humor, and the Open University doesn't provide alcohol service."

"Are they going to make me drink for the initiation? I don't have a head for the hard stuff and beer puts me to sleep. I'm the family wimp."

"Nobody is going to force you to do anything," Aabina told him, nodding with satisfaction as the arrow on her tab indicated the narrow entrance of a Frunge greenery bar. "If you've never been in one of these places, don't try ordering any grains to go with your drink."

"I wouldn't dream of it," Samuel muttered, following after the Vergallian ambassador's daughter as she pushed back her cowl and forged a path through a particularly dense stand of tall, leafy plants that were practically begging to be pruned with a machete. "Who picks these places?"

"Sam, Abs," Czeros greeted the newcomers as they finally broke into a small clearing. The Frunge ambassador was sitting at the head of a metal table crowded with students nursing drinks. "When I heard you were being initiated I couldn't resist dusting off my old school tie and volunteering as the toastmaster."

"But you didn't attend the Open University," Samuel replied as he squeezed into the narrow space on the bench indicated by his mother's friend.

"Most of the student secret societies on the tunnel network have reciprocity arrangements," Czeros explained. "It always pays to mention being a member if you run into diplomatic trouble on some world. You never know if there might be an alum present and it shows that you aren't a loner."

"Abs?" Aabina hissed, fixing the ambassador with a frosty glare.

"Ambassadors are the highest rank of alumni, and as such, I'm allowed to assign one permanent nickname per event I attend. From this day hence, thou shall be known as Abs to all and sundry—in secret, anyway. Now stop procrastinating and place your orders," Czeros concluded, conjuring up a holographic menu that was composed entirely in Frunge. "The manager, an old drinking friend, has color-coded the items you can imbibe without internal damage. The white entries are safe for you, Sam, and the purple ones are for Abs and the other Vergallians."

Samuel took no time to decide. "I guess I'll try the only white one."

"Wise choice. Abs?"

"I'll have what Ajeida is drinking," Aabina said, pointing at a pale pink concoction that the Vergallian across the table was sipping through a straw. "You must have started early. Did we miss anything?"

"It's traditional for everybody to arrive before the new initiate for the maximum impact when the blindfold is removed," Czeros told her pointedly.

"When I saw where the lift tube let us out I thought it would be better to skip that part. A hooded female leading a blindfolded male down that corridor—"

"Would have blended right in," the Frunge ambassador interrupted. "Young people these days don't know how to have fun. Why, at my initiation, somebody put a dyeing agent in the punch bowl that turned everybody's hair vines orange. It took forever to grow out."

"Doesn't that mean that you marked yourselves as secret society members?" a Dollnick student asked.

"Secret, shmecret. The important thing is to network and learn how to share your burdens." Czeros stopped and took a grape from a fruit platter and fired it down the table at a student's head. "You, the Horten who keeps pouring her drink out on the ground. It's wasteful and it's bad for the plants. If you can't tolerate booze, order juice or water, but don't pretend to be drinking while you're staying sober in hopes of gaining an advantage. It's unsportsmanlike."

"What did I order?" Samuel asked.

"It's an Earth wine, the only one they had on the menu. It tastes watered down so you'll probably like it."

A waitress with her hair vines coiled in a tight bun so they wouldn't catch on the dense foliage of the green bar brought a tray full of glasses. "One Human wine, Two Vergallian Pinkies, refills for everybody else."

"I didn't order a refill," a Drazen girl protested.

"Drink up," Czeros ordered. "No internships for teetotalers."

"Paying internships?" a Frunge student asked eagerly, then slammed back a shot of clear fluid. "Is there something open at our embassy?"

"Planning on replacing me, sapling? Oh, don't look so upset. You kids really can't take a joke. Stop in on the first of the new cycle and give the embassy manager your transcript. I'm sure we'll find something for you."

"But how about the rest of us?" the Drazen girl asked, eyeing her unwanted drink dubiously.

"The Humans are hiring for all positions," Czeros told her. "Just sign up for their civil service exams."

Samuel choked on his wine. "What?"

"Really?" a Dollnick student asked. "They not only hire outside of the lead diplomatic families but outside of their species as well?"

"There must be some mistake," Aabina said, retrieving the EarthCent announcement on her tab. A minute later she concluded, "It really doesn't restrict the species of the applicant."

"They probably didn't specify the species so that our artificial people could apply," Samuel said. "I'm sure there must be something in there about at least being human-derived."

"No," the Frunge ambassador told him. "I received an intelligence brief about your new civil service tests this morning and that point was quite clear. Any member of the tunnel network can sit the exam."

"But that's crazy. We'll end up with a diplomatic service run by aliens."

"Is this pay scale in creds?" asked the Drazen girl who had complained about the refill. She looked up from her own tab. "Who could live on these salaries?"

"InstaSitter pays more, and the benefits are better too," a Horten student contributed.

"Tricky," a Verlock student commented. "Open to all, desired by none."

"Does EarthCent have an initiation?" a Grenouthian student asked. "When I started an internship at our embassy, they made me carry a Booler egg in my pouch until it hatched."

"Thank you for reminding me," Czeros said, "I'd almost forgotten the most important part of our evening."

"Song, song, song," the students all chorused, pounding the table and staring expectantly at Samuel.

"I have to sing?" he asked, and took a large gulp of the watery wine, more to wet his throat than for courage. "I can do the theme to 'Let's Make Friends.'"

"You have to sing your EarthCent anthem," Aabina said.

"We don't have one," Samuel told her, a declaration that was met by the students moaning and casting fearful looks at Czeros.

"What a funny coincidence, EarthCent having no anthem and my being here," the Frunge ambassador said. "In my capacity as the senior alum at this meeting, I will extend my protection to our young initiate and assume the burden of singing an anthem. Feel free to join in."

Czeros leaned back in his chair, opened his mouth, and began an awful creaking sound that sounded like a structure being buffeted by high winds and on the brink of collapse. The two Frunge students present came in on harmony, and everybody else placed their hands over their ears and activated the noise-cancellation option on their implants. It only helped so much.

Twenty

"This chair is too big," Bork teased the EarthCent ambassador after taking the Verlock's assigned seat.

"This chair is too small," Ambassador Crute complained, making a comical effort to fit himself into the Horten's chair.

"This chair is just right," a voice came out of nowhere as the Chert ambassador announced his presence.

"Early is on time," Ambassador Srythlan announced himself as he shuffled into the new conference room. "Please vacate my seat, Ambassador Bork."

"Are all of these puzzle pieces real or is this some kind of printed coating?" Ortha inquired, leaning over the table and trying to insert a fingernail between two adjacent shapes while waiting for the Dollnick to extract himself from the chair. "I do believe they are real. Did it come assembled?"

"Joe and the boys put it together," Kelly informed the Horten ambassador, knowing that Ortha had really been digging to find out if she had accepted alien help. "Everything you see here was manufactured and installed by humans, except for Dring's globe," she added, pointing out the pièce de résistance suspended above the table.

"I'm honored you chose a Dollnick subcontractor to cut out the existing wall," Crute couldn't restrain himself from saying. Then, realizing he was being ungracious, the ambassador added, "These small renovation jobs are the worst. Too much for a handyman, too small to bring in a construction management firm. Where did you find the labor to fit those panels?"

"Daniel imported a construction crew from one of the sovereign human communities."

"Are those seams supposed to be horizontal?" Ortha inquired.

"It's the new style," Kelly replied quickly. "Who are we missing?"

"Not me," declared the Grenouthian ambassador as he entered from the embassy reception area rather than the door on the corridor and quickly found his seat. "Comfy."

"Good morning," Czeros croaked, sinking gratefully into a chair. "I'm sorry if I sound a bit hoarse in translation. I was called upon to exercise my singing talents for an extended period not many hours ago and I seem to have overdone it."

"Secret society meeting?" Bork asked.

"Samuel's initiation," the Frunge ambassador con-firmed, and the others all nodded their understanding. "I don't suppose there's anything to drink?" he added hope-fully.

"The caterers will be serving any time now," Kelly told them. "And that shelf on the back wall is for your personal mugs and tankards, if you choose to bring one to leave."

"Like in a Human pub. What a wonderful idea. Given the number of meetings you'll be hosting, my favorite wine glass will see more use here than it would in my own embassy."

"I doubt that," Ortha said under his breath.

"When do you plan the handover?" the Grenouthian addressed Kelly. "Was adding the conference room to the embassy a transition gift?"

"What do you mean?"

"For your son, to smooth the way for him," the giant bunny responded.

"If Samuel is planning to replace me, it's the first I've heard about it," she told them. "My son is welcome to the job if EarthCent sees fit to give it to him one day, but I'm afraid I have another decade to go before I qualify for a full pension, and Sam has just swapped into the diplomatic path at school."

"Ambassador Aainda," Ortha greeted the Vergallian beauty and patted the chair next to his own. "I saved your seat."

"Thank you. Why is the Gem Ambassador waiting outside?" she asked Kelly. "It appears that everyone else is here."

"I don't know," the EarthCent ambassador replied, getting up from her place and sticking her head out in the corridor. "Gwen Two? We're about to begin."

"Of course," the clone said, and slipped her change purse back into one of the large pockets of the latest jumpsuit fashion adopted by Gem professionals. "I was just waiting to give the caterers a little pep talk about the importance of your first hosted meeting, but I'm mortified to see that they're late."

"They've been here over an hour. I took your suggestion to add a kitchen at the same time as a conference room. It's almost a pity that the ventilation system works so well or you'd smell what they're cooking."

"Station building code," the Gem ambassador explained, following Kelly into the embassy. "So many of my sisters work in the food preparation business that I'm familiar with the requirements. Any kitchen in an area accessible by multiple species and not specifically designated as a private residence or a food court must employ a negative pressure system to minimize airborne odors."

"No wonder the kitchen was so expensive. I got three quotes but they were all within a few creds of each other."

"Did the contractors know each other?" the Gem ambassador asked suspiciously.

"The truth is, I was focused on getting the conference room right," Kelly admitted, taking her seat between Bork and Czeros. The Gem sat to the left of the Dollnick, the Chert deigned to turn off his invisibility projector, and all of the diplomats turned expectantly to the EarthCent ambassador.

"I swear the food will be out in just a minute," she told them.

"I call this meeting to order," Bork muttered under his breath.

"Oh, right," Kelly said. "First time hosting, you know."

"Who's counting?" the giant bunny said, leading to laughs all around.

"I call this meeting to order," the EarthCent ambassador declared. "I want to start by saying that I've never been comfortable with the whole 'nuisance species' concept. Since I'll be hosting the next three meetings, I looked into the history of this committee, and our station librarian assures me it was mandated by the Stryx. When I mentioned that we never actually talked about nuisance species at any of the meetings I've attended—"

"You mentioned it to the Stryx?" the Dollnick interrupted-ed.

"To Libby, yes. It's not like she doesn't listen in anyway."

"Did you make it clear that you weren't requesting additional work?" Crute continued.

"I don't think I gave that impression," Kelly replied slowly. "Libby did say that the station manager had been receiving quite a few complaints since Baa took up residence, but that's sort of understandable, given the history most of you have with her people."

"If the Terragram mages had come to us as superior aliens there would be no problem at all," Czeros reminded the ambassador. "They presented themselves to my ancestors as gods."

"In any case, the station librarian suggested I invite any local Terragrams to the meeting and offered to put out the request on a private network maintained by the mages. I asked Baa to attend, but I guess she's running late."

Kelly found herself speaking slower and slower by the end of this statement because she couldn't help noticing that the ambassadors were all regarding her with a mixture of puzzlement and horror. Fortunately, the Gem caterers chose this instant to enter from the kitchen, and the smell of the specialty desserts Donna had ordered for all of the species present wafted over the conference table. Any incipient move to call for an early recess to the meeting was nipped in the bud.

Ten minutes later, the Verlock was the sole ambassador who hadn't cleaned his plate, and that was only because he was such a slow eater. The other ambassadors were enjoying their beverages and relaxing in their species-specific chairs, and the gentle rise and fall of the giant bunny's chest made Kelly suspect that the Grenouthian ambassador had dozed off with his eyes open. Just when she was about to ask if anybody had new business for the committee, Donna entered from the reception area, leading a tall stranger.

"This is Raa," she introduced the alien, who was dressed in a one-piece garment that bore a striking resemblance to one of Dorothy's ponchos. "Libby confirmed that he's a Terragram mage and he's responding to our open invitation."

The Grenouthian jerked awake, and the other ambassadors all sat bolt upright at this announcement, but the new arrival showed no sign of awkwardness.

"My name is Raa, and if I understood the communication that our Stryx friends injected into my private channel as I was passing through the neighborhood, I'm here to defend my species against being declared a nuisance." The mage looked slowly around the table, giving each ambassador a careful once-over through his vertically slit pupils before continuing in a honeyed voice, "Do any of you have a grievance you'd like to share?"

"Not me," Czeros said immediately. "The Frunge loved our Terragram mage. We have an entire necropolis dedicated to statues of him on our homeworld."

"How about your people?" Raa asked, staring intently at the empty seat where Kelly had last seen the Chert ambassador. "I hope that your long sojourn as refugees has nothing to do with my kind."

"I would never dream of even implying you had anything to do with our troubles," the invisible diplomat replied. "I assure you that I have never made any sort of complaint, nor would I if I had one."

"Second that," Ortha announced.

"Third," the Dollnick contributed.

"Motion passes," Bork muttered to Kelly.

"There's no motion on the table," the EarthCent ambassador said in exasperation. "Please take a seat, Raa. I assure you that there's been some error and that nobody is here to declare Terragrams a nuisance. But it is true that the station management has been receiving complaints about a mage who is living here, and this committee is tasked with fostering better understanding between your species and ours."

"Did you say that a Terragram mage has taken up residency on this station?" Raa demanded. "That isn't possible. The Stryx banned us long before any of your species joined the tunnel network."

"I thought the Stryx only banned harmful—oh," Kelly cut herself off. "Well, the ban must have been lifted because Baa has been here for almost a year now and she works with my daughter in the fashion business."

"Baa?" the mage repeated incredulously. "As in, 'Pay the tithe or bad things will happen to your crops and livestock' Baa?"

"She's not like that," Kelly protested. "Besides, it turns out that she was acting under compulsion."

Raa appeared to be skeptical, but rather than making an issue of it, he inquired in a conciliatory tone, "Does your species always make a practice of serving the food before the guests arrive?"

"I'll check with the catering staff," the Gem Ambassador volunteered, and practically fled into the kitchen.

"Salt cod?" the Verlock ambassador offered the mage, holding up his last piece of dried out fish. Kelly would have sworn that Srythlan sent her a slow wink when Raa turned away with a disgusted look.

"It's not that anybody objects to your people, per se," the EarthCent ambassador told the Terragram mage. "They just feel that you might have handled first contact situations with a little less, uh, divinity."

247

"You try reasoning with a primitive species sometime and see how it works for you," Raa retorted. "I've been in hundreds of pantheons, and if there's one thing I've learned, it's that you can't tell the natives what gods you are."

"I'm not sure I understand."

"I'm absolutely sure that you don't," the mage replied, glancing impatiently towards the kitchen. "Do you think it matters to me whether I'm taken as the god of death or the god of knowledge? I'd happily serve in a pantheon as the god of fingernail clippings if it would fill a temple with worshippers, but you have to play to the audience."

"Or, perhaps you might consider a career that didn't involve acquiring worshippers," Jeeves said, floating in from the embassy reception area with Baa in tow. "I'm sorry we're late but we had a fashion emergency that I'd rather not get into."

"Is that you?" Raa demanded of the female mage, coming to his feet. "I thought you were with—"

"Don't speak his name in my presence or we'll find out which one of us has lived too long," Baa interrupted. "And I want you all to know that I'm attending under protest."

"I'm sorry," Kelly said. "I didn't know that Jeeves would force you to come. I thought you'd appreciate a chance to make your peace with the ambassadors."

"It's not them I'm upset about, it's him." Baa glared at the Terragram mage standing on the other side of the table. "I have half-a-mind to tap into the station grid and—"

There was a ripping sound as Raa tore off his poncho, which was apparently held together by one long Velcro strip, and then he extended his arms and fanned his feathers. Kelly felt her heart miss a beat at the dazzling display that made the most colorful peacock look like a female cardinal by comparison. A bright, pulsing orb tore free from Baa's chest and began floating across the space that separated the two Terragram mages.

"Don't let it reach him!" Jeeves shouted at the ambassadors. He interposed himself between Raa and Baa's heart, which launched into a series of evasive maneuvers in an attempt to reach its goal. "I can't hold her heart back forever. Throw him out."

To Kelly's surprise, the Grenouthian ambassador was the first to spring into action, bodying up against Raa and pushing him a step back from the table. The Terragram was forced to choose between maintaining his plumage pose and protecting his abdomen, and with a snarl, he brought in his arms and began conjuring a flame. Before he could set the bunny's fur on fire, the Verlock ambassador lumbered between the pair, and the flames did his leathery skin no more harm than a lava bath.

"I'll get you for this," Raa shouted as the Dollnick ambassador wrapped all four of his arms around the mage's torso, hoisting him from the floor and preventing him from fanning his feathers again. Bork and Czeros each grabbed one of Raa's legs, and together the three ambassadors carried the would-be god of Baa's love to the door and tossed him out into the corridor. The instant the door slid closed, Kelly shouted, "Security lock-down," and a shiny energy barrier she never even knew existed materialized over the doors.

Aainda hurried to catch the slumping Baa, and with Kelly's help, held the mage erect until Jeeves finally succeeded in herding the wayward heart back to its owner. The female mage came to with a start, shaking her head to dispel the cobwebs.

"What happened?" Baa asked.

"Raa made a play for your heart and we stopped him," Jeeves informed the mage.

"We?" she asked, looking around at the ambassadors who hardly seemed to know what to think themselves. "Where is he now?"

"Libby?" Kelly asked. "Is Raa still in the corridor?"

"He attempted to damage station property so Gryph removed him," the station librarian answered. "Raa and his ship won't be bothering anybody in this galaxy anytime soon."

"We did it," Ortha declared, exchanging the Horten version of a high-five with the Chert ambassador, who had also been conspicuously invisible during the action.

"I can't believe I helped bounce a Terragram mage," Czeros said, though the radiant smile on his face proved he had no doubts over what had just happened. "Do you think it's possible to get a copy of the security imaging, Ambassador McAllister?"

"Second the motion," Bork added immediately.

"Third," the Grenouthian ambassador said. "I'd settle for the part where I threw Raa across the room."

"Libby?" Kelly asked again.

"I'll send a copy to all of your respective embassies," the station librarian replied.

The Gem ambassador emerged from the kitchen carrying some type of puff pastry that had risen so high that she could barely see around it.

"My sisters consulted the universal dessert cookbook and this is the only dish that was recommended for Terragram mages," she said. "What happened to Raa?"

"I'll explain later," Kelly said to the clone. "Baa will be taking his place."

"And that looks scrumptious," the mage said, though she still seemed a little bit hazy and allowed the Vergallian ambassador to support her during the short walk to the table. "Does anybody else want some?"

An hour later, the embassy was packed to standing room only, making it difficult for Kelly to circulate and greet all of the grand opening guests. As she made her way around the conference room table, she encountered a knot of Grenouthian reporters armed with immersive cameras interviewing their own ambassador about his part in ejecting the Terragram mage.

"It helps that we've been working together on committees for years," the ambassador was explaining. "Of course I was the first to react, but what else would you expect?"

"Is it true that flames were shooting from the mage's eyes?" the reporter asked eagerly.

"If there were flames on the security imagery then I will remember them in great detail. I withhold comment until I get a chance to review the footage."

A few steps further on, Kelly encountered a pair of Drazen reporters demanding details from their ambassador.

"I believe my years of battle reenactments proved their worth," Bork said. "Have you ever seen my rally cry from the Battle of Scort Woods? Sadly, the production was abandoned when the Hortens released their own version, but I could send you an outtake."

After greeting a few more guests, Kelly headed back for the embassy reception area and almost bumped into Baa, who was deep in conversation with the Dollnick ambassador.

"Spare me all the whistling around the bush, Crute," the mage was saying. "Jeeves has me locked up in an exclusive contract for all enchantments related to apparel and weapons. What is it exactly you're asking for?"

"My third wife doesn't get along with the first two," Crute said in a rush. "I need a love potion for family harmony."

"What you need is to build her a nest of her own," Baa retorted, catching Kelly's eye and shaking her head.

"There's my mom," Dorothy told the Vergallian ambassador, who had already relayed more advice for a successful pregnancy than any of the girl's family and friends, including the Farling doctor.

"Just two more," Aabina insisted, blocking Dorothy's escape with her own body. "This one is really good for the tendons. Now stretch against the wall with your palms flat on the surface and raise yourself on your toes. Come on, you won't remember if you don't do it."

"I'm already standing on my toes. That's what heels are for."

"I wore heels throughout my first pregnancy and my daughter is shorter than I am," the Vergallian told her. "I found out too late that there's a statistical correlation."

"How is that possible?"

"The beauty of correlation is that causation doesn't come into it."

"What are the four of you so busy discussing?" Kelly asked her son, who together with Vivian, the Frunge ambassador and the Drazen head of intelligence, had taken over Donna's display desk and were running some sort of projections.

"Czeros has been giving me some advice on career options in diplomacy," Samuel replied. "I guess I kind of thought that EarthCent was the only possibility, but he and Herl have been pointing out that only a small fraction of their own diplomatic corps is employed on Stryx stations."

"And Herl had some great advice about the intelligence field," Vivian added. "I'm thinking of doing an internship for the Drazens."

"Is that possible?" Kelly asked Herl.

"Given the working relationship between our intelligence services, I think it would make a reasonable next step," the spy master replied.

"Over here, Kel," Joe called to his wife from behind the table where he and Paul were mixing drinks. "Some turnout."

"It's been quite a day," Kelly said, slipping in behind the improvised bar and discovering that it was the least crowded spot in the embassy. "I had been afraid that all of the ambassadors would run off right after the meeting, but it turns out they're all being treated as heroes for ejecting a Terragram mage."

"I saw the security imaging," Joe said, then grimaced as a Drazen approached the bar and ordered a Divverflip. "Can you get this one, Paul?"

The younger man sighed and donned heavy rubber gloves to handle the toxic ingredients.

"I couldn't believe how fast it all happened," Kelly told them, reviewing the experience in her mind. "One second, Baa was staring at that other mage like he stood her up for the high school prom, the next second her heart had left her body for a display of feathers. How could a species evolve like that?"

"Didn't you find it a bit suspicious when Jeeves yelled for help?" Joe asked.

"He was busy trying to keep Baa's heart from reaching Raa, and—now that I think of it, he didn't even go super-sonic."

"It certainly hasn't hurt her popularity with the other species," Joe commented. "Normally I could tell you where Baa was in a crowd like this because everybody else would be giving her as much room as possible."

"Libby?" Kelly subvoced. "Was bringing Raa to the meeting a setup?"

"You did ask why we insist on a committee to deal with nuisance species."

"That's just because I was hosting. I must have been to a hundred of these at the other embassies and usually we just talk about the park decks or some benefit concert. I thought this was one of those cases where the committee kept the same name even after the purpose evolved. And you didn't answer my question."

"I'm just glad that Jeeves has found a vocation that suits him," the station librarian said of her sole offspring. "Some of the first-generation Stryx were beginning to believe that his interest in humanity was just an excuse to avoid doing multiverse math, but he's developed quite a way with people for one so young."

"You mean, quite a way with manipulating people," Kelly muttered, not realizing that Jeeves had floated up to the bar.

"For fun and profit," the young Stryx told her. "And before you go attributing all sorts of good intentions to my actions, I'll have you know that Baa is a critical part of my business plan."

"See what I mean?" Libby whispered over Kelly's implant. "He's even learned how to lie convincingly. That usually takes us tens of thousands of years."

"But I thought you guys never lie," Kelly subvoced back.

"We never get caught. It amounts to the same thing in the end."

Career Night on Union Station is getting a sequel because I'm addicted to my own characters. You can sign up for notification of the next EarthCent release on my website, IFITBREAKS.COM. I also post an updated cast of characters and prior book synopsis to the website with every new release to get readers back up to speed.

For readers suffering from EarthCent withdrawal symptoms, I recently released **Turing Test**, a novel about a team of AI Observers visiting Earth in the present day to assess our humanity. Strangely enough, the Observers are more human than we are. Due to reader demand, I've written a sequel, **Human Test**.

If you believe there is still a place in science fiction for stories that aren't all about death and destruction, please help to get the word out. Posting an Amazon review on the first book of this series, Date Night on Union Station, will help new readers discover these books, even if you only write a few words.

About the Author

E. M. Foner lives in Northampton, MA with an imaginary German Shepherd who's been trained to bite bankers. The author welcomes reader comments at e_foner@yahoo.com.

LARP Night on Union Station is getting a sequel because I'm addicted to my own characters. You can sign up for notification of the next EarthCent release on my website, IFITBREAKS.COM.

About the Author

E. M. Foner lives in Northampton, MA with an imaginary German Shepherd who's been trained to bite bankers. The author welcomes reader comments at e_foner@yahoo.com.

Other books by the author:

Meghan's Dragon

Turing Test

EarthCent Ambassador Series:

Date Night on Union Station

Alien Night on Union Station

High Priest on Union Station

Spy Night on Union Station

Carnival on Union Station

Wanderers on Union Station

Vacation on Union Station

Guest Night on Union Station

Word Night on Union Station

Party Night on Union Station

Review Night on Union Station

Family Night on Union Station

Book Night on Union Station

LARP Night on Union Station

CPSIA information can be obtained
at www.ICGtesting.com
Printed in the USA
LVHW091558121021
700244LV00001B/6

9 781948 691130